IF HE'S NOBLE

HANNAH HOWELL

ZEBRA BOOKS
KENSINGTON PUBLISHING CORP.
http://www.kensingtonbooks.com

ZEBRA BOOKS are published by

Kensington Publishing Corp.
119 West 40th Street
New York, NY 10018

All Kensington titles, imprints, and distributed lines are available
at special quantity discounts for bulk purchases for sales promotion,
premiums, fund-raising, educational, or institutional use.

Special book excerpts or customized printings can also be created
to fit specific needs. For details, write or phone the office of the
Kensington Sales Manager: Attn.: Sales Department. Kensington
Publishing Corp., 119 West 40th Street, New York, NY 10018.
Phone: 1-800-221-2647.

Zebra and the Z logo Reg. U.S. Pat. & TM Off.

First Printing: August 2015
ISBN-13: 978-1-4201-3503-9
ISBN-10: 1-4201-3503-1

eISBN-13: 978-1-4201-3504-6
eISBN-10: 1-4201-3504-X

10 9 8 7 6 5 4 3 2 1

Printed in the United States of America

MIDNIGHT LOVER

Just as Primrose was about to doze off over a particularly dry treatise on the good and bad of planting flowering vines, a soft sound caught her attention. She looked at the door and saw the latch slowly lifting. Then, so abruptly it startled her into nearly dropping her book, the door opened, Bened slid inside, and then he silently closed and latched the door. He turned and grinned at her like a naughty boy. It was a look that should have been ridiculous on a man of his size but she found it charming.

"Are you certain you were not seen?" she asked quietly as he walked toward the bed shedding his clothing with each step.

"Very certain." He yanked off his boots and underdrawers and stood there proudly naked "Gardening? I would have thought you did not need to read such a book."

"There are always new things to learn although this is clearly written for beginners. Yet, despite that, I have found several interesting tips to make use of. Odd for my uncle to have spent coin on it as he is no beginner, either." She glanced at the proud proof of his intentions and then rolled her eyes. "You have no modesty at all, do you?"

"Not a drop," he said cheerfully as he climbed into bed beside her, turned on his side, and studied her nightdress. "You, however, may have too much."

Before she could protest that assessment, Bened was removing her nightdress. Primrose had barely a minute to be embarrassed by her nudity and then he pulled her into his arms. The moment their flesh touched, she no longer cared about having no clothes on. . . .

Books by Hannah Howell

THE MURRAYS

Highland Destiny
Highland Honor
Highland Promise
Highland Vow
Highland Knight
Highland Bride
Highland Angel
Highland Groom
Highland Warrior
Highland Conqueror
Highland Champion
Highland Lover
Highland Barbarian
Highland Savage
Highland Wolf
Highland Sinner
Highland Protector
Highland Avenger
Highland Master
Highland Guard

THE WHERLOCKES

If He's Wicked
If He's Sinful
If He's Wild
If He's Dangerous
If He's Tempted
If He's Daring
If He's Noble

VAMPIRE ROMANCE

Highland Vampire
The Eternal Highlander
My Immortal Highlander
Highland Thirst
Nature of the Beast
Yours for Eternity
Highland Hunger
Born to Bite

STAND-ALONE NOVELS

Only for You
My Valiant Knight
Unconquered
Wild Roses
A Taste of Fire
A Stockingful of Joy
Highland Hearts
Reckless
Conqueror's Kiss
Beauty and the Beast
Highland Wedding

Silver Flame
Highland Fire
Highland Captive
My Lady Captor
Wild Conquest
Kentucky Bride
Compromised Hearts
Stolen Ecstasy
Highland Hero
His Bonnie Bride

Published by Kensington Publishing Corporation

Chapter One

Spring, Western England, 1791

"*Sir* Bened Vaughn." Bened grinned, savoring the sound of the words. "May I assist you, *Sir* Bened? Would you like some wine, *Sir Bened?*" He laughed softly. "That will never grow old."

Bened rode deeper into the woods, deciding to take the shortest route to the village where he planned to rest for the night. If he had known that all he had to do was take a bullet for some spoiled, inept heir to a title to get his own honors, he would have been leaping in front of the fools years ago. Even the few times he had been hired to watch over some young gentry man, he had never considered the possibility that he could end up with more than just a very decent wage for the work. Then again, the previous gentry lads he had watched over had not been as dim-witted or reckless as this last one. Young Lord Percival Dunstan, an earl's only heir, should never be allowed to leave his ancestral lands again.

Over the last few years of doing such work, he had also become a very wealthy man, or wealthy enough in his eyes and most of his family's. Now, with this latest largesse, he could settle somewhere, stop making a living chasing foolish young gentlemen around and trying to keep them alive. It would please his mother beyond words. After he took that bullet, a wound that had kept him bedridden for a few weeks, she had decried his choice of work loudly and consistently.

"Smudge! Where are you, you obstinate beastie?"

Bened reined to a halt and stared in the direction of that angry feminine voice. The accent was definitely that of a well-born woman. What was some gentry lass doing deep in the forest with night coming on fast? Aside from making a lot of noise, he thought, as he heard a loud thrashing around in bushes followed by a faintly shocking litany of curses that would make a stable boy proud.

He sensed no threat so patiently waited for whoever was stomping through the woods calling for a horse, the same speckled gray mare he could see calmly grazing several yards away to his left. When a small, bedraggled woman stumbled out of the shadows of the thick trees, Bened actually caught his breath, surprised by the sight of her as well as his reaction. His heartbeat picked up its pace. Something it had never done at the sight of a woman. Certainly not for one like her. She was not the type of woman who usually caught his interest or attention.

She was short, delicate of build, yet shapely in a way that would please any man. Her hair was a mass of long, thick blond curls now cluttered with twigs and leaves. A look of angry frustration did nothing to dim the innocent beauty of her heart-shaped face. The flush of anger coloring her cheeks actually looked good on her fair skin. She was the perfect example of a gentle-bred Englishwoman except for the pistol she held aimed at his heart.

The pistol looked too big for her small, long-fingered hand but that hand did not tremble. Bened still experienced no sense of a true threat from her; saw no dangerous enemy before him. He supposed it made sense for the woman to have a pistol while running around in the woods and to point it at some stranger she met. It was, in truth, the only indication that she had recognized the precarious position she was in. He frowned at how fiercely she squinted at him and realized her eyesight might not be very keen.

"Do you intend to use that?" he asked as he very carefully dismounted.

"Do not move."

"I mean you no harm, m'lady."

"How do you know I am a lady?"

Bened bit back a smile as she growled softly and rolled her eyes.

"That was not what I meant to say," she grumbled. "I meant how did you know who I am?"

"I do not. I but assumed your rank because of how you speak and the fine quality of your clothing. I am Sir Bened Vaughn." He stepped closer to her.

"You are moving again."

"I know." He took one swift, large step and snatched the pistol from her hand.

"I told you to stop moving!"

"And I told you that I mean you no harm but I do prefer not having a pistol pointed at me."

"Fine. I quite understand that but I need you to hold still. Considering your size, I suspect you have large, booted feet and I have lost my spectacles around here somewhere. I would rather you did not find them by stomping on them."

Suppressing a sigh, Bened stepped even closer, ignoring how she tensed, plucked the spectacles caught in the button loop of her coat, and gently put them on her. They made her dark blue eyes look even bigger. She was adorable, he thought, as she blushed and arranged her spectacles as she obviously preferred on her small straight nose. Adorable did not usually stir his interest but it appeared to be making an exception for her.

"Thank you for finding them," she said in a prim voice. "Where were they?"

"Caught in the button loop on your coat."

"Oh." She blushed even more. "That is somewhat humiliating." She held out her hand. "I am the Honorable Primrose Anabelle Matilda Dunmore Wootten of Willow Hill." She grimaced. "Long name, I know. Had to honor the paternal aunties."

"Ah." Bened nodded. "Understood. 'Tis why I was saddled with a second name as well—Madawg."

"Ma-what?"

"Mah-dawg. My maternal uncle's name. My brothers were given it as well."

"How many brothers do you have?"

"Six. I think my parents hoped the man would feel honored enough to will his cottage and land to one of us but, five years ago, even though the man was fifty, he had the bad manners to wed a much younger lass and now has three sons of his own."

"Oh." Primrose saw him grin and had to smile. "How very rude of him. Well, a pleasure to meet and speak with you, Sir Bened, but I must be on my way. As soon as I can find my horse," she added in a soft mutter.

"That horse over there?" Bened pointed toward the dappled gray and almost laughed at the way she blushed and scowled in the direction of the animal, then muttered a few curses he pretended not to hear.

"More humiliation," she grumbled as she walked toward her horse.

By the time she reached her horse, intensely aware of the big man walking by her side, Primrose began to try to think of the best way to leave. This man had been very helpful so she did not wish to offend him in any way. Since he made no move to leave, she then began to worry that she may have stumbled into some more trouble. There had been a lot of it on her journey, much more than she would have considered normal and it had begun to rouse her suspicions. Yet, even as she thought that, she could muster no fear, felt no threat from him at all.

He was a big man, something that did stir a trickle of alarm, but it was easily shrugged aside since it was the only thing about him that did. He was quiet, even moved quietly, and being near him calmed her. His features were somewhat harsh, but he was handsome despite that. His silvery blue eyes encircled by thick black lashes were spellbinding. Primrose noted that his clothing was not the height of fashion but it was well made, the cloth of very good quality, and the fit well tailored. Those eyes and that deep, smooth voice with the faintly musical lilt of Wales in it were his best features, she decided. Neither, however, explained why she was drawn to him, comfortable around him, and intrigued by him. She decided that was a puzzle best saved for solving later.

"May I have my pistol back?" she asked, silently cursing her own stupidity for letting him get hold of it.

Bened studied the pistol he still held and then looked at her. "Why? And exactly why are you riding about the forest all alone?"

"I am in search of my brother. He needs to know that our father has died." She stuck out her hand, sighed with relief when he placed the pistol in it, and carefully put it back into her coat pocket.

"You could not just send a message to him?"

"I did but never got a reply. He loved Papa and would never have missed his funeral. Yet, he did and that was when I decided to go after him. He was not where he said he would be, so I suspect he does not know about our father's death yet. His friends said he had abruptly left their house with no true explanation why and that they have heard nothing from him since then."

"How do you know where to look for him then?"

"Simeon is the sort of man people notice." She frowned when he shook his head. "What?"

"That is a poor way to track a person down."

"It has been working well enough thus far."

"But it will fail if your brother takes even one short route where no one sees him."

"Then I will need to find the trail left by his horse."

"You know how to look for that?"

"I do and Simeon's horse leaves a very distinct trail."

"Distinct in what way? An odd gait?" Bened could see that she was reluctant to tell him and wondered why.

"Simeon can be whimsical and he had his horse shod with shoes that have stars on them. So his trail shows stars in it." She nodded at his look of astonishment. "I know. I told him it was such things as that which made people think him a lack-witted dandy. He knows that and finds it amusing. Papa was much the same."

Bened did not like to think that a young woman with poor eyesight who set out alone to hunt her brother down was the most sensible one in the family. "You cannot continue riding about the countryside alone looking for people who may have seen your brother or for a trail of stars in the dust."

When the man put it just that way, it did sound idiotic, which annoyed her. Primrose searched for a mature, sensible way to defend her actions. It was, by all the rules of society, indefensible. No lady of good birth should ride about England unaccompanied, unchaperoned. The need to find Simeon and to flee her aunt's many plots had allowed her to ignore all that. Facing this big, calm man who expected her to explain herself, it was suddenly not so simple.

"Someone had to find Simeon. He is needed back at Willow Hill. Badly needed." She turned to her horse, intending to mount and ride away before he could press her for more answers.

"Then we will find him."

"We?"

Primrose watched him smoothly mount his large black gelding. A part of her wanted to thank him for offering to come with her, repeatedly and loudly, but she resisted the urge. This concerned her family and her future. It was not right to place her burdens on the shoulders of a complete stranger, no matter how broad those shoulders were.

"Yes," he said, looking down at her with those calm silvery eyes and then nodding toward her horse. "Mount up, m'lady, and we shall hunt down that brother of yours."

"This is not your trouble, Sir Bened," she said, even as she mounted her horse. "This is all part of a familial contretemps and you must not feel compelled to get tangled up in it just because you have a chivalrous nature." She frowned at him when he laughed.

"Chivalrous, am I? That opinion would amuse my kin. Nay, m'lady, I am but a man who has too long worked at watching over others. You need watching over whether you wish to admit to it or not. I am also very, very good at following a trail and need no stars in the dirt to do it." He leaned toward her to add quietly, "I am also very good at knowing when danger and an enemy draw near. I have a strong feeling that you may be in need of those skills, m'lady."

"I truly want to say I do not need them but"—Primrose sighed—"it would be a lie, I think. I have not much enjoyed traveling about alone, either. 'Tis not accepted anywhere. And, I am not Lady Primrose, you know. Just an honorable, so you do not need to keep saying *m'lady*."

"Easier than saying *m'honorable*."

Primrose laughed. "True, so just say *miss*."

He nodded and took the lead as they rode back to the road. Bened would have preferred riding through the woods but he hoped he might find her brother's trail on the road. What he really needed was more information from her and a sedate ride along a road would make talking easier. Bened was certain there was more to her hunt for her brother than a need to tell him about their father's death.

"You say your brother is very noticeable," he said. "In what way?"

"He dresses in a way to catch the eye. Some would call him a fop or a dandy but he never goes quite that far. Simeon does love color though and lace. He is also, well, pretty. Women would notice him were he to dress in rags. He has a face that looks both softly beautiful and yet manly. Brilliant blue eyes and what some call guinea gold hair, which is long, thick, and has soft waves in it. I have watched perfectly sensible women go all foolish over him more times than I can count. If I did not love him so much, I would probably want to kill him for so outshining me."

Bened laughed. "I have kin like that."

"I do not understand why he left his friends as he did, not even telling them where he was going."

"One does not always tell one's friends everything. Mayhap it concerned a woman."

"It could be as simple as that yet he would have told them enough so that they would have guessed why he was being so reticent. They have all known each other since the cradle, are as close as any brothers could be. They were almost worried by the time I left them for they had begun to realize how little they did know."

"And they just allowed you to ride away alone? None of them offered to be your guard? Just how old is your brother?"

"Nine and twenty. Six years older than me. Two of the friends he was visiting are wed and new fathers. They could not go off adventuring." Primrose sighed. "I did not even think to ask the others. They are good enough men to have thought of it after I left but it would have been too late by then. And, to be fair, I am not sure they even considered that when I said I had to find Simeon, that I actually intended to do so myself."

Bened said nothing but decided Primrose had been surrounded by people who had had little to do with the darker, harsher realities of life. It was often a problem when dealing with the gentry, especially those who spent much of their lives in the country. He studied Primrose as she rode beside him with an admirable skill. He suspected she was naïve but not blindingly so. It was something he was counting on because using his skill to keep her calm and unafraid could not continue indefinitely. It was good now, allowing him to gain information and some trust, but could quickly exhaust him. That would hinder his ability to hunt down her brother, something he believed was imperative.

It was growing dark by the time they reached the village where he had planned to stop for the night. Bened was relieved to find there were still two bed-chambers available, side by side, which would help him keep Primrose safe during the night. After washing the travel dust off, he went down the stairs and ordered them a meal as well as a private parlor.

Taking a seat at the table in the private room, Bened sipped at his ale and thought about what he was doing. He realized he was acting just as he did with the lordlings he had watched over for the last few years. That might prove to be the wrong way to behave with a baron's daughter. A woman who went out on her own to hunt down her brother undoubtedly had a very independent nature. Such a woman would object to him trying to lead her about.

He thought on what little she had told him and frowned. There was something she was hiding from him. Bened was certain of it. Primrose was hunting her brother for more reasons than to inform him that their father had died. That was not enough cause for a gently bred female to set out on a journey on her own. Bened was determined to find out exactly what had made her so desperate. Every instinct he depended upon was telling him that she was in trouble and he needed all the information he could get from her if he was to protect her adequately. It surprised him a little when he realized just how determined he was to do that.

Primrose finished brushing the travel dust from her gown, hung it up, and dug a clean one out of her bag. She pushed aside a pang of disappointment over the fact that she had brought only a few serviceable gowns. The strange urge to look nice for Sir Bened was unexpected. She was not even sure she could trust him. He could be the chivalrous man she had called him but she no longer so readily believed such people exist. Recent events had shown her that her judgment of people was not as sound as she had once believed.

She had certainly misjudged her aunt and uncle. When her father had generously allowed them to move into the dower house when her uncle had lost his money through bad investments, she had soon deemed them both to be foolish, rude, and somewhat mean-spirited. Having had as little as possible to do with them from then on, she had not altered her opinion of them by much. Then her father had died and her aunt and uncle had moved into the manor to, as they told anyone who would listen, care for young Primrose until her errant brother returned. She had quickly decided that her aunt was still rude and mean-spirited but that the woman's foolishness was mostly an act. Augusta was cunning, coldhearted, and dangerous. Although she had no proof of it, Primrose was certain Augusta had killed her father.

The pain of that loss struck her hard and Primrose nearly collapsed beneath the smothering waves of grief roiling inside her. Her father had been six and fifty years of age when he had suffered his fatal heart seizure. It was not something that should should have raised any questions. Then her brother had not returned home, not even for the burial, and Primrose had begun to grow suspicious. The air of contentment, even smug victory, Aunt Augusta had assumed grew more noticeable as the woman took over more and more of the running of the manor. She had pushed aside all Primrose's attempts to become the lady of the manor as was her right, and not always with tact or even subtlety. It was all just another good reason to find Simeon as soon as possible.

She had hesitated even then for she had been afraid of setting out on her own. It had quickly become clear that she had no one she could really trust, no one who could go against Augusta anyway. Only her father's man of business could still be trusted but she knew he would have done all he could to stop her. Every other person with any power who had been close to her father or worked with him had fallen away over the last year. That had been strange but she had always assumed it had just been because they had all been getting older and traveled less. Now she began to think her aunt had been slowly but surely isolating them. Why the woman would do such a thing was the question, and none of the answers Primrose came up with were good ones.

Shaking off her grief and pulling free of her meandering thoughts, Primrose quickly braided her hair and secured it with a ribbon. Bened had said he would get them a meal and a private parlor and she had already left him waiting on her for too long. Her stomach rumbled to remind her of how long it had been since she had eaten so she hurried out of the room.

With every step she took, Primrose plotted out what she would say to the man. She needed to thank him for his help and then send him on his way without offering any offense. The man had been all that was kind, assisting her when she needed it and clearly prepared to keep doing so. It was tempting to let him continue as she had no wish to keep traveling around alone searching for her brother, an adventure fraught with danger. She would not drag Sir Bened into the middle of it and put him in danger as well. There was also the fact that he was really a stranger to her and every female was told from a very young age that she should beware of any strange men. Before she had a chance to even ask the maid where Bened was, the young woman waved Primrose to the battered door from near the foot of the stairs.

The scent of a rich stew and warm bread scattered her thoughts as she entered the private parlor. Primrose clapped a hand over her stomach when it roared its approval. Sir Bened stood up, pulled out a chair for her, and Primrose was quick to sit down. The maid hurried in with more stew and bread and Primrose silently cursed when her stomach rumbled again. She ordered mulled cider for her drink and turned her full attention on her meal.

"This is very good," she said when they were alone again after the maid brought her cider. "Thank you."

"You are welcome." He pushed aside his empty bowl and sipped his ale. "'Tis but mutton stew."

"True, but it is hot, filling, and done very well."

"What are your plans for the morrow? Do you have a destination set?"

Primrose stuffed some stew in her mouth to smother the curse she wanted to spit out. The man was evidently going to ask her every question she had hoped he would not ask. She had to find her brother but truly had no plan beyond that. Even she knew that would sound foolish and reckless.

It was certainly the latter but desperation drove her. Since she did not want to tell him the cause of that desperation, she feared he would think her a witless fool.

"I am following the sightings of my brother," she finally said.

Bened sat back in his chair and studied her as he sipped his ale. He had not known her long at all but, despite the way they had met and what she was doing, he had talked with her enough to know she was not lacking in wits. Just following a trail marked by people who had caught sight of her brother, however, was an idiotic plan. The way she was avoiding meeting his gaze told him she was hiding something. He suspected it was all the true reasons she was riding around the countryside on her own in a desperate attempt to find her sibling.

For a moment he wondered if he should even push for the full truth, getting himself more involved than he was now. His family had stumbled into a lot of trouble and danger in the past few years, mostly when trying to help someone else. This business with Miss Primrose carried the same feel. She hid it well but he could sense her desperation, her worry and fear. The part of him that reacted to such emotions was reaching out to her to calm and soothe. If he did stay with her, offer her his help, he was going to have to learn to rein it in or he would exhaust himself before they ever found her brother.

He watched her nervously glance his way as she helped herself to some bread, spreading a thick layer of butter on it, and he inwardly sighed. There was no chance he would be able to let her ride off alone. There were too many dangers out there for a woman alone, especially a pretty little one like her. Instinct told him he was about to step into a tangled mess but it also told him he would never rest easy again if he turned his back on her and left her alone.

"You are not doing this simply because your brother did not attend your father's funeral."

Primrose tried to keep her expression calm with a hint of confusion. "I do not know what you mean."

Bened leaned forward, set his tankard down, and crossed his arms on the table, determined to get the full truth from her before they went one step further. "You are not some witless twit of a lady so cease acting like one."

"Thank you, I think."

"You are not one to leave hearth and home, ride out completely alone, and search the whole country for your brother in some blind, confused way."

"I love my brother and am worried about him."

"I am certain of that. Just as I am certain you know full well how dangerous it is to do as you have been doing. There is good reason women do not travel alone. So, tell me, what drove you from your home? What has truly set you on the road alone to seek out your brother?"

Chapter Two

Primrose stared at the man who watched her closely with those sharp, silvery blue eyes and the lies she was composing in her head died a swift death. He would not believe any of them. She would just embarrass herself by even trying to divert him with lies. Somehow she had given herself away and revealed her desperate need to find Simeon.

The question was, could she trust him with the truth? Perhaps he was working for her aunt. Even as those thoughts ran through her mind, she discarded them. Her judgment of people may have failed now and then, but the feeling she had was that Sir Bened Vaughn was just what he seemed to be—an honest, decent man who only wanted to help her.

"Staying at Willow Hill without my brother taking his place as the baron would not have been wise," she said.

"Ah." He nodded. "Someone stepped up to try to fill the gap left by your father's death and your brother's absence."

"Yes. My aunt and uncle. Papa had allowed them to move into the dower house when Uncle lost all his money. Bad investments he said, but I have since discovered it was from gambling losses. Papa found out shortly before he died and he was furious. He intended to cut my uncle off from any connection to him, Willow Hill, and Wootten funds if the man gambled again. I think Uncle Rufford was gambling again. Some items of value had gone missing and each report only angered my father more."

"And then your father died."

She slowly nodded as she fought to push aside her grief again. "And within a day my aunt and uncle were fully moved into the manor."

"Do you think they may have killed your father?"

"I think it but I cannot prove it. One moment they are all arguing, the next Papa is clutching his chest and falling to the floor. By the time I reached his side, he was already dead. He was not a young man but he had always been healthy and there had never been any sign that his heart was causing him any trouble." She clenched her hands into tight fists as she remembered that night, all the soothing words her aunt had spoken even as the woman's eyes had gleamed with triumph. "I checked my supplies of foxglove, both in my herb room and in my garden, and found none missing. I tried to examine what Papa had eaten or drunk but my aunt had already had it all disposed of."

"So they killed him because he was about to toss them out to fend for themselves."

It made her heart ache with sorrow to hear that truth stated so clearly. "I fear so. I should have seen it, should have been able to see something that warned me."

"Why? Your father did not and he knew his brother better than you did. Had many more years of experience with the world as well." He reached across the table to pat one of her clenched hands, her grief so deep and real he could almost feel it. "Few see the threat when it is family, even when it is family they have never much liked or trusted." Finding that he liked the feel of her small, soft hand beneath his a little too much, he removed his hand from hers and sat back in his chair again. "The closer the connection the less chance the victim will think that person can ever be a true threat to them."

"I still find it difficult to believe Uncle Rufford could be part of it but he must be. His own brother, one who was always willing to help him." She sighed and shook her head.

"Something that undoubtedly ate at the man. But, your aunt was not blood. She may be the strong one in that marriage."

Primrose thought about that for a moment and nodded. "I believe she is. I first thought her just a foolish, mean-spirited, vain woman but had recently begun to see that she is actually very cunning, greedy, and cold. But, as I said, I found no proof to use against her. 'Tis but a feeling I have, one that is a certainty that she had a hand in my father's death. It is possible she got some foxglove from some other garden or what she needed from some physician."

"You know your herbs and medicines."

"A hobby. And when you learn about what can

help heal, you also learn about what can also harm or kill."

"But she would have to know what to get and how to prepare it."

"Any of the many books I have would tell her that and everyone knows it is a poisonous plant, just not always how and why."

"Do you think she might try to be rid of you next, if only because you have the knowledge to guess what she has done?"

"You don't question any of this, do you?"

Bened shook his head. "Too many times a younger son or some other relative has grabbed both title and land through the all-convenient death of the heir. One of my cousins was caught up in such a mess about six years ago. She helped an earl whose uncle not only cuckolded him but wanted him gone so that he could lay claim to it all. He tried to kill the earl at least five times. The man even tried to murder the earl's newborn son but had to settle for making the man believe the boy was dead. Put the babe with a woman dying after birthing her own stillborn babe but my cousin was there and saw it, saving the child."

"Was that the Earl of Collinsmoor?"

"Aye. You have heard about that?"

"A tale like that travels far and wide. Every time he or his wife is seen, it gets repeated."

"That does not surprise me. An earl, an unfaithful wife, a missing heir, and a mad uncle." Bened grinned. "Who could resist chewing on such a meaty tale?"

Primrose could not resist returning his smile. "Very true. It also had a happy ending. The perfect touch." She cocked her head to the side as she grew serious again. "So, his uncle was mad?"

"What else would you call a man who cuckolds his own nephew, plots to be rid of his own great-nephew by leaving the babe to die with some poor woman in a tiny, poor cottage, and makes plans to wipe out his entire bloodline from the nephew to his own wife and daughters."

Shock froze her in place for a moment and then she lifted one unsteady hand to push back a lock of hair that had slipped free of her braid. "Insane indeed. I do not believe my relatives are insane, not even Aunt Augusta. Cold, sly, greedy, bitter, but not mad." Her eyes widened. "You think she means to kill Simeon?"

"And you do not?"

She had to think about that for a moment. Although her desperation to find Simeon had mostly been born of her aunt's plans for her, now she wondered if she had nursed a fear for his safety as well. If her aunt did not think Simeon could be controlled or ignored, she would see him as a threat. Augusta had been around enough to know her chances of getting Simeon under her thumb were very small indeed. It was now clear how Aunt Augusta dealt with anyone who threatened her comfort and her place in society.

She took a deep breath to steady herself and said, "None of this is your trouble, however."

Bened watched her straighten her spine so that her slender body was perfectly erect in her chair. She clasped her hands together in front of her. Her expression was one of a cool, composed courtesy but he could see the uncertainty shadowing her eyes and sensed the taut fear she struggled to control. She was brave but that would not help her fight the dangers she would encounter if he let her continue on alone. Such things required an experience and hardening that she simply did not have.

"It is now," he said.

"Why? You do not know me."

"True, but I know you need help. I also have some experience in hunting people down. I have been honed in battle and have a way of knowing when the enemy is near."

"What does that mean? What exactly is *having a way of knowing?* You have a skill for tracking people?" She had to admit that it would be a useful skill to have access to.

"Do you know whom the Earl of Collinsmoor married?" Bened decided he might as well speak the truth now rather than have her discover it later and run from him at just the time she needed him close at hand the most.

"The woman who found his son, Chloe Wherlocke. Oh. *She* is your cousin? They say some odd and, perhaps, unkind things about her and the Wherlockes, I am sorry to say. But, you said your name was Vaughn."

"Two branches of the same tree, the roots of which go back to the first Duke of Elderwood, maybe even further. I suspect that talk you mentioned is of the many eccentricities in the family, perhaps even whispers of witchcraft." He shrugged. "Old talk. At least it remains but gossip now and not nearly as dangerous as it used to be."

"Are you about to tell me that it is all true?" Primrose supposed she ought to be alarmed but she found herself fascinated, almost eager to have some of the rumors she had greedily listened to confirmed.

"Not sure what you have heard about us, but, aye, we could rightfully be called an eccentric lot. We are *not* witches, however, or tools of Satan, or wizards, or whatever else some call us. We are gifted." Seeing only curiosity in her expression, he felt something inside him relax and continued. "Nearly every one of us can do something very unique, something most others can never do. Unfortunately, many find such gifts frightening, even a sign of evil."

"Is your gift frightening?"

"Nay. I but have a gift for sensing the enemy, some approaching danger, and can track down near anything or anyone." He decided not to mention his ability to calm people as that could be something she might not so easily accept. "I *will* find your brother, although, from what you have told me, it does not appear that he is trying to hide."

Primrose laughed. "True, but, if, and I do not have any proof to say anything, but if my aunt is thinking to be rid of the heir and somehow Simeon catches wind of it, he will hide. He will do it very well, too. As I told you, some people think him a worthless fop, but he is actually quite brilliant. My mother once told me that she thinks all brilliant people are a little odd because their minds are so busy. She saw my father's love of fine clothes and occasional foolishness as the way he escaped all those deep thoughts." She smiled. "I cannot say I believe that, yet both Simeon and Papa could be foolish one moment and then fall into a long discussion of something so deep and complicated it was beyond understanding. At times you would even have to remind them that they needed to eat a meal."

Bened nodded. "I have some kin who are much the same."

The hairs on the back of his neck rose and Bened tensed. He could hear no one approaching but he knew someone who meant them ill was near at hand. As he abruptly stood up, he patted the pocket of his coat, pleased that he had decided to keep his pistol with him.

"What is wrong?" Primrose asked, fighting the fear that threatened to swamp her as his expression darkened.

"Not sure. Stay right here," he ordered, and left.

She stood up and then sat right back down. The urge to rush after him was surprisingly strong but she knew it would be best to do as he had commanded no matter how much being ordered around annoyed her. She had no skill for fighting or dealing with any sort of real danger. All she could do if she insisted on being with him wherever he had run off to would be to impede him in whatever he had gone to do.

Drumming her fingers on the table, she wished she knew what was happening. He had told her he had a gift for sensing an enemy. Although she was not sure she believed in such gifts, there was always the possibility they existed. Her father had been fond of saying anything was possible. The question that needed answering was had he sensed his enemies or hers? And just who were her enemies? Next time she would ask a few questions before he ran off.

A moment later she realized that she had accepted his presence in her search for Simeon. It annoyed her to have to admit that she needed a man to help her but she was neither too proud nor too stubborn to accept the facts. Her reputation might be utterly ruined if it was discovered that she had traveled around with a man who was not related to her, but traveling alone could as well plus cost her a great deal more. She had already seen that in the looks men had given her, heard it in the crudeness of comments directed at her. Even if Bened did not possess the skills he claimed, he could prove to be a fine shield against such harassment. She only needed to recall the last time she had stopped at an inn to admit that she needed one. Primrose just hoped her new shield did not get badly dented by whatever or whomever he had just charged off to confront.

Bened cursed as he stared at the empty stalls that had once held his and Primrose's horses. It was bad enough her horse had been taken while under his watch but to lose his own was embarrassing. He then turned to stare at the cowering stableboy. The youth did not look as if he had put up any fight at all while someone had taken the animals.

"Where are our horses?" he demanded.

"They been taken back by the ones ye stole them from," the boy replied, the tremor in his voice stealing some of the bravado he was attempting to display.

"Is that what they told you?"

The youth nodded. "Said they were taking them back to the lady what owns them."

"And how much did they pay you to believe that lie so readily?" The way the youth clapped a hand over a pocket in his stained trousers gave Bened the answer he needed. "Those horses were not stolen but now they have been. Be grateful I am not in the mood to watch you hang for helping them, boyo. Now saddle me a horse so I can go and get my horse and her ladyship's horse back." As the white-faced boy hurried to do as asked, Bened added, "And if anyone tells you such a tale again, you might consider fetching a magistrate to sort it out first instead of just taking a few coins and handing over two fine horses. You might also pause to consider the fact that few horse thieves are young well-bred ladies, nor do they stable their stolen horses at a busy inn and then go pay for a room and a meal."

As Bened headed out he studied the trail left by the horses. Three men had taken them and were headed back the way he and Primrose had come. It appeared the ones chasing her had outrun her or, worse, had been waiting here for they had figured out where she was going. He doubted Primrose knew she was being chased but he had suspected it, just as he suspected there were still a few things she was not telling him.

Without his gift, he would never have found the men for the sun had set, leaving only faint moon-light to reveal the trail left. Fortunately, that trail appeared as clear as a signpost to him. Within an hour he had found the men. They sat around a small fire just off the road, thinking the trees hid them well enough. Bened slipped off his horse, secured it, and crept up behind the men. It surprised him that they had not gone very far but then realized many others would stop when it grew dark too.

Quietly he untethered the horses he had come after so that he would be able to flee quickly with them if he had to. Whoever had hired these men and set them on Primrose's trail had wasted their money. They were crude lackwits. Did they truly believe no one would set out after them for the theft of two finely bred horses? Not only had they left a clear trail but they had not even gone very far before stopping, then lighting a small fire to mark where they were for anyone who did choose to chase them down. The fools were not even keeping a close watch on their valuable prizes.

"I be thinking we should have gone farther down the road," grumbled the biggest of the three men.

"No one's even going to know the horses are gone 'til the mornin', Will." The man who spoke scratched under his ragged beard. "That lad will nay be warning anyone."

"Not sure I trust that old bitch we just risked a hanging for either."

"She is paying us well."

"True, but I do not much trust her, neither," said the thin man with the long, visibly filthy blond hair.

"No need to, Ned," said the bearded man. "Three of us against her and one servant. And we got the horses, so the lass and that big feller she has with her now will be easier for the old crone to catch."

Bened, fearing that one of the men might glance his way, moved to hide, using the horses as his shield. He was eager to leave but wanted to hear what the men had to say. Information was often the best defense and Bened was certain the old crone the men did not trust was Miss Primrose's aunt. He was also sure that little Miss Primrose Wootten was still holding on to a few secrets.

He briefly considered hurrying right back to the inn to ask her a few tough questions but decided that could wait just a little while longer. The opportunity to find out who was pursuing her was too good to pass up even though he suspected exactly who it was. Over the past few years he had come to the conclusion that some of an heir's deadliest foes slithered out of his own bloodline.

"Might be best to just send her word about our success," suggested Will.

"Then how do we get paid?" asked Ned.

"By not being cowards and facing the bitch. She be just an old woman, fools."

"She is nay that old and in fine shape," said Will. "She is also mean as a badger, sly, and cold, Mac. Do not forget she is paying us to stop a sister from finding her own brother and is chasing that boy down like he is a rabid cur what needs shooting. I be thinking we have been dragged into some family battle and that is always bad. Real bad."

Mac should listen to Will, Bened thought. Stepping into the middle of a family battle, especially one over money and land, was the action of a reckless fool. Bened just wished he could avoid it but a pair of big dark blue eyes were tethering him to this trouble. At least he was on the right side of the fight.

Cautiously, he began to move the horses away from the campsite. His horse, Mercury, had no saddle, nor did Smudge, but he did not need one. Once he gathered up the horses from the stables, he could ride Mercury and lead the others.

He reached the patiently grazing horse from the stables, secured the three horses together so that they would remain that way during his ride back to the inn, and then crept back to the campsite. While keeping a close watch on the three men, still arguing, for any sign that they sensed his presence, Bened untethered their horses. He walked back toward where his horses waited, paused and picked up three stones, then turned to look at the men's horses. Offering up a silent apology to the animals, he hit each one in the rear flank with a stone then turned and ran for his horses, the sounds of chaos caused by three men trying to avoid being trampled and yet gather up their panicked horses following him.

Leaping onto Mercury's back, he headed back to the inn, moving as fast as he dared while trying to keep the three mounts close together. The stable-boy still looked chastened and afraid when he led the horses into the stables. Although Bened did not think the men would risk coming after him all the way to the inn, he decided to stand guard in the stables for about an hour. He then proceeded to give the boy a few lessons in the harsh realities of life. Once certain no one was coming after him and assured the boy would let him know if those men came sniffing round again, Bened left the boy with his ears probably still stinging from the his lecture and headed into the inn. As he moved toward the parlor, he planned what and how much he should tell Primrose.

"Are you really thinking of going to see that bitch?" Will asked Mac as they all secured their saddles on their horses.

"Why not? Need to tell her that we failed and convince her to let us try again."

"Well, I am nay going."

"Me neither," said Ned.

Mac looked at both his companions in shock and then his mouth twisted in an expression of disgust. "Are you really that afraid of an old woman?"

"Not her exactly," said Ned, "but of what she might have done to us because we failed."

Mac mounted his horse and glared at his men. "Cowards."

"I think you should consider nay facing her with bad news."

"Damn me, Will, when did you become such a wretched coward you tremble in your boots over facing some old lady?"

Will shook his head. "Not a coward. She gives me a real bad feeling, Mac. Real bad. If you have to go, that be your choice, but watch your back. Watch it close. Me and Ned will wait for you at the Cock and Thistle."

Still shaking his head, Will rode off. By the time he reached the agreed upon meeting place, he found himself wishing he had stayed with his friends. He became all too aware of how deserted the meeting place was. No one would be near at hand to see or hear anything. He was utterly alone. Slowly dismounting when the carriage arrived, Mac fought back a sudden urge to leave and go share an ale with Will and Ned.

"You failed," the woman said as she paused in the doorway of the carriage before stepping down the steps lowered by her servant.

"That huge feller she has with her now found out we had taken the horses and took them back. Everything else went as it should. I do not know how he even discovered the horses were gone before morning. We should have had at least until the sun came up. But we will be ready for him next time."

"There does not appear to be a *we* any longer. Just a *you*."

"My men are waiting for me to join them. No need of us all riding here."

"This *huge feller*," she said as she finally left her carriage and stepped closer, "who is he?"

Mac shook his head. "No idea, m'lady. He just appeared at her side. Lad at the stables said he was called Sir Bened Vaughn."

She frowned. "I do not recognize the name yet something about it nudges a memory. What matters now is that you failed. I do not accept failure, sir."

When a hand grabbed his hair from behind and a knife blade was pressed to his throat, Mac cursed himself for scorning Will's and Ned's unease. The woman studied him as if he were some strange insect that had dared to intrude upon her stroll through her gardens. "Meet your replacement."

Even though he knew he had no chance at all of

escaping his fate, Mac fought but the brutal slice of the knife over his throat quickly stopped him. His last thought as he fell to the ground, his blood flowing out of him at a rate that would end him swiftly, was that he should have treated Will's concerns with more respect.

Augusta Wootten grimaced and looked over her cloak. The blood from the wretched fool lying dead on the ground had sprayed far and wide. She could see a few spots on her cloak. Tsking with disgust, she took off the cloak and tossed it over Mac's body before looking at her newest hirelings. The man cleaning off his blade and his two cold-eyed companions looked far more capable of doing what needed to be done.

"Get rid of that," she said, waving a hand in the direction of the body, "and then we will discuss what needs to be done next."

"Should we hunt down the other two?" asked the leader as he sheathed his knife.

"No. Who would they talk to about this without risking arrest and hanging? There are more important matters to attend to now. If we happen to stumble across those fools, we will deal with them then, but there is no need to waste time hunting for them."

Carl Mullins watched the woman walk back to her carriage and her waiting servant and then signaled his men to help him carry off the late Mac.

"I do not trust that woman," his man Tom said.

"Good," replied Carl, "then I know I can count on you to help us watch our backs."

Tom grunted. "She will see us done the same way as soon as she gets what she wants."

"This is why we will disappear before she gets her hands on the prize she seeks. All we need to do is keep a very close eye on when that is about to happen."

Chapter Three

The word Primrose had just read fled her mind before she even began to read the next one. It had surprised her to find four books set proudly on a shelf in the private parlor near the fireplace, but she suspected guests had left them behind. Books were valuable but not so much so to some people that they would turn around in their journey to retrieve one. At least none of them appeared to be from some village lending library for such places could not afford the loss.

Her mind was too full of questions and concerns about one Sir Bened Vaughn to stay fixed upon the words in a book, however. Why had he not yet returned? It was dark now. The man might be all he claimed but she could not believe even a highly skilled tracker could find anyone in the dark.

It hurt to think of Smudge being gone from her life, lost to her forever. The mare was a cherished gift from her father, who was also lost to her now. Primrose could remember the day her father had given her the horse. She had been so sad for over a month, ever since her first horse had broken its leg and needed to be killed, ever since she had been thrown from the animal and hurt her head. When she had come to, it had been to the loss of her beloved horse and trouble with her eyesight, a trouble that had lingered. Then her father had given her the dappled gray, laughing when she had squealed in surprise for she had not even known why he had brought her into the stables. She could still recall admitting that she had not seen the yearling, had seen only a smudged image of something that moved.

There had been the hint of tears in his laughter after that but she had pretended she did not hear it. Her father had brought in physician after physician to try to fix her eyesight. She had felt his grief over what had happened to her and done her best never to complain. Her sight might have never gotten better but it had not gotten any worse, either, and she had made herself find some comfort in that. The part of her that suddenly wanted her eyesight to be perfect again because of a broad-shouldered knight made her angry with herself. If Sir Bened was worthy of her good regard, her poor eyesight should be of no concern to him.

Annoyed by her wandering thoughts, she moved to get herself more of the mulled cider the maid had left on the hearth so it would keep warm by the fire. Primrose knew all of society would be shocked to find out she was traveling, unchaperoned, with a man she had only just met. Then again, the fact that she had been traveling alone would have shocked them too. Society, she thought, was far too easily shocked.

Those in society also had evil little minds, she decided as she retook her seat and sipped at her drink. Why else would they immediately assume that she had been soiled just because she traveled alone or with a man not related or married to her? Evidently they thought women too weak and foolish to behave with propriety unless under the strict watch of some relative. The fact that so few women were deeply insulted by that opinion puzzled her. And did men not get insulted by the implication that they were so weak and immoral they could not contain their lusts when alone with a woman?

"Does not matter how unfair, insulting, and ridiculous it all is," she muttered. "I was ruined the moment I rode away from Willow Hill alone. Having Sir Bened at my side only adds a few more stains on my tattered reputation. It is a small price to pay for finding Simeon and letting him know what sort of danger he is in."

She sat up straight when she heard the faint echo of the sound of greetings exchanged and the inn workers responding to a new arrival. Primrose prayed it was Sir Bened. Now that he might have returned safely she realized just how deeply afraid for him she had been.

The door opened. Bened stepped in and shut the door behind him. He watched her, smiling faintly but with a look of caution in his eyes. Primrose did not even consider the good or bad sides of what she did next as she stood up, ran over to him, and hugged him. To her shock it was not just relief she felt as her body was pressed up against his and his strong arms wrapped around her. Beneath the lightness of the relief she felt over seeing him return unharmed, a warmth spread through her. Innocent she might be, but Primrose was almost certain that heat was born of desire. Blushing, she stepped back.

"My apologies," she murmured when he grasped her hands to halt her retreat. "I fear I did naught but sit here and fret after you left to find the horse thieves and the relief I felt to see you return safely proved stronger than good sense and good manners."

"I did not hear myself complain," Bened said.

Primrose laughed but knew it was a shaky sound. She had not put on her gloves and she could feel the warmth of his large, lightly calloused hands spreading through her. It troubled her when she found it took a great deal of effort to move her gaze from his mouth and look into his beautiful eyes. The warmth of his gaze only increased the growing urge she had to throw herself back into his arms, to feel that warm, strong body pressed against her again. She nervously cleared her throat and tugged her hands free of his. The disappointment that came over her at the loss of the warmth of his touch worried her.

The man was a sore temptation, Primrose decided. It was odd for she was not one who was often tempted by a man, certainly not by just looking at him. Bened was not a man who drew the sighs of delight from many women as her brother Simeon did. There was no prettiness to Bened, just strength. He was handsome but not exceptionally so, his cheekbones a little too sharply defined, his skin good but a bit too swarthy to please some. His thick long lashes surrounding his beautiful eyes and, perhaps, his attractive mouth were the only hints of softness on his face.

His mouth was what kept drawing her gaze and she was not sure why. It was a little wide but that suited his square face. The bottom lip was fuller than the top, which she supposed was what gave it that tempting softness. Finally she found one reason she was attracted to that mouth. She wanted to taste it, to see if it was as warm and soft as its appearance promised it would be. And that was not an urge she should give in to, she told herself firmly.

"There is cider being kept warm on the hearth or I can order you something else. An ale?"

He should have grabbed the chance to kiss her when he had it, literally, in his hands, Bened thought. It would have been a mistake, though. Bened had seen the glint of interest in her eyes but knew she was not ready to give in to it yet. He was still no more than a kind man she did not really know, not even for one full day. Although he badly wanted to taste those full lips of hers, he knew he had to be patient. If nothing else, she was an innocent, well-bred young woman, most likely completely untouched.

"What I would truly like to have is some coffee but I doubt there will be some here," he said.

"Actually, they do have it." She smiled at his look of delight mixed with surprise. "There are several prominent gentlemen in the area and they learned to love the brew whilst at the university and when in London. They give the inn the beans and the tools to make the brew. All they ask is that the inn charge to cover the cost of any they brew for another guest and let them know when the sack of beans they give the inn reaches a certain level so they know to bring more or buy more. They come every Wednesday evening to talk and drink coffee. The innkeeper is actually considering buying his own and just selling the men a coffee when they come in but no longer having to worry about figuring out what to ask for each drink or if he can even list it on his offerings."

"Then I should like a coffee, please."

Primrose hurried off to get him one, eager to leave his presence for a little while. She needed to cage the urges he stirred inside her before she embarrassed herself by revealing it all to the man himself. He did not need to discover her weakness.

By the time she returned to the private parlor with the maid who brought them both a coffee, Primrose felt more at ease. She added a little cream to hers and sipped it as she waited for him to tell her what had happened. A chat with the people fixing the brew let her know that Bened had returned the horses but then everyone had become distracted by their own pleasure over how he had not demanded any punishment for the young lad who had allowed the horses to be taken.

"It was said that you retrieved the horses," she said, carefully looking him over. "It appears you did so with no harm to yourself, as well, which is a happy circumstance."

"I certainly think so." He smiled when she laughed for she had a pleasant laugh, one that was light and carefree, inviting others to join in. "They were idiots. Your aunt did not hire the best," he added, and silently cursed when she paled.

"You believe my aunt hired them?"

"I do. They spoke a lot of an old lady, a crone,

even though one said she was not so very old and kept herself in fine shape. They did not trust her."

"But they did not mention her by name?"

"Nay, they did not. Not whilst I was there to hear it. Yet, do you have any other woman you think would be trying to stop you from finding your brother?"

Primrose sighed. "None yet but I hate to think she would do this."

"I believe you told me she was cunning, mean, and cold."

"And very greedy, with a large opinion of her place in the world and society."

"Sounds like a woman who could easily believe she has a right to ensure that she remains in that high place she thinks she deserves."

"It does."

Bened could see how his news upset her and fought the urge to take her into his arms to comfort her and ease the pain he could read in her eyes. He knew what would happen if he held her in his arms again. The feel of her slim, pleasantly curved body pressed close to him was still all too clear in his mind. He wished he could have found a gentler way to tell her what he knew but then decided there really was no gentle way to tell anyone such news. Betrayal by a member of one's own family cut deep, even when one did not particularly care for that person. Too many of his own family had learned that lesson all too well.

"As you said, however, they mentioned no name. Did not even mention what she looked like."

"Now you try to comfort me. Do not. I need to accept this. It could easily be a matter of life and death. All that stands between her and becoming a baroness with a fortune and some fine lands is Simeon. I have to think of him and not my poor bruised feelings."

"You also stand in her way, do you not?"

"Not as much as my brother does."

"True, but I have the feeling she may have plans for you as well. She has to know how you care for your brother, would search for answers if anything happened to him. That is not something she would ignore. Do you think she knows you suspected her of killing your father?"

Primrose nodded, remembering all the tears and recriminations Augusta had heaped upon her when she had guessed that her *darling niece* could think such a cruel thing about her. There had also been a lot of sorrowful talk of how much she had loved Peter Wootten, what a kind, sweet man he had been, and how much she owed him. Primrose had not believed a word of that but it had worked to end her intense search for some proof that Augusta had killed him. Augusta would not leave that to chance, however. That explained the sudden appearance of Sir Edgar Benton, the man her aunt insisted she marry.

"She had guessed," Primrose finally answered.

"And claimed to be hurt and upset, crying about her undying love and gratitude for your father."

She blinked at him in surprise. "You have seen this play before?"

"It was easy to see. It means, however, that she knows you suspect her. She will not chance that her act worked. Did she do anything to try to get you out of her way before you left to hunt for your brother?"

"She tried to marry me off to a Sir Edgar Benton, a neighbor and longtime friend of my uncle."

"Ah, an old friend. And he was old, was he not?"

"Nearly two score years older than me. But that was not my biggest objection. Many women marry men much older than they are. The pool of unwed men who are considered acceptable through birth and fortune is a very small one. But this man is a horrid little fellow. I doubt there is a vice he does not indulge in. My uncle is about the only one for miles around who will even speak to him." She sighed, finished her coffee, and set her cup down. "I also discovered that he was covering some gambling debts of my uncle's. I was payment for that debt."

"Sold you off. And she thought that enough to keep you quiet?"

"Once wed to him, I would become as ostracized as he is. I would be going nowhere and seeing no one. I think he may also have caused the death of his last wife. Rumor is rife that he beat her to death even though he claimed she fell down the stairs. I did my best to avoid it happening but soon saw that my agreement might not be needed in the end. That is when I decided I really needed my brother to come home. Yet now I fear I would be sending him into the lion's den."

Bened finished his coffee, set his cup down, and leaned toward her. She sat in the chair opposite his and he could see how uneasy talk of her aunt's plans made her. This was the reason she had taken such drastic action. There was not even the risk to her reputation for her to consider for the marriage would destroy it anyway. Augusta Wootten was indeed a dangerous woman. Bened suspected the woman was as cunning as Primrose thought, so cunning that she was going to be difficult to stop.

"And there was no help from your uncle?"

"None. Augusta is the backbone in that marriage. He has none. He is a weak, foolish man. He gambles and makes no secret about his infidelities. Not once did he do any work while living off my father's largesse." She shook her head. "He is truly useless. If he knows what she plots he does not care, or might even approve, just doesn't have the spine to do it himself. The only regret he showed for the death of his brother was to whine about what a pittance was left to him in the will. A will even I have not read yet," she murmured, and frowned, then shook the concern of that aside. "There is nothing in him, if you know what I mean."

Bened nodded. "So you do not see him as the dangerous one."

"No. To be dangerous requires some work and that is one thing my uncle never does."

He reached across and patted one of the hands she had clenched into small fists on top of the table. He could tell by the brief look of surprise on her face that she had not realized she had done so. Bened was sure he had the full truth now, although he was not sure she fully believed the threat she faced. Whoever this Sir Edgar Benton was, he would have to be dealt with for Bened suspected the man would not quietly accept the loss of such a young, nubile bride.

"One thing I do have experience with is greedy, murderous relatives." He was pleased when she laughed for he knew it had been a rather harsh thing to say even as the words left his mouth.

"I truly do not wish to think of them that way but I must."

"You must. Even if something proves me wrong. There are, by my count, three people who would benefit if your brother was gone and at least one who would benefit if you were both gone."

"Three?"

"Your betrothed. He is out the payment of a debt and a young bride."

She slumped back in her seat and rubbed her hands over her face. "And it is my aunt who would benefit from both Simeon and me out of her way."

"Exactly."

"Do you think the men you took the horses back from are still going to be a problem?"

"I have no idea, but, if not them, someone else will be. Sadly, there are many more rogues to hire if she dismisses them for failing her."

"Oh, dear. Augusta hates being failed, detests any failure at all. It is the one thing that reveals that ugly side of her she usually keeps so well hidden. It enrages her. Once I saw that I began to wonder how my uncle had survived being married to her for so long. He fails her all the time."

"She needs him for some reason. Maybe to hold her place in that society that is so important to her. Maybe she likes the fact that she is the power in her marriage and knows she would not find that anywhere else."

"You clearly do not even consider the fact that she might actually love the fool, do you?"

"Not for a moment but I could be wrong. Yet I find it difficult to believe a woman who does what I think she is doing is capable of such an emotion."

Suddenly Primrose felt exhausted. It was all too much. The worry she had suffered while he had been chasing horse thieves combined with the knowledge about her aunt bled all her strength away. It was weak and cowardly but she had no wish to talk of it, or even think of it anymore for now. She forced herself to her feet and brushed down her skirts.

"I thank you for getting Smudge back. I would have been heartbroken to have lost her. I am also very glad you were able to do so without injury. And now, I believe I will retire. Suddenly I am very tired despite the brew I just drank. Good sleep, Sir Bened."

"Good sleep, Miss Primrose."

Bened watched her leave and sighed. He hated the fact that the hard news he had had to deliver had crushed her so. He knew that was part of the exhaustion she claimed. It bruised the spirit to learn your family wanted to hurt you, would betray you that deeply and completely.

Deciding he needed to clean up and get some rest himself, he ordered a bath and went to his room. As he passed the door to Primrose's bed-chamber, he heard a sound that made him pause and his hand was on the door latch before he could stop himself. She was crying. He forced his hand away from the latch. She had a right but he did not have the right to intrude. He also knew that, if he went in the room, his plan to comfort her could all too easily turn into so much more.

Shaking his head and wishing he could strangle Augusta Wootten, he went to his room. The hot bath brought to him calmed him and slowly his need to rush to Primrose's side faded in strength. It was too soon to push himself into her life in that way.

There was also the fact that Primrose was not a woman you bedded and walked away from. Bened knew that before he drew too close and gave in to the desire that she could stir in his blood, he had to make up his mind about just what he wanted from her aside from a long night of lovemaking. The Honorable Primrose Wootten was a woman you did not play with. She was well bred, rich, and far above his touch for a start, despite his new honors. If he took her as his lover, he would have to take her as his wife. That was not something a man did without a great deal of thought. Bened could only hope his attraction to her gave him the luxury of having time for such deep thinking.

Primrose slowly got off the bed where she had collapsed upon entering the room only to indulge in a long weep. She washed her face and then proceeded to get ready for bed. There was nothing she could do to change her circumstances. Or her family. In truth, the only real family she had left was Simeon. He was all she should give any thought to. Her aunt and her greed could not be allowed to hurt him.

Crawling back into bed, she found herself thinking

of Sir Bened and softly cursed. Despite her best intentions there was obviously one distraction she could not shake free of. She desired the man and desire was obviously a tenacious beast that would not be ignored. The only thing she needed to consider was whether or not she would do anything about it.

If she did she would destroy her reputation. Then again, she mused, her reputation was already at great risk and would be destroyed anyway if word got out that her aunt and uncle had betrothed her to Sir Edgar Benton. She could cling tightly to what scraps she had, thus allowing her to deny any accusations with complete honesty, or she could accept her ruin and do what she wanted. It was very tempting to do the latter but she knew she had to resist that temptation until she had thought the whole matter through very carefully.

There was always the chance that news of the crimes of her aunt and uncle would shroud her own and allow her to continue as she had before her father's death. Such a circumstance depended far too much on luck and the whims of society. What a baron's daughter had done or was suspected of having done was of more import to gossips than what crimes her aunt and uncle had committed. Society would consider her taking a lover as gossip far more tempting to repeat and salivate over than the fact that her aunt and uncle were guilty of murder and had plotted to murder the baron's heir and daughter, or even to marry her off to someone all of society had turned their back on simply to pay off her uncle's gambling debts.

She closed her eyes and sighed. There were too many roads to turn down. She needed to make up a list of the benefits and consequences and go from there. It might be wise to remind herself more often of just how little she knew of Sir Bened and how short their acquaintance had been. The fact that she trusted him, liked him, felt as if she had known him forever, was just her lonely heart playing tricks on her. It was not possible after barely one full day of acquaintance.

"But I do know him," she whispered, and opened her eyes to look at the door. "I know it is foolish after so short an acquaintance but I *know* him."

Try as hard as she might she could find no disagreement with that statement in heart or mind. Every instinct she had said he was a good man, one she could trust, and that her desire for him was not some trick brought on by a need to have someone strong to lean on. She knew she was not so weak that a man's offer of help would make her ready to give up her much-prized chastity.

Flopping onto her back, she stared up at the ceiling. Having that coffee had probably been a mistake. Now her mind was far too busy for her to sleep. Learning that part of your own family wanted you dead did not help either.

Was she leading Augusta to Simeon? Was that why the woman was following her and trying to make it so she could not reach her brother? Did the woman already know how to find Simeon or have some other plan she and Sir Bened had not yet uncovered? The thought that her aunt would kill her brother terrified Primrose. Somehow she had to find him before that woman did. And warn him.

She had to wonder what Simeon would think if and when she found him and had Sir Bened at her side. Simeon was an amiable man not given to fighting and posturing, but he was her only brother and now the head of their household. It was quite possible he would react as many a father would if he found his daughter had been riding all over the countryside with a man. Primrose shook that thought aside. It was a problem she could deal with when she had to.

A yawn swept over her and she realized she was finally feeling sleepy. Since she had settled nothing in her mind, she had to wonder why. Then she realized that she had indeed made a decision. She knew Bened, in her mind, in her heart, even in the very blood in her veins. His interests and opinions might still be a mystery as was his family and history, but she knew the soul of the man as if it was clearly visible to her. He was a good, honest man. Now she just had to decide how deeply she wished to be involved with him.

It made her a little giddy to realize she was considering taking a lover. Shocking that she would do so soon after meeting him but then she was no longer a young maid. Many thought of her as a spinster. Such a step would have serious consequences concerning the rest of her life. Giving a man her body would mean giving him her heart. Primrose had no doubt about that even if she had never done such a thing before. She could never become so intimate with a man without her heart becoming involved. Men could have such relations with women and maintain their distance. Thus, she had to consider that she would run the risk of getting her heart broken. Before too much longer she had to decide if Sir Bened Vaughn was worth the risk.

Chapter Four

Stepping out of the dress shop into the late morning sun quickly had Primrose squinting. She stared down at the ground until the sting of the bright sunlight eased a little and then started to look around for Sir Bened. He had said he would wait for her just outside the shop, his reluctance to enter it so visible, she had been amused, but she could not see him anywhere.

After Primrose bought some ribbons, the previously reluctant clerk had suddenly become very talkative. Primrose had gathered a lot of information but was not sure what use she could make of it all. Yet now she knew for certain that her brother had passed through this village. She just wished he had lingered for a while. Instead she was going to have to follow him again and try very hard to catch up to him. She always seemed to end up where Simeon had been not long after he had left the place. If this had been a game, she would have quit playing it long ago.

Keeping a close eye out for Sir Bened, she walked

toward the inn where they were staying. She worked hard to convince herself that everything was all right but there was an unease beginning to knot her stomach. It was strange for Sir Bened to wander off with no word to her. He was very set in his determination to save her, protect her. The man would never simply walk away without letting her know where he was headed, she was certain of that. So where was he?

Perhaps some woman had lured him away, she thought, recalling the looks the women had given him from time to time, and then stumbled slightly at the pain that thought caused her. Yet she had no claim on him. He had stuck by her side because he was convinced she needed protection as well as help in finding Simeon. The stab to the heart she had suffered when thinking he had left with a woman told her that some part of her did indeed think of him as hers, that she had some claim on him. Telling herself not to be a fool, that she had only known the man for a day, helped not at all.

Pausing at the front of a pub, she wondered how big a mistake it might be to go inside to look for Bened. Then a noise from within the shadowed alley between the pub and the cooper's shop caught her full attention. She had seen enough arguments between the men working at Willow Hill to recognize the sounds of fists hitting flesh.

Stepping just inside the alley, Primrose pressed herself up against the stone wall of the pub. Three men were confronting Bened. She winced each time one landed a blow on him although he was holding his own against such poor odds. When one pulled a sword she nearly called out but then

Bened drew his own sword. A movement caught her eyes and she watched as one of the men was very slowly inching his way around to get behind Bened. The moment he was past Bened she pulled her pistol and aimed it at him.

The man held a knife in his hand and Primrose braced herself to shoot him before he could use it on Bened. Then he saw her and the smile he gave her was so cold she shivered. He was far enough away from her that she could not see him all that clearly, although his grin was easy enough to spot. A faint light shone through the window of the building behind him making a precise silhouette of his form, and she used that to keep her gaze, and her pistol, fixed on him.

"You mean to shoot me, lass?" He tossed his knife from one hand to the other and back again, displaying his prowess with it. "One chance before I reach you. Head or heart?"

She saw how the light revealed that his legs were braced apart, in a fighting stance, that faint light shining between them. "I do not think I like those choices."

"Only ones you got, lass."

She aimed at his head and then drew that aim downward until it rested just above the light shining between his legs. "Not the only one. Might not kill you though you will probably wish it had. You could also bleed to death as you wail about your lost pride."

Bened stumbled and nearly got himself skewered when he heard Primrose's voice from behind him. The man facing him with a sword was good, seeing his brief distraction, and quickly taking advantage.

Bened suspected all that saved him was that he had a lot more practice and more recently than he suspected this man had. He drew his pistol, needing to hold at bay the two men he was fighting long enough for him to chance a glance behind him.

What Bened saw made his blood run cold and not simply because the third man had managed to slip up behind him. Primrose stood there aiming her pistol at a man who had evidently intended to stab him in the back. He hoped the man could not see the cloudiness of her gaze or her fear. The threat she tossed out in a calm, cold voice made him proud even as he bit back the urge to order her to run.

The men in front of him demanded his attention and he swiftly pushed them back with pistol and sword. They all knew the pistol held only one shot so was only a threat until he fired it, that he would have no time to reload it and fire again before they could bring him down, but, for now, the threat of being the one who got shot was enough. What he needed to do was push the men in front of him so far back and in such a way that it kept them back long enough for him to help Primrose.

"Sir," Primrose said when the rogue she faced slid a step closer to her. "Do not move."

"Pretty wee thing like you will not shoot a man."

"Are you willing to bet your life on that?"

Primrose was proud of how cold she sounded despite how she was inwardly shaking with terror. The very last thing she wished to do was shoot the man but she was determined to do it if he threatened Bened again. It would haunt her forever and she knew it, but she would find that far easier to deal with than seeing Bened stabbed in the back.

Just as she began to believe the man would allow her to keep him at bay, he lunged at her. She shot him before she even finished the thought of doing so. Her aim was a little to the right so, instead of the horrible wound she had intended to inflict, she caught him in the upper right leg. It still took him down but she doubted he would stay there long.

With a flurry of sword work, Bened wounded both men facing him. They retreated and he took the chance to hurry to Primrose's side. The man she had shot lunged for him and Bened kicked his arm. The snap of a bone and the man's scream assaulted his ears. That and the gunshot would, he hoped, draw a few people to the alley to investigate.

"Can you reload your pistol?" he asked as he placed himself between her and his attackers.

"I can."

"Then do so as swiftly as you can. These men are not the sort to be down for long."

"I know." She took a deep breath to steady herself and began to reload her pistol.

A gunshot and a man's scream should bring people running, she thought as she fought to do what she had to with care yet some speed. Relief nearly sent her to her knees when she accomplished the chore and could stand and face the enemy along with Sir Bened. Her attempt to stand at his side was swiftly and very firmly thwarted, however. Bened just kept shifting that big strong body of his to keep himself between her and their attackers.

Before either of them could do another thing, six men raced into the alley, stopping just inside as they studied the scene. That hesitation gave two of the men who had tried to kill Bened a chance to run, however. Two of the men who had rushed to their aid went after them but Primrose doubted they would be successful in capturing the men. The one she had shot had no chance to attempt an escape and was being yanked to his feet by two others. The remaining two approached her and Bened.

"Are you hurt, miss?" asked the older of the two.

"No," she said. "You arrived in time."

Bened nodded and slung his arm around Primrose's shoulders, ignoring her start of surprise. "And we are grateful for it. I am not sure how much longer I could have kept them from robbing us and putting their filthy hands on my wife."

Primrose was surprised at how smoothly Bened lied to the men who had rushed to their aid. She had to admit it was a good lie, though, as it nicely explained what was going on in a way that would probably prompt very few questions or doubts. The man they had wounded just glared at them. He was clearly no more eager to explain what was really behind the fight than they were. She also tried to ignore the small thrill of delight that went through her at hearing the words *my wife* on Bened's lips.

She leaned into him, turning her face into his chest so that the men he spoke to could not see her expression. The last thing she wished to do was to spoil Bened's game. It could prove as much help to the men who had attacked him as it did her and Bened but there was nothing to be done about that. They simply did not have the time or the proof to drag out the whole true story.

What troubled her most was that her aunt had sent her hirelings after Bened. The woman had seen what a problem he would be and set out to be rid of him. This attack had been intended to kill him and that terrified her. Primrose began to try to think of ways to get him to leave but doubted any of them would work. She would do her best, however. There was no way she could allow her difficulties, her family's battles, to cause him to lose his life.

By the time the men left, dragging their prisoner off to the magistrate, Primrose was feeling a bit weak. The fight and the fear caused by it had sapped all her strength. She allowed Bened to lead her to the inn where they had booked two rooms for the night. The solicitous way the maid treated her as she brought them some tea and food told Primrose that word of the attack was already spreading. She frowned at Bened who appeared to be finding it funny.

She glanced at the other couple in the private parlor, and said softly, "Such a smooth liar you are, Sir Bened. I was most impressed."

"At times it is the only smart thing one can do. Did you want us to tangle them up with the truth?"

She sighed. "No, yet I feel a bit guilty for lying to men who had come to help us and accepting the sympathy of that maid when nothing happened."

"Then think of it as sympathy handed out simply because you were in danger and you were. Maybe not the one I implied, but there was a real threat to your life."

"It was mostly to your life. I but happened to stumble into it. She wants you gone."

"Which tells us quite a lot."

"What? That my aunt, whom I had long dismissed as a nasty, vain fool, is actually a cold-blooded killer?"

"Forewarned is forearmed."

"Are you going to heed the warning?"

"I have or I would already be dead."

"I cannot allow you to put your life at risk for me."

"Ah, I wondered if that was where you were headed. It is not all for you. I cannot leave you to her mercies. It would shame me for life if I did so. I am a man who has always watched people's backs. It is who I am. I find their enemies before their enemies can find them. Do you know how it came to be that I, the son of a farmer, got a knighthood, was named a baronet, and was gifted with a small piece of property?"

"I rather thought it was because you have relatives with much higher honors."

"There is that and I am certain it helped the man who pushed for this honor for me, but I got it because I was protecting an earl's son. Took a bullet for the idiot. And, believe me, it was not what I had planned when I moved to save him. Never expected more than my pay but he was the earl's only heir. And we should all pity him for that," he added, and took a drink of his ale. "Whenever my family has need of someone to help them track a person or go against their enemies, they come for me. That makes me a man whom you will never convince to leave just because things have become dangerous."

She sighed and slumped in her chair. "So you will stay and if the worst happens to you, leave me to have that on my conscience forever."

"Your conscience is clear or should be. None of this is your doing. You merely wanted to find your brother to tell him of your father's death."

"And to flee a marriage I did not want so there was some selfishness involved," she reminded him.

"From what you told me of the man chosen for you, you would have been foolish not to try to get as far away from that risk as possible."

"There is nothing I can say to make you change your mind, is there."

"Nay, not a thing." He studied her for a moment. "And you can just forget trying to lose me by running off."

Startled that he had guessed what she had been thinking, she stared at him. "Those familial gifts you spoke about? One of them is not the ability to, well, read my thoughts, is it?"

"Nay, that curse settled on the head of the clan, the Duke of Elderwood."

"Truly?" she whispered. "He can see inside a person's mind?"

"Hear what is there, aye. And it is not the wondrous thing you appear to think it is. It is a curse. Modred is a young man but he hides in that castle of his because being amongst people can be a pure hell on earth for him. The few in my family who have been gifted that way often end up insane or kill themselves to end the noise. It is sad for he is a good man."

"When you explain it that way, I can see what you mean." She frowned. "His name is Modred?"

"I fear so."

"That seems a bit like adding insult to injury."

He laughed and nodded. "It does. But, as I said,

he is a good man and, amongst the family are ones he can be around without discomfort. They do their best to visit with him as often as they can."

"Can he be around you?"

"He can be around most of my family and he now has his aunt Dob there to train him in silencing the world. One day he might be able to make short visits to the world outside those walls."

"Then I shall pray for him to gain that freedom." She helped herself to one of the small sandwiches the maid had brought them.

"You accept what I say very easily."

"Well, as was said by Shakespeare in *Hamlet,* 'There are more things in Heaven and Earth, Horatio, than are dreamt of in your philosophy.' Papa also said to keep an open mind and never cease to question and learn. He felt the way to judge what was good or bad was to ask oneself, 'What harm does it do to the innocent?'" She shrugged. "I heard that from the time I was a small child and it stuck with me."

"Not a bad piece of wisdom for a parent to leave a child with."

For a while they just drank their tea and ate the sandwiches. Try as she would, Primrose could think of nothing to say to convince him to save his own life and leave her to face her own troubles. She understood why he would not. For him it was far easier to stay and face the danger than to run for his life and leave her to face it alone. That probably tasted of cowardice to him. The newly dubbed Sir Bened Vaughn would never give in to cowardice.

She watched the other couple sharing the parlor get up to leave. They walked by with their arms wrapped around each other's waists and the man was whispering in the woman's ear. If the woman's blushes were any indication, those words were very heated ones.

"Newlyweds," she said after they were gone.

"Or ones having an affair."

"Cynical man. Why would you think such a thing?"

"Because I believe her husband has just come looking for her."

Primrose suddenly became aware of a loud disturbance outside the door. She listened closely and heard a man demanding to know where his wife was, that he had watched her come into the inn to meet her lover. He also went into great detail about what he planned to do to the rogue who had stolen his wife from him. She had to give the angry man credit for being creative even if it was in a bloodthirsty way.

"That is just sad."

Bened laughed but never took his gaze from the window overlooking the stables. "True more often than not."

"What are you looking at? Have my aunt's men come back for you?"

"Nay. I am watching a lover flee the scene of the crime he did not have time to commit."

She breathed a sigh of relief then frowned. "He did not even stay to try to help her."

"She has a better chance of soothing her husband than he does."

If the loud voices she heard were any indication, that soothing was going to take a long time. Then there was the sound of a blow and a scream of pain. She did not even have time to get to her feet before Bened was up and out the door. Off to protect someone else, she thought as she stood up and followed him.

The young woman who had been cooing and flirting with her lover a short time ago now lay on the floor weeping. Bened was holding a big, homely man back by the arms and talking to him in a low, hard voice. Primrose turned her attention to the woman as it appeared no one else cared to interfere. She crouched next to the woman, wincing when she looked up for she was going to have a badly bruised eye soon.

"Does he hit you regularly?" she asked, and watched those bruised eyes narrow in a sly way.

"He beats me all the time, m'lady," she said in a trembling voice.

"Do not lie to me. He should not have hit you as you are much smaller than he is but do not try to turn this into a lie that will stain his name forever. But you are hardly innocent in all of this. If you did not want him, why did you marry him?"

"He has his own shop."

That was probably the most honest the woman had been in a long time. "A poor reason to tie your life to a man you obviously do not want."

"What do you know with your big, handsome gent? Not all of us have such choices." The woman used her own skirts to wipe the tears of pain from her face. "I had to think of my future."

Primrose stood up, took the woman by the hand, and helped her to her feet. "Then stop trying to destroy it."

Once she knew no one had forced the woman to marry her big husband, Primrose lost all sympathy.

She still thought the man had not been right to strike someone so much smaller than he, a woman not trained in the ways one can defend oneself or the strength to use them, but it appeared her erring was not even done out of love. She had not even asked after her lover.

It was several moments before the pair were calmed enough to leave. By the looks on the faces of the others at the inn, they had not been surprised by the scene they had witnessed and Primrose sensed sympathy lay with the husband. All she hoped was that the man would not hit the woman again no matter how hurt and angry he was. She headed back into the parlor to get her coat.

"What did the woman have to say?" asked Bened.

"She chose that man because he has a shop but she neither likes nor respects him. Oh, she did not say so, but you can almost feel it. He should not have hit her as she is smaller and weaker, but she chose him and should at least try to care for more than his shop. It is something one sees too often. My father was very firm with the people who live at Willow Hill but even his rules and punishments could not completely put an end to it." She picked up her coat and turned to smile at Bened. "And what did that big shop owner have to say for himself?"

"Not much but he was ashamed of himself and that is good. Fool loves her."

"And I think that is probably the saddest part of it all. I must seek my bed. It has been a very long day with too much excitement, I think."

"There is one thing I meant to say—I think your aunt may already know where your brother is."

A chill went through her and she stared at him, dreading learning how he had come to that conclusion. "Do you think she has killed him?"

"Nay or she would not still be around to cause us trouble. Yet, I have been careful to leave no easy trail for them to follow but they still find us. I do not believe it is because they are good trackers but because they are close on your brother's trail, they might even know where he is heading."

"That would explain why he never lingers in one place for long and the direction he has taken."

"You have some idea of where he is going?"

"I think he is headed to Uncle George's, my mother's brother. He lives but a few miles from your cousin's castle with his companion of thirty years. Atop a hill surrounded by fields. No one can creep up on him. Simeon would think it a good place to hide. I just worry that he is bringing more trouble than he knows to Uncle George's door. Then again, our uncle is an old soldier and no weakling. He would be insulted if we thought him too old to protect his sister's child." She watched him closely as she added, "His companion Frederick is also an old soldier so neither one is without some skill at defending themselves or someone else."

"That will make it a lot easier when we end up there then."

"So, do you want to just head there?"

"I think it might be a good plan." He lightly brushed his fingers over her cheek. "Go and get some rest. We can decide in the morning."

She nodded and headed for her bedchamber, asking the maid to lead her to it. The madness her aunt had pulled her into was exhausting her and she thought a lot of that weariness was of the spirit as well as from an unending fear for her brother. Now she had to be afraid for Bened. Her aunt had clearly decided that he was a problem and wished to be rid of him. How could she have missed this evil in the woman for so long?

As she undressed for bed and washed up, she thought back over the years she had known the woman. The hints of Augusta chasing her and Simeon down had been there but Primrose had never thought her aunt would become murderous. She doubted her father had, either. Even when in the midst of a temper, they had never considered her dangerous. Selfish, greedy, vain, and far too aware of her consequence, something the woman thought was greater than it actually was, but never the sort they needed to watch their backs around. They were paying dearly for that blindness now. She just hoped Simeon was not still blind to the danger their aunt had become.

Lord Simeon Wootten stretched in the bed he shared with Lucy, the inn's maid. It had been too long since he had enjoyed a woman, or even a night of comfort in a good bed in a warm inn. His body still ached from his time spent with his aunt and her men but not so much that he had been unable to enjoy himself for a little while. He sat up and was pleased to see that his clothing was neatly placed on a chair. He did not wish to show up at Uncle George's home looking shabby and travel-worn.

A soft rap came at the door and he slipped out of

the bed, yanked on his drawers, and went to open it just a little. The stableboy he had paid to watch for anyone asking after him stood there. He sighed, knowing that his moment of peace was about to end.

"Someone has asked after me?"

"Aye, m'lord. Some woman."

"Did you see her?"

"Nay. She stayed in the carriage and sent her man to speak to me. He was tall, thin, and had silver hair. Big long nose, too."

"Jenson. Damn."

"I think he slipped into the stables and had a look around while the old woman talked to me."

"So they might know I am here."

"That gelding of yours be easy to spot."

"True. Ajax is a fine steed." He fetched a coin from his money purse and handed it to the boy. "Time for me to be leaving, I think. Get Ajax ready and leave him where I showed you."

The moment the boy was gone, Simeon hurried to dress. He watched Lucy slowly wake up and stretch out her luscious body before smiling at him. It was tempting but he did not think she was worth dying for. He smiled and shook his head, ignoring her pout. If Jenson had seen Ajax and told Aunt Augusta, he could be facing a hard run for his life.

Collecting up his possessions, he paused to kiss Lucy good-bye and then slipped out of the room. He headed for the back stairs, keeping a close watch behind him. Just as he slipped into the shadowed opening of the back stairs he heard someone rap on one of the doors. A careful look around the corner of the wall revealed a man he did not recognize talking to Lucy. Not waiting to see how that went, he hurried down the stairs and slipped out the kitchen door.

Weaving his way through the alleys of the town, he caught sight of his aunt's carriage and ducked into a dress shop. With a cap hiding his hair, he strolled over to the counter and looked at the ribbons displayed there. There were some red ones he knew his sister would love and bought three. That made the girl behind the counter more than willing to keep his visit a secret if asked. She even showed him how to leave the shop without being seen.

It still took him an hour to get to where the stableboy stood with his horse. He attached his bags to the horse and mounted it before handing the boy another coin. If he had known how many people he was going to have to bribe to keep his passing through a secret, he would have brought a chest of coins.

He turned his horse toward the direction of his uncle's home and rode off, staying away from the main roads and doing his best to remain out of sight. It worried him that his aunt believed killing him would gain her anything. The only way that would be true was if something had happened to his father. Simeon felt a pang in his chest as he feared that may be the case. He also worried about his sister's fate.

Primrose did not know just how much Augusta disliked her, never had. His father and he had done their best to shelter her from the worst of it. That might have been a mistake, he thought. It had been, and still was, difficult to resist the urge to ride for home and see just what was happening but he had to remember that he was the last of the Woottens of Willow Hill, the last one to carry on the barony and the name, something his father had considered very important. So, for his father's sake, he prayed for the safety of his family and fought to stay alive.

Chapter Five

"Are you certain?"

"Very certain, miss. I would have noted a gentleman as fine as the one you have described and I saw no one like that."

Primrose stared at the woman. She was a little plump with shapely curves, just as Simeon always liked women to be. There was little doubt in her mind that this woman had *noted* and was worldly enough to have done a great deal more if the chance had arisen.

"Yet I followed his horse's trail right to this inn."

"If he was here, it must have been on the day I do not work."

The words *you are a liar* were hot on her tongue when Bened grabbed her by the arm and dragged Primrose out to where their horses waited. She did not know who she was most angry with, the lying woman in the shop or Sir Bened.

"She *knows*. She *saw* him," she protested even as she mounted her horse.

"Yes, she does," he agreed as he mounted Mercury

and started to ride out of the village, pleased that Primrose followed him with no further protest. "She was also not going to tell you a thing."

"Why? I told her I was his sister, gave her my name, which she clearly recognized, and assured her that I meant him no harm. Simeon would not hide from me."

"But he is apparently hiding from someone, which I find very interesting."

"Oh." She frowned and thought on the failed interrogation of the woman at the inn, as well as what Bened had said just before she had retired last night. "So you were right to think my aunt is actually following Simeon's trail, not ours. And my brother has become aware of her pursuit."

Bened nodded as he thought over all the reluctant, even missing, witnesses they had sought out. They would find Simeon's trail only to end up being told that no one had seen the man, a man whose own sister said was very noticeable. Or they could not locate a person, when everyone insisted they would know about any stranger coming through the village. He hoped they were just hiding and not been silenced.

"I do think he has discovered someone, aside from you, is following him and that person is not looking to keep him safe until he can return to Willow Hill. He is the one trying to hide his own trail."

"So he must know he is in danger now. That is a relief. Yet, why has he not tried to reach me? If he knows the enemy is on his trail he must also know that I am."

"He may but who does he trust to give you a

message? Much safer to just tell everyone not to let anyone know that he has passed their way. Then they cannot be tricked into revealing anything to the enemy instead of the friend."

"Silence is golden."

"Certainly safer."

"Do you think I now waste our time hunting for him?"

"Oh, nay. He will discover that soon enough and will then try to safely meet with you. We stay on his trail to give him that chance. The fact that he now works to hide his trail tells me that your aunt and her hirelings have gotten too close from time to time. Your brother is in dire need of some ally, someone to watch his back."

Those words both pleased and frightened her. She had not wanted to stop looking for Simeon so was happy Sir Bened agreed that they should continue. If he had decided she should stop and go home or someplace he decided was safe, they could have come to a parting of the ways. Primrose knew that she could not stop now, she had to find Simeon and, if he already knew he was in danger, she had to stand with him. Although grateful beyond words for Sir Bened's aid, this was a family matter and when Simeon faced the threat from within their own family, she had to be at his side.

"This has turned out to be a very tangled web you have gotten tangled in," she said.

"Nay, I am not leaving."

She scowled at him. "That was not what I said."

"Aye, it was."

"Well, then, it is a reasonable thing to contemplate."

"It might be reasonable if and when we certainly

find your brother. I untangle myself now and you return to riding about alone. Not a good plan. The theft of your horse was not the first attempt to stop you from continuing in your search, was it? Just why were you separated from your horse when I found you?"

Primrose silently cursed. She had hoped he would not ask that question. Before it had been because she had not wished to drag him into the mire with her. Now it was because he would just use the information to strengthen his opinion that she could not continue alone, that even if Simeon was sitting right around the corner, it was not safe for her to turn that corner alone.

"Some hunter shot at his game too close to me and it startled Smudge."

"So she tossed you."

"I fell, lost my grip when she bucked in alarm."

Bened gave her a look that silently asked just how gullible she thought he was. "Of course. Tell me, how close was this shot?"

"Not close at all. It hit a tree several feet behind us."

"Would it, perhaps, have been a tree you had just ridden by?"

"Perhaps he mistook us for game?"

"Strange-looking game. Sounds as if he might need spectacles too. Very strong ones. Or he was a man who had little practice shooting at moving targets or one who even thought you might pause for a moment to admire the tree." He could not fully suppress a smile when she growled at him.

"If someone was trying to kill me, then why did he leave me lying in the road? I would have been a very easy kill. As it was I had only just roused myself when I heard a carriage coming. I got out of the way then."

The image of her sprawled in the road while a carriage raced toward her chilled Bened to the bone. "He did not check on you because he believed the carriage would finish the job he had begun. I believe that if you think back, each and every problem you have had in finding Simeon can be attributed to intentional interference." Her shoulders slumped and he resisted the urge to comfort her. She knew he was right and it was past time she faced the dangerous days ahead of her with a sharp, clear eye.

"She knew what I was about from the beginning. When she did not get blamed for Papa's death, she probably began to immediately plot the many ways she could get rid of me and Simeon." Primrose shook her head. "Long years of resentment and envy have twisted her mind. It was always there. That ability to be rid of anything and anyone in her way or which annoyed her, has always been there. It was just never turned against us before."

"The death of your father made her see the chance to get everything."

"Which makes it even more plausible that she killed him when he threatened to take away what she had managed to hang on to, all through his generosity. And she would only kill the man who held the purse if she believed she could soon get it all."

"True and that is truly a shame. He sounds as if he was a good man."

"He was. He did not much like his own brother and certainly not his wife but he did as he felt honor and family duty demanded and took them in when they were in trouble. That she may have killed him, the one person who actually helped her, only makes her crimes more heinous." Primrose took a deep breath and let it out slowly, releasing the heavy grief that could still swamp her when thinking of her father. "Is your father still alive?"

"Aye, although whenever we all gather he claims we will be the death of him." Bened had to smile when he thought of his father complaining about his lively brood. "I tell him it is our mother we should all worry about since he made her bear so many big fellows."

"No sisters?"

"Only the women my brothers have chosen. Good choices each one. And six nephews. Only one niece."

"And very spoiled, I suspect, with so many watching out for her."

He laughed as he thought of little Angharad who, at just five, was already ruling the whole family. One tear fell from her big brown eyes and every male Vaughn within reach groveled to make her smile. "Oh, very spoiled indeed but, fortunately, she shows signs of having a very good heart, so we do worry when she wields her power over all of us."

He abruptly shut up before he rambled on about his large family anymore. It suddenly occurred to him that he was boasting a little, perhaps even trying to catch her interest with the size and closeness of his family. Considering all she was facing now, he decided it might be just a little cruel to continue.

A movement in the trees on the left side of the road caught his attention and he decided he needed to check it out more closely. "Keep riding and pay no heed to me disappearing for a moment. If anyone notices I am not at your side I want them to think it is but a brief visit to a tree that drew me aside. So stay calm and act as if you do no more than take a ride in the country."

"You have seen something." She forced herself not to look around.

"I think so but cannot see it clearly. Could be no more than a stray cow."

She doubted it, but nodded, and kept on riding, studying the many birds that abruptly flew from one tree to another. Primrose sensed more than saw him leave but kept on riding slowly down the road. To calm herself she told herself that it did not need to be another attack from her aunt's men. Or even highwaymen. It could just be someone who was merely traveling between farms. She prayed that was what it was and began to worry about what Bened was riding into.

Bened slipped off Mercury's back, kept his mount's reins in hand, and crept toward where he had seen the movement as well as the sudden rousing of the birds. That chilly itch on the back of his neck that warned him of an enemy was back. He paused at the top of the rise that bordered the road, hiding himself in the heavy shade of the trees, and watched a man ride quickly along the route to a place where he would be forward of where he and

Primrose would ride. Hoping Primrose kept her pace slow as instructed to, Bened followed the man.

The man dismounted and climbed a tree. Bened cursed. That was going to make it difficult to end the threat the man posed. He pulled his rifle from its place on his saddle and loaded it. It would be a difficult shot but he had taken such ones before. It had served him well in Canada when he had been watching out for the Earl of Collinsmoor's brother. And he could boast of some skill with it. Shooting a man out of a tree was not easy, however, no matter how skilled one was.

Taking aim, he sighed. This was not a part of battle he had ever liked. The only thing that would make it easier this time was that the man was planning to shoot an unarmed woman, to shoot Primrose. This was not a fight for freedom or to take or hold on to land, but a killing driven by one woman's greed. Bened did not think he would suffer the usual touch of sadness he did after such a shot.

He heard the slow approach of Primrose's horse and watched through his sights as the man tensed and settled in to make his shot. Anger swelled in Bened. Primrose had done nothing to her aunt, had suffered the woman's presence in her life because that is what family did. Charity might gall some people but it did not often inspire murder and this is what this was.

The moment the man adjusted his aim and stilled, Bened fired. He watched the man's body jerk and tumble from the tree to lie still on the ground. Bened waited for that regret he always felt at taking a life and it did not come. He hoped it was because this man had been willing to murder an innocent woman for a few coins and not because he was growing hardened to such killing.

He returned his rifle to its sheath on his horse, mounted Mercury, and rejoined Primrose. It touched him when she reached across the space between him and squeezed his hand. The sound of a shot was enough to tell her what had happened and he was glad she did not ask any more about it.

Primrose felt her heart clench with sorrow and pain. This man had killed for her. A part of her wanted to know how he felt about that but she silenced it. She knew little about men who did battle but she suspected it was not something they easily shrugged aside when that fight caused a death, not even when there was no real choice in the matter. She had caused him to get blood on his hands and she cursed her aunt for driving them to this point.

It was almost an hour before Bened spoke, surprised at how comfortable the long silence had been. "I think we shall have to spend the night outside," he said.

"Sleep on the ground?"

"Aye. We will never make the next village until after dark and I do not want to ride into a village when there are so many shadows to avoid or peer into."

"Ah." She frowned and looked around. "I have never slept outside."

"Never? Not even when you were a little girl?"

"Never. Why should I have? I had a nice room and a warm bed at Willow Hill. Once my mother passed, we never traveled much or far enough to warrant it. Simeon must have since he went hunting or fishing with Papa."

"You never went hunting or fishing, either?"

"No. Is that something I should have been doing? Once I heard it required such things as worms impaled on hooks, I had no interest in it. I preferred just going on nice long rides with Papa and, sometimes, Simeon. We never rode long enough to need to sleep out on the ground, either."

"Not to worry. I have done it many times and in several countries so I can set us up comfortably."

Primrose frowned and looked around as he led them off the road to a small glen. It was pretty and the ground looked clean. It also looked hard. It was not until he began to spread out the roll of bedding he had been carrying on the back of his horse that she recognized the enforced intimacy of what they were about to do. It was not until he went to her horse and pulled off another roll of bedding that she realized that had somehow appeared since she had left Willow Hill.

"When did I get that?"

"In the last village," he answered as he spread that bedding out not far from his own. "I became aware of the lack and knew that at some point we might have to camp."

"I must give you the money I have. It has occurred to me that you have been paying for everything yet I have brought money for this journey. And I can see you thinking of how to refuse it. Do not bother."

"It does not make a man comfortable to accept money from a woman."

"Not even when it is her business that has given them the need for it?"

"I do not need it."

There was the definite hint of manly insult behind those words and she almost smiled. Men's pride could be a strange thing. No woman would concern herself. If two women traveled together, both paid a share. Somehow she had to make him understand that that was all she was doing, carrying her own weight as much as she was able.

"I began this journey. You are here because you know I needed someone to protect me and help me find my brother. I was fully prepared to pay my way for the whole journey. All I mean to do is give you that money. If naught else, it will make it easier for us to continue to afford the rooms and meals we keep having to pay for at the inns along the way. It is not even payment for being my guard, just a sharing of costs. If I was traveling with a woman, a friend, it would not only be readily accepted but expected."

Bened sat back on his heels and looked at her. He realized they were having a clash of pride. She needed to help pay and he needed to be the one who took care of her. Yet, she was right, if it was two women, or two friends, or even two relatives, a sharing of the actual cost of the journey would be welcome, even expected. He would just make very sure that he used only half, no more and no less.

"Then set it with my belongings and we will split the costs for the rest of the journey."

She wanted to point out that he should take what was owed for the journey costs thus far but bit back the words. It was all the concession she would get and pushing harder would then start to prick his pride. Nodding, she hurried to collect her funds and tuck them into his saddle packs. By the time she returned to his side, their bedding was set out. It did not look much more welcoming than it had rolled up and sitting behind the saddle but she promised herself she would not complain.

His reasoning for the need to spend the night on the ground was sound. Villages at night were a warren of shadowy places where their enemies could easily hide. If her aunt's men had arrived first they would also know the grounds they fought on much better than Bened did. He always reconnoitered when they entered a village and entering it at nightfall would make that almost impossible and dangerous.

Despite her good intentions, she could not fully repress a grimace when she sat down on the bedding he had laid out for her. There was no softness despite the thick bottom blanket and the grass. Men did this a lot, she reminded herself, and she would do her best to endure it. She forced herself not to think about what might be crawling through the grass beneath her bedding and watched him prepare a fire.

"Shall I collect some wood? One thing I do know is what is good for burning. Papa used to have us sit out at night so he could teach us about the stars and we would often make a fire even though the light from it could sometimes make seeing the stars a little difficult. At least you could hurry back to it when you got cold, though."

"A supply of wood would be helpful."

Bened watched her wander off and held his smile inside until she was out of sight. She did not like being ignorant of sleeping outside and all it entailed. He suspected she was one who did not like being ignorant about anything. The talks in which she told him about her father, even her brother, revealed two very intelligent men with a greed for knowledge, who did not exclude her from that part of their lives.

She had had a good family and her aunt had taken one of the biggest pieces away already and was aiming for the rest. It had to hurt yet she had held strong through each new discovery about the depth of the betrayal of one of her own. What he did not understand was how, with so many smart people in the family, no one had noticed the adder in their midst. All he could think of was that, they themselves being incapable of such a thing, they had never considered the woman's envy and anger a true threat to their very lives. Such naïveté had buried too many people.

He was pleased when the wood she brought back proved her claim that she knew what was good for burning. Then he caught sight of the plants she carried. "What are those?"

"Medicinal plants." She hurried to her bag, dug around inside, and pulled out several little cloth bags into which she put the plants. "They have gone to seed so I am hoping if I can get them home, I can plant them in the garden. I hesitated for a bit as I rather like wandering through the woods hunting for plants I need and then preparing them but there are so many, I will still be doing that a lot."

"There are enough wooded areas near your home for that to be useful?"

"Yes. When my father discovered my interest in plants, especially herbs and medicinal ones, he told the ones who care for the lawns and all, to stop clearing out around the trees that surrounded us, to let it go wild. He said we had all the lawn we needed so why use so much time to try to make a wooded area look so prim. They did and now we have quite a few acres that have gone back to what they should be. Papa was especially pleased when he discovered such a thing also provided us with wild mushrooms. That required a great deal of study as some of the ones that are poison look a lot like the ones that are good." She carefully tucked the little bags back into her satchel.

"I think your interest in herbs and plants is a bit more than a hobby," he teased.

"I will confess that I can become quite lost in coming up with a new, useful potion, lotion, or tisane. My father and brother would bring me books or even plants when they traveled. Sad to say, not all the plants took as they came from far warmer places but the books were often a wonder."

"So you know more than one language." He watched her blush and look uneasy.

"I do know several."

"Do you know the Welsh tongue?"

"No, I fear not although I do know a little Scottish Gaelic. Mama was a Scot."

He nodded. "Another language too few are using anymore." He set up a roasting spit and then sat back. "I need to go ahunting for our meal. I have seen the signs that there a lot of rabbits about so I should not be away long. Anything makes you uneasy, just let out a hearty scream. That sound carries far and wide in areas like this."

"I do not suppose you saw any signs of pheasant or quail."

He laughed. "Nay, but I will be quick to grab one if I see one. Roasted rabbit is not bad."

"Oh, I know that, although we usually have it in a stew or some kind of meat pie."

"They are more tender that way." He stood up and fetched his rifle, carefully reloading it. "I actually prefer to hunt rabbit with bow and arrow but do not carry such a weapon around with me."

"Dead is dead when it concerns a rabbit, I would think."

"True. It is just that the arrow is easier to remove and makes no sound. The sound of a rifle shot carries far. Remember, as loud as you can make it, scream if you think there is any threat near at hand."

"I will."

She watched him walk away and the moment he was out of sight she began to feel uneasy. When she wandered the woods it was in the daytime with the full knowledge that her home was but a fast run away through the trees. Most of the time, she was able to keep it in sight as she wandered. She had never been alone in a strange stretch of woodland, far from anyone she knew, with night coming on. Primrose sternly told herself to find her backbone and stop fretting, and then turned her mind to what she would do with the seeds she had just collected.

Chapter Six

As the sun went down and a chill entered the air, Primrose moved closer to the fire and warmed her hands. She had never greeted the night outside unless with her father and brother. As the birds grew quiet and the light faded away, she was not sure she wanted to. There was a great deal to be said in favor of a roof, four walls, and a proper bed.

When Sir Bened returned to camp with a fat, dead rabbit, she decided there was also a big advantage to not actually seeing all the preparations for the meals she ate. She kept her gaze averted as he prepared the animal for roasting and put it on the clever spit he set up over the fire. When she heard him moving around, she forced herself not to look for she suspected he was cleaning up after those preparations needed to ready the animal for cooking.

"Squeamish?" he asked as he sat down across the fire from her.

"Not that I know of. I just did not want to see what you were doing."

"You have spent your life in the country. Surely you have seen an animal butchered?"

Primrose had to think about that for a moment and was a little surprised when she had to say, "Actually, no, not that I can recall."

"You were kept that sheltered?"

She frowned. "Not really. I know farm life, including things about breeding that many think no lady should ever know. Yet everyone was always very careful to never do any butchering where or when I might see it." She bit her bottom lip for a moment. "That is a little odd, is it not?"

Bened had to nod in agreement. "It might be something your father thought no well-bred lady should be subjected to."

"Yet no one hid that what I was eating was raised on Willow Hill land. There was a great pride in the fact that our farms supplied us and the people of Willow Hill so well. I can tell by how you spoke that it is a very odd thing for a countrywoman to have never seen it done so why would my father, country raised, care if I saw it?"

"Many women from the country know nothing of the breeding of stock because someone decided it was not something a well-bred lady should know despite how much of her comfort depended on the value of that stock. I have met gentry women who cannot read, were never taught, because their elders felt it would give them too much knowledge about the evil of the world or of indelicate matters."

"I wonder how many soon worked to gain that

skill and went on to read books that would turn their mother's hair silver."

Bened laughed. "No doubt there are many. The women in my family would certainly do that."

"You have a very large family. I recall that much from the talk I have heard."

And for a woman whose family had dwindled to two he suspected such a thing fascinated her, he thought with a pang of sympathy. "Very large and growing all the time. It is good to see after a lot of hard years when any one of us could find ourselves victims of witch hunts. The gossip might grow irritating at times but it is far less troublesome than knowing at any time you could find your home surrounded by superstitious people with torches."

"Our branch of the Woottens is but a skinny twig. We always seemed to be on the wrong side of things. Catholic when Elizabeth was queen. Protestant when Mary took the throne. With the king when Cromwell came to power and with Cromwell when the throne was restored. By the time Papa was born, his father was all that was left and one of his two sons has bred no children. It is sad to think that one's bloodline is vanishing."

"There is still you and your brother."

"True though I will not carry on the name if I marry and have children, nor can I ever inherit the barony. Of course, if dear Aunt Augusta has her way that will definitely mean the end of the Woottens of Willow Hill."

Bened began to better understand her dogged pursuit of her brother. The unwanted marriage and fear for her brother's life as well as the need to let him know he was now the baron were acceptable reasons for what appeared to be a very reckless act, but this went even deeper. He was certain she had been well versed over the years on the waning of her bloodline, imbued with the need to continue it. Although she might not see it herself, that also drove her to place her reputation and even her life at risk. She could carry on the bloodline herself but, as she said, not the name and the barony although a son of hers might be able to take it on if her brother bore no sons. Because of the man her uncle was, the barony and the name would really die with her brother if he was taken before he could marry and breed a son or two.

As they dined on the rabbit he related a few of the more humorous tales concerning his family. It pleased him when the sadness brought on by recalling how few of her family were left began to fade from her eyes. It was a heavy weight she carried on her slim shoulders. Bened began to realize that, for the first time in his life, he actually wanted to hurt a woman. He wanted to put a bullet in Augusta Wootten.

He also noted that Primrose showed no concern or fear during his tales of his family when he mentioned various gifts each possessed. She was curious, even fascinated, at times but never showed a hint of fear. Even in this enlightened age that was rare.

"Do you have your pistol?" Bened asked Primrose.

"I do. Loaded and close at hand. Do you need it?"

"Nay. Have my own, my rifle, my sword, and a few knives." He grinned at her look of surprise.

"I always travel well armed." He stood up and brushed off his backside. "I need to go and look about but wished to be certain you were still armed."

"Look about for what?"

"Any sign of your aunt and her hirelings. I need to know if they are following us since we had the brief problem with the man while on the road, or if we are just keeping apace with them. Are they in front or behind? Will you be fine waiting here? I will not be long."

"Go. I will be fine," she said, hoping he could not sense the lie.

The moment he disappeared into the night's shadows, she felt the fear begin its slow climb into her heart and mind. It was an old fear, one from childhood that had never faded, was only strengthened when she had become lost in the woods and unable to find her way back to the manor. That had been an odd event for no one, not even her, could understand how she had ended up so deep in the woods between the manor and the church cemetery, or who might have led her there. Fright had stolen her voice and, some feared, her mind. For days she could not even sleep in her own bed, the room too dark, and she would slip down to her father's or Simeon's room to curl up on the floor next to their beds. That had faded, eased enough so that she returned to sleeping in her own room again, but now she wondered yet again who had caused her to suffer so.

It was becoming apparent that there were a lot of puzzles and unanswered questions about her past, a lot of very large holes in her memory.

Primrose knew that many people recalled little of their childhood but surely one should recall the things that left one with a strong fear, a lingering pain, or some other thing that had caused a fierce emotion. She stared into the fire and decided she needed to dig out some of those memories. Something told her they could be very important now.

Bened searched the ground and frowned. Someone had died here and it had been a bloody death. There had been three men standing behind one. That one had struggled but so briefly that Bened had a good idea of how he was killed. Someone comes up from behind, gets a tight grip on him by his hair or collar, yanks his head back, and cuts his throat. Quick, efficient, and bloody. It could explain what had brought him to this spot to look for signs of their enemy. He had seen the ravens around before the sun set, and ravens and death went together like men and women. Somewhere nearby there was a body. He moved carefully in a straight line from where he had found the blood and paused to study some more prints in the ground. A woman had stood there while the killing was done, just close enough to have been splattered by blood.

A few steps more and he found the tracks of a carriage. It had drawn up, sat in place just long enough to make its marks in the ground deep enough to remain for a few days. Bened could easily envision the scene, as easily as if it had been drawn for him by a skilled artist.

Augusta had come here to meet with some of her hirelings, bringing a new crew with her. They had all waited but only one of the previous men had appeared. Bened suspected who it was and wondered if the man's last thought had been how he should have heeded his friends. The new slew the old while Augusta watched. It was a good way to let the new hirelings understand how she rewarded failure. Now he just had to find the body.

Going back to where the killing had taken place, he soon found the prints of two men carrying a heavy weight off into the woods. They had not carried it far. His stomach roiled at the smell and the sound of creatures dining on the dead. Fortunately they scattered when he appeared. There was not much left but enough for him to know it was the one called Mac. The man had certainly been no saint but it was a hard way to end. Shaking his head, he started to make his way back to his camp. Seeing no more recent signs of the enemy nor sensing them in any way, he felt it was safe to rest now.

He stepped into the clearing where they camped and, at first, was annoyed that Primrose barely noticed him, thinking she had been keeping a very poor watch for troubles. Then he saw that she was trembling. As he crouched in front of her, he realized she was crying. The blank look on her face worried him and he grasped her by the shoulders to give her a little shake. She stared at him and slowly her eyes sharpened. Then she hurled herself into his arms, clinging to him in a way that left every inch of him hardening with interest. Shifting to sit more comfortably, he rubbed her back and sternly reminded himself that now was not the time for lusting. She was deeply upset.

"Are you that afraid of being alone in the dark?" he asked.

"Not anymore. I think I will be better soon." Primrose took a few deep breaths and let them out slowly as she pushed away the last dregs of the childhood fear and grief that had grabbed her so tightly. "I know where the fear comes from now."

He brushed her hair back from her face and looked down at her. "What do you mean?"

"I always wondered why I had never really grown out of that childhood fear of the dark. I had no thoughts of things under the bed or anything such as that. It was a blind fear. So I got to thinking of something that happened when I was small, just after my mother died, and the more I thought on it, the more I remembered, especially when I did not allow the fear and sorrow thinking about that time always brings to force me to leave it alone, shake it from my mind."

"What did you recall, Rose?"

She smiled faintly as she rested her cheek on his broad chest and soaked up the pure strength of him. He was calming her as he always did although how he could do so with no words, she was not sure. If it was some gift he had it was a good one. It helped conquer the last of the fear and grief she had been crippled by.

"I was five, nearing six when my mother died. It was hard for she had been a very loving mother. I thought to find some of that when my aunt and uncle came but soon realized there was none of that warmth or softness there. Anyway, one night I woke and ached for my mother as only a child can. I understood death as much as a child that age can but I still wanted to visit my mother. I went looking for Papa but he was lost in his own grief somewhere and I found my aunt in his office. Now I can see her sitting at the desk with his ledgers open in front of her but at the time something like that meant nothing to me."

"What did she do?"

"When I said I wanted to see my mother she smiled. She said she would take me to see her and she did. She walked me through the woods to the graveyard, stood me in front of my mother's grave, and said there was my mother. That she was in the ground and feast for the worms now. Then telling me that we all end up there, some sooner than others, she walked away. No hug for a crying child, which is what I think I had been really looking for."

"She left you in a graveyard at night?"

"Yes, but once I realized I was alone I tried to get back home. I knew the woods but had not realized how different they looked at night. I ended up horribly lost and was crying and yelling for people until my voice died. Then I guess, from what was said, I went away into my head. They found me lying on the ground. I could not speak and when they tried to put me to bed that night I made the only noise I could actually make for months afterward. I screamed. Poor Papa had to sleep in a well-lit room for quite a while before I could be left alone in my own bed. Sometime during those months I completely forgot how I had ended up in the woods at night and anytime I tried to recall I was pushed back by my own fear and grief for my lost mother."

"And so your father could not know just what sort of evil he had let into his house and let it stay," he said as he held her close and rested his chin on her head.

"I know. I think there may be other things. That childhood adventure did, I think, leave me susceptible to burying all sorts of things deep inside and not looking at them again. I am going to start digging them back out. There may be some answers there."

She sat back a little and smiled at him. "Now that I have calmed, it is a relief to know the truth. It always troubled me that I was so childish I had never gotten rid of that fear of the dark, the kind that children have. As I said, I know there are no monsters under the bed or nasty things in the closet or any of that. I should not have been as disturbed by being alone in the dark as I have always been."

"You caught her looking at your father's ledgers. If you had ever mentioned it, I fear you would have had some accident."

"Oh, I did not think of that. She was probably hoping they would not find me, that I would have an accident trying to find my way home. There are certainly enough pitfalls in the woods."

He pulled a handkerchief from his pocket, tilted her face up to his, and began to gently wash the tears from her face. "A lot for a little terrified child."

"If I had remembered what happened earlier my father might still be alive," she said, and had to fight the urge to start weeping again.

"There is no way to know that. And, you were a child. How could a child understand what she was dealing with and explain that to an adult? Then again, it might well have gotten him killed earlier while you and Simeon were still too young to deal with the woman as she helped herself to all that belonged to you."

"There is that. He would have sent them away immediately. But, all that is in the past. As you say, I was but a child. I doubt I could have even explained it all in a way that would have worked to warn my father. I can just imagine it. 'Oh, Papa, I found Aunty reading books and asked her to take me to see Mama and then I got lost and could not find Aunty anywhere.'"

"Which sounds very much like a child of five. Now you can look back, see that she was reading his ledgers, and understand what that meant."

"This plan to set my uncle up as the baron has been one she has nursed for a very long time."

"From the beginning, I suspect." Unable to resist he began to lightly stroke her hair, letting the tips of his fingers drag through the thick, soft curls. "How did your mother die, Rose?"

"She fell and she was with child. Everything went wrong and she ended up miscarrying and bleeding to death. And, oh sweet God, do you think Augusta had something to do with that?"

He shrugged. "Well, it is a possibility."

He saw her mouth tremble and, holding her by the chin, he pressed his lips against hers, not wanting her to begin weeping again. Comfort swiftly changed to desire as he lightly nipped at her bottom lip. She shivered in his arms and her mouth opened slightly. Bened slid his tongue into its heat and savored the taste of her as he held her as close as he dared.

When Bened slipped his tongue inside her mouth,

Primrose thought she ought to be disgusted but instead her whole body grew hot and all she could think of was pressing herself as close to him as possible. The very few kisses she had had before this had never made her feel this way. It was sweet, fiery, heady, and made her greedy for more of them. She murmured her disappointment when he ended the kiss, slowly pulling his mouth away from hers. She was pleased to see that he was breathing heavily for it meant that kiss had moved him as much as it had her.

"That was probably not a wise thing to do when we are about to spend a night together in the woods," Bened said but was unable to resist brushing his mouth over hers one more time.

She allowed him to ease her off his lap. Just when had she crawled into his lap, she wondered, but did not really care. Reluctant though she was to admit it, she knew he was right. They were still new to each other. Realizing that they could stir up so many feelings with just a kiss when they were about to sleep together in the woods, alone, but feet apart, was only asking for trouble.

Primrose sat on the bedding and watched him put his weapons around. He moved so quietly and gracefully for such a big man. It was a joy to watch him. For the first time in her entire life, Primrose found herself curious as to what he would look like without his clothes as he moved around.

Shocked at the path her thoughts had taken, she asked, "Did you find anything out there?"

"I believe we are very safe here. Your aunt has been in the area but there is no reason for her to return. Whoever that man was off the road that thought to shoot at us as we road by, was probably just some ruffian she hired to deal with us so she could continue to hunt down your brother."

"She has to know where he is going."

"I would not be surprised if she does know, but dealing with him before he gains any allies would make everything much easier."

"True. How do you know she was in this area?"

"Recall the men who stole our horses?" He sat across the fire from her and she nodded. "They did not trust her, two of them most adamantly and one more interested in payment due. I believe he went to an arranged meeting place. What I could read by the marks in the dirt is that she pulled up in her carriage, faced him, and three newly hired men came up behind. One of those cut his throat while she watched. Then they dragged his body off into the woods."

"There is a part of me that knows she is a cold woman, perfectly capable of such things, yet I am still shocked. She is not just cold, she is evil."

"Since what she is doing is all to gain a title and money, to make herself more important, then, aye, evil is a word that fits. She also showed her new hirelings how she responds to failure."

"Fear to keep them in line. She is fond of that trick. I now see she used it on me but I have watched her use it on women she needed to hold her place in society no matter how foolish her husband was. Everyone has secrets and she had a very calm, cold way of letting any who thought to criticize her that she knew all of theirs and would have no trouble whispering it into a few impor-tant, influential ears. I always thought that was so malicious. Actually said as much to her and she calmly told me that it was how one held one's place in society. I thought some of it was also a bit of revenge for something bad one of them may have said about her or her husband."

"Not uncommon in society."

"It has never sounded like a particularly pleasant place, or rather group, to me and I have managed to avoid it."

"I was never invited in but from what I have seen amongst the ones in my family who have dealt with it, it is complicated, cutthroat, and often just plain cruel. I have no idea why so many are so desperate to become part of it."

Bened banked the fire, tugged off his boots, and climbed beneath the blanket of his rough-ground bed. He watched as Primrose did the same and chuckled at her grimace. "It is not bad unless you have found a rock."

"It all feels like rock to me but I will manage. I just do not understand why men would actually choose to do such a thing."

"For the thrill of the hunt."

After shifting around a little, Primrose found a reasonably comfortable position and closed her eyes. "I think it must be a great thrill, for after a night on the ground the whole lot of you must be creeping about the woods like crippled old men. I am certain it makes the hunt very challenging." She smiled as Bened's laughter followed her into sleep.

Bened watched her sleep. There were scars on Primrose's mind and heart, ones put there by a cruel woman who thought she deserved more than she had. If the remembering had begun, there would be a few hard days ahead. It pained him to think it but the world would be a better place without Augusta Wootten in it.

He was just slipping into sleep when she whimpered. He looked at her and saw tears leaking from beneath her closed eyes. Bened sighed and tugged his bedding closer to hers. It would be uncomfortable but he could not leave her hurting like that so he put his arm around her, tugged her close, and calmed her. To his surprise she made a sound as if something pleased her and huddled even closer, resting her head on his shoulder. It was going to be a long night, he thought, as any urge to sleep was pushed aside by other basic urges it would take time to quell.

Chapter Seven

Bened glanced over at Primrose and grinned. She was looking very flushed and he doubted it was because she had woken up in his arms. It was a warm day and he knew women's fashions, even the plain serviceable gown she wore, were not the most comfortable attire to wear for a long ride in the sun. The look on her face told him she really wanted to complain but was biting her tongue. The touch of amusement that brought him was a welcome relief from the tight knot of desire he had suffered from for most of the night while thinking far too much about the kiss they had shared.

"'Tis nearly midday," he said, "and I would like to pause for a bite to eat."

Primrose tore her gaze from the cool temptation of the river she could see through the trees. "Oh, that would be lovely. Someplace in the shade. And I will take some time to wash off the dirt."

"What dirt? You look quite fetching. There is a pretty gloss to your skin from the sun."

"You mean the dew?"

"The what?"

"The dew. That is what my mother used to call it. She said women did not sweat, they became dewy. It will be nice to wash away the dew and the dust of the road with some cool river water."

"Huh. Dew. That is a very ladylike way of speaking of it. But, I am not sure you should go to the river. We are too close to your aunt's trail, which appears to matching right along with ours. Might not be safe. River is not too safe, either."

He watched her out of the corner of his eyes as he spoke. She bit her lip and looked at the river. He was teasing her and it astonished him. It had been years since he had done any teasing, especially with a woman. Bened found that he was enjoying himself.

"It is not dew," she snapped as she dismounted the moment they halted beneath some trees. "It is sweat. I am sweating like a hard-run horse and I wish to wash it off. And my feet hurt. They feel as if they are twice the size they were when I put my boots on. I want to put them in that water. 'Tis calling to me." She yanked a small towel and some fresh stockings from her bag. "I am going down to the river," she added in a tone that practically begged him to argue with her.

"Go then. Answer the call. Or, you could just allow your feet to answer it."

"Oh, hush," she grumbled, suddenly realizing that he had been teasing her.

It was difficult not to run to the river as fast as she could. The sun had felt so nice at the start of the day but had quickly grown to be a torment as the day grew warmer. Her feet hurt so much inside her boots she was surprised she could still walk. Shedding her boots and stockings as quickly as she could, she waded into the water and sighed with relief.

Bliss, she thought. The cooling effect of the water quickly spread through her body. Since she had no intention of putting the same pair of stockings back on, Primrose grabbed one, soaked it in the water, and, as discreetly as possible, began to wash up.

For a minute, she thought seriously about shedding all her clothes and sinking her whole body into the water. Then good sense prevailed. She was out in the open, at a river she had little knowledge of, and in an area that could be a lot more traveled than she knew. It would be beyond reckless to sit in the water naked as the day she was born. Anyone could come along. The fact that she would have even considered such a shocking action told her that she may have been traveling around by herself for far too long.

Just as she was buttoning the front of her gown again, she saw a young maid holding a basket hurry down the hill to stand at the river's edge. Thinking the girl had come to eat her lunch by the river, Primrose wondered if there was a chance she could buy whatever the maid had in the basket. Patting the skirts of her gown to see if she had any coins in her pocket, Primrose watched the maid open the basket, pull out something white and wriggling, draw her arm back, and hurl it into the river.

It yelped as it hit the water and Primrose leapt to her feet. She did not think twice but plunged into the river and walked as quickly as she was able to in the water toward the animal that struggled to paddle back to shore. Then she felt the current.

It was tugging hard at her feet. Keeping her eyes on the little animal fighting so valiantly to stay alive, she reached beneath the water to tie up her skirts and free her legs before pushing farther into the river. Primrose was afraid she was going to have to swim into the swift current and was bracing herself for plunging all the way into the water when she heard a bellow from the shore followed by a lot of splashing. A heartbeat later Bened stood beside her, glaring down at her.

Bened finished washing the travel dust off and had to admit that it felt good. He also understood why Primrose had wanted to put her feet in the water. It had been a while since he had enjoyed anything so simply pleasurable as tugging his boots and hose off his feet and setting them in the cool water.

He frowned in the direction of where she had gone to the river's edge. She had had long enough, he decided. It was not wise for her to be out anywhere alone. No matter how hard he had tried, he had been unable to shake Augusta. He knew she was hunting Primrose's brother but that would change quickly if the woman got word of her niece's presence in the area.

Primrose would be almost as big a prize for the woman as Lord Simeon. She could not get hold of all she wanted without putting the girl out of her way as well as the son. Bened did not know what the woman got out of marrying Primrose to a filthy, aging roué but he suspected it was a lot more than Primrose thought it was. The very last thing he wanted was for Primrose to be in the hands of a woman who could do to a child as she had done.

Stepping out of the river, he wiped his feet dry with his hose and then rinsed them out in the water. He looked at his shirt and rinsed that out as well. The question was, did he go back to the horses to get a new shirt, or just go find Primrose. He grinned, tossed his shirt and hose over his shoulder, and set off down the river to where she was cooling her feet. They would be traveling together for quite a while, he told himself, so she should learn to see him in the rough as soon as possible.

The moment he saw her, he tossed his wet clothes onto a rock and ran toward her. She was standing in the river. Then he saw that she was actually moving into deeper water where the current would be more dangerous. He yelled at her but she did not turn back so he went into the water after her, his heart pounding as he feared he would not reach her before the current swept her to her death. When he reached her side, he beat back the urge to just pick her up and take her back to shore. She was close enough to grab now if the need arose.

"What the bloody hell are you doing?" he demanded, the fear that had choked him fading as he saw how she was standing steadily in the water of a river notorious for catching people in its swift currents and drowning them or smashing them against the rocks a little farther downstream.

She ignored him and grabbed hold of his hand. "Hold fast to me so that I can stretch out and reach that poor thing."

All Bened could see was a small animal's head bobbing on the water. It was not getting any closer to them but he knew it was paddling furiously against the current that was trying to pull it deeper into its flow. He looked at Primrose who was hanging on to his hand and reaching out to it. He braced himself and switched his grasp from her hand to her wrist, then reached beneath the water with his other hand to grab hold of her tucked up skirts, struggling not to think of her bared legs hidden by the water. Now that he knew she was safe he was a little too interested in the way her wet gown clung to her full breasts. He did not need thoughts of her bared legs adding to that distraction.

"You are trying to save a rat?" he asked.

"It is a puppy. She just threw it in the river."

Primrose feared it was taking her too long and she would soon see the animal pulled off downstream to its death. She reached out as far as she could, confident that Bened would hold fast. Her fingers brushed over the animal's small head and then she clutched the loose skin at the back of its neck. It did not struggle against her grip and she yanked it free of the current, clutching it against her chest as Bened wrapped an arm around her waist and carried her back to the riverbank.

They had just reached the shore when she abruptly realized he was bare-chested. And a magnificent chest it was, she decided. Broad, a small patch of curly black hair in the middle of whatever they called a man's breasts, with smooth dark skin stretched over muscle. She was just thinking of rubbing her cheek against it when he set her down on her feet. The direction of his gaze reminded her that her skirts were kilted up, exposing her bare legs, and she quickly lowered them, grimacing at the feel of the wet material against her skin.

"That river has killed a lot of people," Bened said, resisting the urge to flex some muscles when he saw how intently she was staring at his chest, "and you just walk into it to save a rat."

"It is a puppy!" she snapped, finally finding the strength to reluctantly tear her gaze away from his chest and look into his face. "*She* threw it in the water." Primrose glared at the maid who was wise enough to quickly avert her greedy gaze from Bened's chest. "Took it out of that basket and just hurled the poor thing into the water."

"My mistress told me to do it. This one is for the river, is what she said. She saw it was a runt and only had one eye and told me to be rid of it," the young maid said.

"Then she should have done it when it was first born, not waited until it was weaned," said Bened. "Snap its neck. A quick death before it is old enough to know what life is. This rat—"

"Puppy!" Primrose yelled.

He ignored her. "—was aware and drowning is a bad death. They have time to try to fight it."

"No one noticed it until the mistress came to look over the litter when she was told they were weaned. She wanted to see if there was one she wished to keep or if she would just sell all of them. She will just make me come back and try again," she added with a glance at the puppy Primrose was busily rubbing dry with her towel.

"Who deals with the breeding?" asked Bened.

"The stable master does all the breeding of the

dogs. He kept the last one she wanted gone but it was not maimed like this one."

"Tell him what I said about snapping the neck."

"I will, sir." She looked again at where Primrose was working so hard to get the puppy dry. "Keep the basket." She turned and made her way back up the hill.

Bened watched how Primrose coddled the tiny dog, and sighed. He knew they would be lugging the thing along with them and he would have to keep an eye out for its safety as well. If it ever got separated from them, she would insist upon searching for it, ignoring the fact that they were being hunted. As a man who had once saved a three-legged dog from being shot by its owner, he fully understood but it was a very poor time to add a helpless animal to their baggage.

"You have saved it so now we can leave," he said, hoping she would see that they could not take the animal on their journey yet knowing it was a false hope.

Primrose looked around and frowned. "The maid left."

"She left the basket." He sighed when she hurried over to get it and ever so gently tucked the tiny animal inside. "You do understand that we are probably being hunted now as assiduously as your brother, do you not?"

"Of course I do."

He winced for there was a definite tone of insult to her voice. "It is not a good time to be dragging a puppy along with us. They need more care than an older dog. More careful watching. Perhaps we can take a little time seeing if someone else would take it and care for it."

"No." She stood up with the basket on her arm. "They will not do it as well as I can."

Primrose faced him, intending to tell him as firmly as possible that there would be no talk of leaving the puppy somewhere. Then her gaze settled on his chest. She was a countrybred woman and she had seen men's chests before, she told herself, yet his had her heart skipping around in her chest in a way that made her a little breathless. Her palms itched to touch that smooth, warm skin. When the thought of pressing her lips to it, maybe tracing those ribbed muscles on his stomach, popped into her head, she startled herself so much she was finally able to turn her mind back to the matter of the little dog.

"Rose," he began.

"I know puppies are a lot of care, but I will do it. I saved the poor creature. I will care for her. It has been a long time since I have had a dog and I have decided I will have this one." She turned and went to get her stockings and boots.

Shaking his head, Bened knew that was the end of it. He had seen that look in his mother's eyes from time to time when she wanted something and his father had protested. Once that look had settled on his mother's face, his father had just stopped arguing. Most of the time, his mother had proven correct in what she had wanted for it had made life better, cooking easier, and any number of other improvements in the crowded house. Bened was not sure a tiny one-eyed dog would prove of any value, but he had no intention of arguing anymore. He went and got his shirt, hose, and boots.

Once back at the camp, while Bened was donning his shirt and getting out new hose before he put his boots back on, Primrose sought out a sheltered area to put on clean stockings and her own boots. She then stood and wrung out her skirts. Already they were drying but she feared the dress might be ruined. Then she sneezed.

Bened was at her side in a moment. "You sneezed."

"I am not surprised. We are out in the wild and I was just in the water. Between the two there are a lot of good reasons for me to sneeze."

"You could be growing ill."

"Of course, I *could* but I sincerely doubt that I am. The water was not cold and today is quite warm."

"We will stop at an inn in the village."

"Bened, I will not fall into a fever just because I went into the water."

"You can never be sure of such a thing. Rivers are not the cleanest of places."

"That one looked very clean."

"We will stop at an inn so that you do not add the chill of the night to everything else."

He went to tend to the horses and she sighed. Stopping at inns was not only expensive, but they also put them inside a building and away from their horses. She knew he preferred to remain outside as often as possible. Shaking her head, she went and got some food out of her bags.

Bened found her carefully tearing up some chicken to feed the dog. As it had dried, it had actually begun to look less like a rat and more like a dog. Nothing would ever make it a real dog, though.

It was one of those women liked, keeping them on their lap or toting them around in fancy baskets and bags everywhere the woman went. He could admit the dog had charm but he did not understand women's fascination with the creatures.

"Hope you left enough for us," he said, and chuckled when she glared at him.

"Bread, cheese, and more chicken are right over there." She pointed to a bag set only a few feet away. "I am never certain about what to bring along on a journey as I am not sure what holds up well for long carriage or horse rides. There is some ale and a little cider as well but I suspect they are quite warm."

"Those three things do well enough. And warm drink is better than no drink. Cider is more tolerable warm than ale, though."

Primrose smiled in agreement and then stroked the little dog's head. It gave her a timid lick and her heart melted. She took a moment to check the animal's sex and was certain she had a female dog. A name was needed but she knew it would be a while before she came up with one. She was very slow whenever asked to name something. It was probably foolish, but she considered the name very important and wanted it to suit the thing, plant, or animal perfectly, to actually say something about it.

Bened handed her a tankard of cider and sat down beside her to enjoy his light meal. She felt her stomach cramp a little in demand and went to get herself some food. When she sat back down beside him, it was to find him and the puppy staring at each other. The puppy had the remains of a little snarl on her face.

"What are you doing?" she asked Bened in a near whisper, not wishing to disturb the puppy in case it had the idiot notion to attack.

"Determining who is the head of the pack," he replied in an equally quiet voice.

"What pack?"

"The one you just formed by bringing this little dog into it. Dogs need to know who is the head of the pack from the start or you will have a very hard time training them to do anything."

"Where do you get these ideas?"

"By watching animals. Have been surrounded by them all my life. They have their ways. Dogs are pack animals."

"I know that."

"This one is testing its place. Snarled at me and I knew what it was about. It was a challenge."

"And you had to answer a challenge from an animal that probably does not weigh as much as your boot?"

"Laugh if you must, but it is important. We are going to have it with us all along the journey and it needs to know that it should do as I say. And as you say, but that will be no trouble. You just became its dam, you know."

"By pulling it out of the river?"

"Aye. By picking it up when even its animal mind knew it was going to die."

"Animals understand death?"

"Why not? Animals understand the fight to survive, the need to procreate and protect that issue, the need to fight for what is theirs whether it be their hunting ground or their mate. This little one was fighting hard to survive and yours was the hand that reached out to help. That is something this dog will never, never forget. Me? I just showed up, although it helps. I was there when it knew it was safe again. And there we go. Submission."

Primrose looked to see that the puppy had her head down, her eye flicking down and to the side as she obviously tried not to look straight into Bened's who was calmly eating again. "That is it?"

"Aye. That is acknowledgment of the head of the pack. If it was not so exhausted and in the basket, it would probably show me its belly."

"Oh. Its weakest spot. How do you know all that?"

"Told you. Spent my life around animals and they fascinate me. Studied them a lot. You should take note. This is why you should always be careful about what dogs you look at in the eye. Look at the snout first and only after you know it is safe should you try a look in the eye, and do not stare into the eyes for long unless it quickly shows you that it is a submissive sort."

"Or what? What happens?"

"The dog could attack. It will think it needs to protect its place as head of the pack."

"What about cats?" She frowned when he laughed.

"Cats have other cats they tolerate and a tom can get all puffed up and angry around another tom but they are nothing like dogs. They do as they please. You might think you rule, but I doubt that you do. We had cats and some liked me, but I never took much time to study them as I did dogs and horses. Horses need their herd, dogs need their pack, but cats just need a nice sunny place to sleep in as far as I can see. I just knew it could take a much longer time to get even the most basic rules to how cats live. I sometimes think cats live with us because we make their fight for survival easier but not always because they like us."

She laughed. "You might be right about that but I like cats. Unfortunately, Papa did not. Not in his house."

Bened silently promised himself that he would ignore any stray cats and, definitely, any kittens he saw along the way. He would do his best to make sure he led Primrose in another direction. It would cause him a pang or two of guilt if the animal was actually in danger but he would do it. There was no doubt in his mind that Primrose would turn them into some kind of traveling Noah's ark if he was not careful. Her safety had to take precedence.

The ferocity with which he thought that surprised him. He looked at her feeding part of her own meal to the pathetic little animal in the basket and sighed. It showed a good character that she would be so loving to an animal most people would put down as useless. But it was more than that which stirred such a fierce need to keep her safe. He was not sure he wanted to look at the more right now.

She gave out another very delicate sneeze and he frowned. They would be stopping at the first available inn. Sleeping outdoors was safer, giving them more room to get away, but she should not be exposed to the night chill and damp. The way she glanced at him and then rolled her eyes told him she could see his decision on his face and he grinned.

"That look did not make you head of this pack," she said as she went to put things away into the supply bag. "It was just a giving up of telling you that I am not sick and probably will not get sick. A sneeze is not proof of that."

"It was a sign of the plague."

"Oh, for mercy's sake, I will not come down with the plague."

"A sneeze is not something to ignore." He assisted her in securely attaching the basket to the saddle.

"A sneeze is not enough to think I am headed for an early grave, either."

Bened just laughed as he mounted his horse and started out to find the next village and a warm inn. Grumbling about men, Primrose nudged her horse to follow him.

Chapter Eight

"There is no need to rush me," Primrose complained as Bened propelled her into an inn. "It is not as if I leapt into the water in the dead of winter. My skirts are already dry."

"I still cannot believe you risked your life for that rat," he grumbled, and then asked for two bedchambers and to be shown to a private parlor with a fire. He added a request for some food and hot tea even as he ushered Primrose to the parlor the maid directed him to.

The minute they entered the parlor, Primrose took the basket with the puppy in it to the hearth and waited while Bened made a fire. She then opened the basket, took out the little dog to set it in her lap, and rearranged the small scrap of blanket so that it covered more of the rough sides before setting it back inside but leaving the top of the basket open. The puppy took a minute to settle herself then sighed and closed her eye.

Except for the eye socket that had a covering of skin and fur instead of a proper lid, the animal was a pretty little thing. It had long fur, mostly white, with fox-red spots. Her face had that same red fur as a cap on her head and a mask over the eye area but white down the middle. It looked very much like the dogs standing with King Charles in a painting her father had hung in the library.

She ran her thumb gently over the place where another eye should have been and sighed. There was nothing there. This was not something that could be fixed. It was a one-eyed dog. The only other dog she had ever had had also had some faults but she had loved Constantine. He had been her constant companion for three years and then was suddenly gone. Primrose frowned for she did not recall much more than that but she was sure she ought to.

"That is odd," she muttered as she stroked the dog.

"What is odd?" asked Bened as he served her some hot tea. "Odder than nearly drowning yourself to save a one-eyed dog?" He watched her stroke her thumb over the patch of skin where an eye should be again. "Is there any eye there?"

"No, nothing. I did wonder if it was just that the lids had formed wrong but, no, there is no eye at all. I can barely feel the hollow in the bone where it should have formed. What I was thinking was a bit odd was that I can clearly recall my little dog, Constantine, but nothing about why he was suddenly gone. For three years he was always there and then he was not."

"He ran away."

"He must have and yet I barely recall any more than everyone searching for him for a day or two and then nothing." She laughed uneasily. "'Tis as if a door shuts on my memories the moment the grief I feel over losing him begins to rise."

"Because there is something there you do not wish to recall." He sat down beside her.

"That would explain the remnants of fear and horror I felt as I just pushed to try to recover the memory. When I was trying to find some reason for my fear of the dark, the same thing happened. I also discovered that I have a lot of holes in my childhood memories."

"One tends to forget a lot of one's childhood."

"True, but you usually recall the big things. Something made me not grow out of a deep, childish fear of the dark, especially when caught outside in it, but now that I know what it was that caused it, sad and upsetting though it was, the fear will ease. Is that not how we learn?"

"It is indeed." He sat down next to her, slowly reached out so as not to frighten the animal, and scratched one of the puppy's soft ears. "Thinking of how hard this creature fought that current despite being so small, it is even a greater shame that he was born maimed and a runt. He could have grown into a fine hunter."

"*She* would have made a fine hunter indeed. She may make one yet. You cannot be certain a missing eye will affect her as badly as you think. She was born with it, first began to see with it. To her, looking at the world through but one eye is normal."

"Ah, like a three-legged dog?"

"Did you have a three-legged dog?"

"When I was a lad. Best dog I ever had. Good hunter and tracker. Could even run, just not too fast and it was not a pretty thing to see." He grinned when she laughed. "I jest, which would greatly surprise my family, but it was wrong for that woman to order the dog drowned. Some pups come out wrong. You can see it at the start. Look each over, snap the necks of the ones you think will not be chosen or live long or well." He patted her on the shoulder when she made a soft sound of protest. "Quick, clean, and, done when newly born. Not a slow death with each moment left one of utter terror. That is cruelty."

"This time I am happy the lady was so certain of her breeders that she did not bother to check the perfection of the litter until they were weaned and ready to be sold."

"I think that is one of those foolish little dogs ladies love to carry everywhere and yaps a lot."

"Those dogs are untrained heathens. This dog shall be a Wootten dog, well-mannered and intelligent."

"Of course."

He put his arm around her shoulders and lightly hugged her. "Something still troubles you."

"My own cowardice," she muttered. "Who but a coward hides from the truth even from herself just because each time she tries to think on it, it brings bad feelings to life along with the memory. I understand the child doing it but not the adult continuing to do it."

"Your mind protected the child."

"My mind did it?"

"Why not? Minds can do wondrous things. Look at my own family, at the gifts given to us. There are several of us who can know an enemy is near like I can or can have visions of what is about to happen or know danger lies just around the corner. Your mind saw danger in how terrified you had become and decided the best thing to do was to bury that memory so deep it could not slip out and terrify you again unless you actually reached out for it. It protects itself from breaking that way, too, I think. I have been to war and seen similar things. Battle is a bloody, gruesome, noisy business and it can break a man, or woman, even a child caught up in the viciousness of it. But, at times, the mind takes another turn and just tries to protect itself by burying any memory of the event that tried to break it."

"You have given this a lot of thought."

"As I said, I have been to battle. I have held the ones whose minds broke and studied very carefully the ones who got some, well, shield, something that pushes away memories and thoughts of some horror they have seen and so they can keep doing as ordered."

"Ah, you studied them. It was an intriguing puzzle to you," She smiled faintly. "I think Papa would have liked you."

"Thank you, Miss Wootten. That was a fine compliment. Now, I believe food is required." When the little dog lifted her head at the mention of food, Bened laughed along with Primrose.

Augusta scowled at Jenson. She did not completely trust the man but she did trust in his love of his family and believed she could accomplish what she had threatened if he betrayed her. He was needed to do the various chores that made travel more comfortable but he was beginning to know far too much about what she was doing and he was not good enough to completely hide his distaste. She did not think she would allow him to go back to Willow Hill where he would be within reach of too many who would listen to him.

"Carl has told me that my niece and her companion are in the inn at the other end of the village," she said, idly wondering how her fool of a husband was managing without his valet. "I have told them to make her a little visit. Now I just need to find that damned boy."

"You know where he is going."

"No, I have assumed he is going to seek shelter with that perverted uncle of his. What I was about to ask you is if you have seen my niece's lover? Everyone keeps calling him that big feller but I cannot see Primrose taking up with some brute."

"He is no brute. He is a knight of the realm and a baronet. A Vaughn."

"So you recognize the name, too, but do you recall if anything is said about the family?"

"A great deal is said about them and the other half of the family tree," Jenson answered as he brushed the travel dust from her clothes. "They all descend from the Duke of Elderwood. Welsh by blood, although they are spread far and wide now. The Vaughns and the Wherlockes. I do not know much about this one except why he was knighted, actually given the hereditary title of baronet as well, and the man who saw to him getting those honors also gave him a piece of property. So he has gone from a prosperous farmer's son with good blood to landed gentry and a knight."

"What did he do to be elevated so?"

"Saved the only son and heir of an earl, a wealthy, powerful one. Heard that he actually took a bullet for the son. If rumor is correct, that appears to be his particular skill."

"Getting shot?"

"Protecting family members of the gentry. He watched over the Earl of Collinsmoor's younger brother when the lad joined the military and ended up in Canada. There have been others and would be a lot more if he did not seem to be very particular about whom he worked for. Now that he is landed gentry, he may cease to do that although I hear it pays very well."

"So he could be a very good shield for my niece."

"Indeed he could be but I suspect the men you have hired have judged his skill by now."

"Then I may have made a mistake not sending more than one of them to shoot her as she and Sir Big Feller rode here. He somehow found the man I sent and shot him right out of the tree." Augusta walked to the window to stare out into the courtyard of the inn. "He cannot be allowed to ruin my plans. I have been planning this since I realized I not only got the younger son but the useless one. Years, Jenson. I have slowly and carefully worked on this for years and I can see the goal I set myself all those years ago finally in reach. Some yeoman who got himself a minor honor or two will not keep me from it."

"No, m'lady, but if I may say so, thinking of him as merely some yeoman might be a mistake. He is a man who has been to battle and a man with a family notorious for coming to the aid of anyone in the family who needs it. A family with many people in it who have done shadowy things for king and country. I have heard it said that if you attack a Wherlocke, which is what he is, you attack them all and if you hurt one of them they will descend upon you like a swarm of wasps."

"Wasps can be swatted, Jenson."

"As you wish, m'lady."

She frowned, thought more on his warning, and then decided she was protecting herself as best as she could. The man would be silenced as would anyone else who might point a finger at her. That would be the end of it.

"When you finish with that, Jenson, go out and see if you can find any sign that Simeon has passed this way. And do not try to hide anything from me. If you find out something about him, you best tell me."

"Of course, m'lady."

A moment later he set aside his brushes and left the room. Augusta went to look over the work he had done, carefully inspecting each of her gowns he had hung up to air. The man knew well how to care for clothing. It was going to be a shame to have to replace him at Willow Hill. But culling would have to be done for she had no intention of leaving one single person who could speak of her guilt in the matter of ending all the Woottens save for Rufford. The only irritating part of it all was she would have to do the final culling of witnesses herself.

* * *

Primrose woke up to hear a soft growl near her head. She looked to see her new puppy curled up on the pillow next to her head staring at the window and baring her teeth in a soft, continuous growl. She groped for her spectacles on the small chest next to the bed, put them on, and stared at the window. She was on the third floor of the inn so she could not understand what could be out there to disturb her dog. Slipping out of bed, she put on her robe and tried to think of what to do next.

Then the window slid open and her heart leapt up into her throat. She cursed when she realized her pistol was on that side of the room tucked in her bags and so she was effectively unarmed. When a man's leg was swung inside the room, she hastily donned her spectacles, dashed to the fireplace, and grabbed the ash shovel. Standing in front of the fire, she watched the man finish his stealthy entrance into the room. He looked at her bed and frowned when he saw that it was empty, then swung his pistol around until he was aiming it at her.

It was an uneven standoff. Primrose knew she had no chance if he decided to shoot her. Considering all else that had happened to her of late, she suspected that was what he had come to do but hesitated now because he knew the sound of the shot would bring people running. Not that that would do her any good, she thought, as she would be dead.

"Shame, really. You be a pretty little thing."

"Then why do it?"

"Because not doing as she says gets your throat cut."

Before she could respond to that, a small bundle

of white and red fur leapt from the bed straight at the man sent to kill her. Primrose gasped as the puppy bit the man on the ear. He screamed and yanked the dog away, tossing her aside. The puppy landed near the hearth with a yelp and he stood cursing mightily while blood flowed down the side of his face.

Primrose took quick advantage of the man's distraction and rushed forward, swinging the ash shovel at his head. The first blow staggered him and the second sent him to his knees. When he actually tried to stand up she put all of her strength into the third blow and he went down. She stood over him, ash shovel raised high, and watched to see if he was going to move again, frantically trying to think of what her next step should be if he did.

Bened sat up straight in bed and then tried to figure out what had dragged him out of a sound sleep. He had that irritating tingle on the back of his neck and immediately looked toward the window. It was silently opening and he got out of bed, crept over to it, and stared down at the man clinging to the side of the inn and trying to open his window. Bened smiled, opened the window, and punched the man in the face. He then watched as the man tumbled down to the ground.

Brushing his hands off, he shut and latched the window. The irritating tingle was still lurking on the back of his neck despite the fact that his enemy was sprawled three stories down with what Bened knew were probably several broken bones. Then fear rose up so quickly in his chest he gasped. Primrose.

He yanked on his pants, grabbed his pistol, and

hurried to her room just as a man's cry of pain echoed in the hall. Throwing open the door, he stopped and stared. She had been attacked just as he had feared but she obviously did not need his dramatic rush to her rescue. That stung for he realized he had rather fancied playing the hero for her. A man was sprawled on the floor while she stood over him with an ash shovel in her hand. As he waved away the people who had rushed into the hall at the sound of the shot, quietly telling one of them to fetch the magistrate or one of his men, he stepped into the room and shut the door.

Primrose nudged the man on the floor with her foot but he did not even twitch. She then looked at Bened as he walked over to stand by her side. Every thought left her head when she saw that he was bare-chested again.

"What did you do to his ear?" Bened asked as he saw the mangled remnants of an ear on the side of the man's head.

"That was my new puppy's doing." She gasped and ran to the little dog that was just rousing herself. "She leapt right off the bed, sailed through the air, and latched on to his ear." She patted the little dog even as she checked for any injury but found none. "Most of the damage was done when he yanked her off for I think she had those little teeth tightly gripping that ear."

"He is missing a lot of it but I don't see it anywhere." He looked at the dog, which was licking its chops. "I do not believe we will be finding it in the room, either."

Primrose looked at her puppy and grimaced at

the blood splattered on the white fur. "Oh, puppy, did you eat it?" The puppy licked her face. "Oh, no, no, no. No licking with the tongue that ate a man's ear."

She put the little dog down and then hurried over to the washbowl to wash her face. She was vigorously rubbing her face dry when she caught Bened staring at her. Primrose began to feel a little foolish, set the towel aside, and walked back to where the unconscious man sprawled.

"What do we do with him?"

"We wait for the magistrate and his men to take this one and the one who tried to get into my room. They tried to kill us."

"Where is the one who tried to get into your room?"

"Sprawled on the ground." He started out of the room. "There will be a few men marching in and out of here in a few moments," he warned her before shutting the door after him, and she hurried to tug on her robe.

It was more than a few, Primrose decided much later as the last of half a dozen men walked out of her room. She had only briefly been embarrassed by being seen by so many in a state of dishabille, but it was, after all, the middle of the night and her robe was actually very modest. Every single one of them had stared at her dog in surprise when they heard what had happened to the man's ear and then grimaced when told there was no retrieving the missing piece. Primrose had been very hard-pressed not to laugh.

She was just deciding to go back to bed when

Bened walked back into her room carrying all his belongings. "What are you doing?"

"Making sure you are not alone," he replied as he set his bags down in the far corner of the room. "Even though you are protected by a man-eating dog, the animal cannot stop a bullet. You did very well, so did the rat . . ." He paused for her protest.

"Puppy," she said, and then muttered a curse when he grinned.

". . . but I think you know there was a measure of good luck involved."

"A very large measure. You also arrived very quickly."

"Not quickly enough to have stopped him from shooting you if you had not awakened and got out of the bed."

She shivered. "Very well then but where will you sleep?"

"I can sleep in the chair."

She looked at the small chair near the fireplace. It was a good size and cushioned but it would make a horrible resting place for such a big man. "No, you will end up all cramped and crooked if you try to sleep there. You take the bed."

"I am not taking the bed from a lady."

"Fine. Then you sleep on top of the covers and I will sleep beneath them."

He thought about that for a moment, knew it was going to be a torment to be so close to her all night long, but nodded. "Agreed." He frowned when he saw her crawl into bed and the puppy leapt up to join her. "The dog sleeps with you?"

"Yes, my man-chewing beast sleeps in the bed. I do not think she takes up much room."

He shed his shirt, yanked off his boots, and grabbed his blanket. "Odd that she went for his ear. Most attacking animals go for the throat."

Primrose could not help it, she giggled. "I think that was what she was aiming for but it appears her having one eye does indeed cause a problem and her aim was off."

Bened laughed as he settled into a comfortable position while trying very hard not to brush up against the temptation that was Primrose. "It did the job."

"It certainly did, although it is a bit disgusting that she then ate it. I shall have to come up with a suitable name for her soon. Sleep well, Bened."

He smiled faintly as she said the same to him. Sleep would be a long time coming when so close to her, his every breath filling his senses with her sweet scent. The fact that he only had to turn to be able to take her into his arms was a truly hellish temptation. It was going to be a very long night.

It was time to consider gaining a few allies, he thought. He had family close. In fact, he was sure Argus's new country manor was not far away and could be gone to without veering off the route they needed to follow. Argus himself might not be able to assist him but he would know where everyone else was and who might be close enough to help him keep Primrose safe until her aunt was defeated. There were many ways his family could help without becoming some private army riding at his side.

The woman was getting tired of the chase and,

perhaps, a little desperate. The attacks were more frequent now. Since he took care of the man on the road and now the two who had come to the inn, he was a little worried about what she would send against them next. None of those men were the same ones who had attacked him in the alley.

He needed some people to help him, ones who could keep a close eye on his back for him. The decision to seek out someone in his family made, he closed his eyes and tried very hard to clear his mind of any thought of turning, taking Primrose into his arms, and showing her how pleasurable a little loving would be.

Primrose heard his breathing even out in sleep and carefully turned to look at him. After she turned her head on the pillow she felt her little dog curl up against the back of her neck and smiled. Her protectors.

She looked over at the big man sleeping by her side and felt her heartbeat race. Primrose knew that if she reached out for him he would take her into his arms and share another one of those wonderful kisses with her. He would want to share far more, too, and she was not certain she was prepared for that yet. The desire he stirred inside of her was something she liked and wanted to savor but she was a complete innocent when it came to what men and women shared in a bedchamber. She was not certain what made her hesitate to reach for him more: the idea that she would somehow disappoint him with her inexperience or that she would give her heart to a man who had not asked for it yet.

These matters should not be so difficult, she

decided. Men found no difficulty learning all about passion from a fairly young age but then they were not the smaller part of the twosome, not the one who had to be entered. It was all so much more for a woman, she suspected. Women had a more difficult time separating the passion from love. A man could share passion with just about any woman, even if he did not actually like her very much and certainly never considered anything more with her than a romp between the sheets. It must be nice to deal with someone in such a deeply personal way with such ease.

A decision had to be made, she thought as she closed her eyes against the temptation of his bare chest. If they were going to be sharing a room for the rest of their journey, she had to know her course. It was time to make up her mind if she would just reach out to experience the passion she knew without doubt she could share with him and accept all the risks such an action would carry, or if she would bury that desire and save herself for some man who might actually want to marry her.

Chapter Nine

Something warm and soft was rubbing against his chest, Bened realized as he slowly climbed out of a deep sleep. He gazed around the room he was in and wondered where he was for a moment before the last clouds of sleep cleared his head and he remembered. He was in Primrose's room.

Cautiously he looked to his side. Despite the covers separating them he could feel her warmth. She was curled up against his side with her cheek resting on his chest. One small hand was resting on his stomach. Peering over the top of her head was the puppy. His arm was still asleep because she was lying on it.

He took all that in even as his body hardened with need. It was time to move away but he was trapped. Slowly he tried to slide his arm out from beneath her soft, tempting little body, stopping when she stirred. He was holding himself very still as he watched her eyes slowly open. Instead of the shock he expected, she looked beautifully flushed with sleep as she smiled at him.

"Good morning, Bened."

"Morning," he said, and, because he just had to, he leaned in and kissed her.

What he had intended to be just a fast stolen kiss quickly became a slow, deep tasting. He knew she was innocent but the way she returned his kiss told him she was also a swift and eager learner. He was aching with his need for her by the time the kiss ended and he buried his face in the warm curve of her neck.

He wanted to make love to her, possibly for days without resting, but he was not sure how to take that next step. Primrose was a well-bred lady who could sit higher at the table than he did and was, without a doubt, a complete innocent. That was not the sort of woman he had ever dealt with before.

Primrose murmured her appreciation as he nuzzled her neck and warmed it with soft kisses. Although she had lost some much-needed sleep trying to make up her mind about him, the decision had come immediately upon waking up next to him, feeling his big, strong body next to her, and looking into his beautiful eyes. Reckless it might be, but she knew that, if she did not learn the secrets of passion in this man's arms, she would regret it for the rest of her life.

She moved the hand she had rested on his taut stomach, lightly caressing that warm skin and tracing the trail of hair that went from it down to the top edge of the covers. And beyond, she thought, suddenly intensely curious about what was beneath the covers.

"Rose," he murmured against her mouth as he brushed a kiss there, "I need to leave this bed or we will not be leaving it anytime soon."

"Is that so?"

"Very much so. We might be spending the day in this bedchamber if I do not move and move quickly."

"Do you want to move?" she asked as she continued to caress his stomach, slipping her hand closer and closer to the barrier of the blanket.

He groaned, picked up that tormenting little hand, and pressed a kiss into her palm. "No, I do not want to move but are you sure you know what will happen if I do not?"

"Mmm. Yes, I believe I do."

"You are an innocent."

"Yes."

"And far above my touch."

She looked at his big hand, which was moving up and down her arm in a slow caress. "Obviously not."

He was surprised into laughing. "This is the point of no return, you know. What will happen ends your innocence and that can never be given back."

"Do you truly want to keep discussing this and trying to talk me out of it, or just get on with it?"

"It is something you should think about."

"I have been. I have discussed it with myself for most of the night. Discussion over." She placed her mouth on his and was pleased when, after a brief hesitation, he kissed her.

As his mind clouded over with his need for her,

Bened thought that if he did this, he could be affixing himself to her for life. That was often the result of bedding down with the innocent daughter of a titled man. She might not have any parents left but she did have a brother and an uncle. When no great fear of that reared its head, he ceased to think of anything save for the taste of her, the feel of her in his arms pressing her lithe body against his.

Primrose lost herself in the heat of his embrace. His strength surrounded her but did not threaten her in any way. She reveled in it. His kisses clouded her thoughts and made her ache for something more. Passion, she thought dazedly, was a powerful thing.

A brief check in her blind desire came when he began to tug off her nightclothes. She had never been naked in front of a man but she was now, before she could decide if she wished to. One glance at his face as he looked her over ended her unease, however. His appreciation was clear and she almost started to preen before him but he pulled her back into his arms. The feel of his warm skin against her cleared her mind of such thoughts in a heartbeat.

The gentle caress of his big hands moving over her body was so wonderful that it did not trouble her that he was touching what had never been touched by a man before. She just wanted him to keep touching her, wanted him to keep sparking the fire running through her veins with every stroke of his fingers. By the time he began to follow the caress of his hands with kisses, she was more than eager to enjoy that as well. She did not tense until he slid his hand between her legs. That much intimacy was a shock but that shock lasted only a short time for his touch began to build an ache in her that pushed aside all concern and embarrassment with greedy demand.

When he slid a finger inside of her, then another, the intrusion was both strange and exciting. Primrose might have been innocent in body and deed but not in knowledge. She knew he was doing what he could to prepare her for his possession. When just the thought of him pushing that hard length she could feel rubbing up against her thigh into her body dimmed a little of her hunger for him, she pushed it aside.

Only once, a married cousin had told her since she had just had her eighteenth birthday and could find herself headed to the altar at any moment. Lily had insisted that if the man knew what he was doing, it only hurt once and only for a short time. If the way his kisses and caresses were making her feel was any indication, Bened knew what he was doing and Primrose allowed her body full rein over her actions. Soon she was arching into his probing fingers, clutching at his shoulders as he kissed her, and feeling a desperate need stirring to full life inside her. She even murmured a faint protest when he took his skillful fingers away.

What took their place a short time later pulled her free of her blind desire for a heart-stopping moment. She fought against the urge to brace herself and tense but was not completely successful. Bened began to murmur soft words of encouragement and flattery against her throat and suddenly she felt a growing fear inside her wash away. She relaxed in his hold and her passion began to climb again.

Bened feared he was sweating all over her as he struggled to keep her calm. She had been all fire and need in his arms until he had actually begun to join their bodies. Then the fear of it had reared its ugly head. Having his gift react while in the middle of trying to bed a woman he had ached for, almost from the moment he met her, had the effect of dimming his own passion a bit but he now saw the good of it. She was all soft and welcoming in his arms again. He murmured an apology as he thrust through her maidenhead and she gasped with pain but even her pain faded quickly.

A heartbeat later that need to calm also faded. He felt his passion roar back to full life, freed from the restraint of his concern for her. He kissed her as he moved, determined to do his best to make her first time with a man memorable by giving her the gift of release. When he knew he would not last much longer, he slid his hand between their bodies and used his fingers to stroke her into joining him in passion's fall from the heights.

Primrose was still trembling from the wave of pleasure that had swept over her. It had so stunned her that she had briefly feared she would faint. The strong body of the man who had so sweetly revealed passion's secrets to her lay weakly against her, yet, even now, he thought to protect her from the weight of him, using his arms to hold him up so that he did not fully rest on top of her. She winced a little as he separated their bodies and all too quickly became aware of a faint soreness between her thighs.

Seeing the wince, Bened went and fetched a wet cloth to wash her with. He grinned as she blushed bright red when he did so. Rinsing out the cloth after cleaning himself off, he moved quickly to crawl back into bed and take her into his arms. He might not be ready to offer her any vows or promises but he would let her know that he was not going to just take what he needed and leave, that he had not only enjoyed what they had shared but was more than ready to keep on sharing it.

Once back in his arms, Primrose was no longer concerned about their nakedness, simply enjoyed the feel of their skin pressed close together. She knew she ought to care about the fact that she was now completely ruined but she did not. This was what she had wanted, and still believed that she would have always regretted it if she had not tasted it. She ignored the part of her that suffered a severe pang of disappointment over the lack of any declaration of love or promise of a future. That was not what she had been seeking.

"I would like nothing more than to spend the day here with you but we need to go have some food and get back on the road," he said as he kissed her cheek.

"Aunty knows where we are."

"Exactly. A part of me would like to hunt her down but I have no idea how many men she has at hand and that would leave you unprotected. It is why I have decided we are going to pay a visit to some family of mine and see if there are any of them who can join us. More eyes to keep a watch for the woman or her hirelings."

"Are you certain they will help?"

"Very certain. It will all depend upon who is around or close at hand. Even if they cannot help me in the way I would like, they will help me in any way they can." He brushed a kiss over her mouth and slowly sat up. "I truly would love to spend the day, or even a few days, right here, but we cannot risk it. And she is still hunting down your brother."

Clutching the covers to her breasts, Primrose sat up. "I know. I am going to take a little time to send a post to Uncle George. I am sure that is where Simeon is headed and, if my brother is still unaware of what is on his trail or why, Uncle George can warn him when he gets there."

"Excellent idea," he said as he climbed out of bed and reached for his clothes.

As he dressed he realized that he was both pleased and disappointed that she had not given him any idea of her feelings for him or pushed for any declaration from him. It was foolish for he had no intention of doing so, returning either words of affection or offering promises. He knew he had feelings for her, probably deep ones, but now was not the time to speak of such things. They were running for their lives and he knew that could confuse one. It could easily be that which drew them so close and once the threat was gone, that closeness would fade. Any decisions on the future had to wait until their lives were back to normal. He hoped she had similar thoughts for the very last thing he wished to do was hurt her.

* * *

Primrose handed her letter to the boy with a few coins and sent him off. There was a chance she and Bened would reach Uncle George before Simeon did, but she had decided that it was best to warn everyone anyway. She looked around for Bened and saw him leading the horses out of the stable. He was so beautifully big and strong. She had spent all morning struggling to decide what feelings she had for him and if she had any chance of stirring any feelings deeper than passion in him. No answers had come to her.

Life was just too frantic and dangerous at the moment, she decided. She did not trust what she felt. Kept asking herself if she was just enamored of him because he was her shield, her savior, and was helping her try to save her only brother. Desire she could trust. It was not a deep emotion but a bodily need. She had heard of enough women who indulged their desires without getting overly attached to the men who fed them to realize that not every woman gave her heart right along with her body. Before she offered up her own heart she wanted to be very, very sure that he was the man who had actually won it.

She secured the basket with her puppy in it to her saddle and watched Bened grin when the dog's small head popped out and the animal looked around, growled softly at the stableboy, and then disappeared back into the basket. On the other hand, she thought, if Bened made any more jests about her man-eating dog, she might decide he was not worth all this fretting she was doing about the true state of her emotions.

"That's a relief," he drawled as they rode out of the inn yard. "I feared your man-eating dog was about to snack on the stableboy."

"She is not a man-eater. She would never have eaten that bit of ear if it had not been in her mouth. And it would not have been there if the fool had not yanked her off while she was latched on so tightly."

Bened laughed. "I am certain that when that man gets asked what happened to his ear, your dog will immediately grow ten sizes in the telling."

Primrose smiled. "I know. So, you do not think they will be hanged?"

"No. They are locals and we were not hurt, they were. It becomes their word against ours. The one I knocked to the ground broke both legs and the other is missing most of his ear. Since I got the feeling they have grown up in this village, it is very likely it will be decided they have paid enough for their crimes. It will all depend on whether they have caused trouble for any of the villagers as well."

"That seems wrong since they had every intention of killing us for a few coins."

He shrugged. "The villagers do not know us."

She nodded and sighed. It was not right but it was often the way of things. It would not even be reported to anyone higher up than the local magistrate. The very last thing any village wanted was to have it known some of their local men had killed two of the gentry. Since the men had failed then no one would see the sense of bringing that sort of trouble down on their heads. And, it was also her aunt who was really the one behind it all yet she still rode around free.

"Do you think my aunt is still close?" she asked.

Bened could feel an itch on the back of his neck but could see nothing threatening and he nodded, deciding the proximity of the woman who wanted them dead was what caused it. "Do you think she will give up?"

"No. I think she has been planning this for a very long time. When small actions gained her nothing she decided to be bolder. Killing my father with no repercussions following probably made her think she could do as she pleased."

"Even if you had found what she used, it might not have been enough to stop this. Poisoning is very difficult to prove unless you actually catch the killer with the poisoned item in hand while her victim dies at her feet. The fact that she is a gentle-bred lady would only mean you had better have very hard proof."

She noticed how he kept looking around as he spoke and asked, "Do you sense someone?"

"I do but I see nothing and can get no sense of what direction the threat may be, which means it may not be very close. Just remember, if I suddenly disappear from your side, just keep riding along as if nothing alarms you."

Primrose nodded but the tension that held him ramrod straight in his saddle, his hand resting on his rifle, soon leeched into her. She looked to her left and realized they rode along the edge of a cliff. Looking down made her dizzy so she quickly turned her gaze elsewhere. A moment later she saw something glint up in the trees just ahead. "What is that?" she asked. "Up ahead and to the right a little. I saw something glint in the sun up in that old oak tree."

Bened looked in that direction, swore, and drew his rifle, but he was too late. The crack of the rifle shot echoed through the air. Smudge suddenly reared and, to Bened's horror, Primrose went flying out of the saddle to land at the very edge of the cliff. She clutched at the ground but could not get a firm hold. Before he could race to help her, she lost her tenuous grip and slid over the cliff. He swung around, aimed at the man he could see scrambling down the tree, and fired. The man was still falling as Bened threw himself from his saddle and raced to the edge of the cliff.

His heart was in his throat as he searched for her body on the rocky ground at the bottom but saw nothing. He was heartily cursing himself for missing the danger even though he knew he had felt it, had been looking for it, and had just not had enough time to find it. Then he heard something scrape against the cliff wall. He looked down at the length of the wall and nearly shouted in relief. Primrose was clinging to a ledge, her body half on it and half off. The noise he had heard had been her pulling herself up onto it.

"Bened?" she called as she cautiously stood up on the narrow ledge she had half-landed on.

"Here." He lay down on the ground and held his arm down. "Can you reach my hand?"

Primrose reached up as far as she could but only brushed his fingertips with her own. "No. Just a few inches too far away. Maybe I can . . ."

"Nay, do not move. I will fetch a rope."

He took the one on his saddle and found her gloves. Tying the rope around himself, he then tied her gloves on the other end and tossed the rope down to her. It was not until she affixed the rope around her small waist with a skillful knot that his heart ceased beating so fast his chest hurt.

"As I pull, use your feet and hands to save yourself from banging into the rocks."

"Is the man who shot at me gone?"

"Aye." Bened glanced toward the tree and saw that the man had not moved. Either his shot or the fall had probably killed him. "Very gone."

The moment Primrose reached the edge of the cliff Bened grabbed her and yanked her into his arms. He just sat there holding her close and savoring her each and every breath for several minutes before he turned his attention to untying the rope around her waist. He carefully looked her over for any injuries, relieved to find only a few scrapes and bruises he suspected she would know better how to treat than he did. He could have lost her this time, he realized, and knew that the devastation he would feel if that happened had nothing to do with the dangerous circumstances and everything to do with what was growing in his heart.

Primrose checked her horse over and found a deep graze from the bullet along the mare's right flank. It explained her panicked reaction. After fetching some things from her bags to treat the wound, she mounted her horse and silently followed Bened as he continued along the road. Even though her curiosity urged her to look, Primrose kept her gaze averted from the body sprawled beneath the tree. A faint odor on the breeze told her the man who had tried to kill her was dead and she had no wish to put that image in her mind to haunt her later.

"So are we still going to go to your family?" she asked as she slid her hand into the puppy's basket and stroked its soft ears to comfort her nerves.

"Aye. Aside from the fact that I cannot keep strewing dead men over the English countryside without having some sheriff or magistrate coming to find out what is going on, that one came too close to being successful. Your aunt is also sending out men to kill us at a faster rate."

"Because we are getting too close to finding Simeon?"

"I think so. I suspect he is aware of being in danger and probably knows just who it is, but she could yet catch up to him. The last thing she wants is you interfering with that in any way."

"I pray you are right about Simeon. There is always the chance that she is trying so hard to be rid of me because she has already succeeded in getting rid of Simeon."

"I just cannot get myself to believe that she has yet been successful in doing that. You said your brother was a very clever fellow, right?"

"He is. Sometimes confusingly so."

"Then he has to have begun to see that he is being hunted. That is probably why he left his friends with no word of where he was going or why. He suddenly figured out what was happening with your aunt and ran."

"From your mouth to God's ears. He is, after all, the one she really needs to be rid of."

"She needs to be rid of everyone who has had a

hand in this. When she hands her idiot husband the barony, she has to be certain there is no one left who knows what she has done or who could even guess what she has done. Anyone she has chased and anyone who has worked with her. There will be a cleansing done when she has rid her world of you and Simeon."

Primrose shuddered. "She truly has shrugged off any reins that held her back."

"She has and that makes her a very dangerous woman."

"Are you certain you wish to bring such a woman anywhere near your family?"

"They will be fine. I suspect a few already know we are coming, maybe even why."

"Maybe one of them can tell us whether or not Simeon is still alive."

He reached across the space between them and patted the hand she had clenched so tightly on the reins. "There may be one there who can do just that. Trust me, there will be some help they can give us and they will do so freely."

Simeon cursed silently as he pressed himself deep into the shadows near the far end of the alley. This time he had gotten the warning too late. He was not sure how he could get away without being seen. His aunt had her men everywhere and he could not let the woman get her hands on him again. Brief though it had been, those few moments in her company had been hell.

The sound of a door opening just to his right startled him and he warily looked at the young woman's face as she peered out and found him. He was tensed for her to cry out a warning when she held one finger up to her lips and silently told him not to make a sound. Then she signaled him to come inside. She was a pretty little thing with her thick black hair and crystal blue eyes but he did not think she was offering him any more than a handy shelter.

He slipped in and started to speak but she clasped a hand over his mouth. "Follow me," she whispered so softly he had to strain his ears to hear her.

There was no reasonable other choice for him so he followed her. She led him down a dark hallway to some stairs. Once in the cellar, she moved to a heavy set of shelves holding a lot of wine. She started to pull on it and he hurried over to help her, although it moved very smoothly after the first resistance. Behind it was a stone cave or cell. There was a small bed and table and he noticed someone had added a washing-up table with a jug and bowl as well as a chamber pot. A tray of food and drink was set on a table with one chair pulled up to it.

"What is this place?" he asked.

"It used to be a priest hole. Now it can hide you from the one looking to kill you, m'lord."

"How do you know someone wants to kill me?"

"I saw it. I am a Wherlocke, you know."

He was not sure what he was supposed to glean from that so he just nodded. She studied him as if waiting for some reaction to her name and then looked amused. Simeon was not accustomed to women being amused by him but tried not to feel insulted.

"A country lad, are you?" she asked as she walked into the cell and uncovered the plate of food. "No real dealings with the city or society?"

"Not much, no. A bit when I went to Oxford but, otherwise, I was learning to be the baron. I left Oxford after a year for they said I had outpaced them and there was no need for me to do any more than return for each exam. I did." He shrugged.

"Aye. I saw that you were a smart lad. But she wants you dead. She wants that clever mind of yours destroyed and gone forever. Seems whatever power lets me see what I do does not like that waste."

"Are you a seer?" he asked.

"A seer?" She laughed and then nodded. "I like that word. A seer. Aye, I see things. All manner of things whether I wish to or nay. Did you think I made a habit of opening doors to strangers, or even wonder how I knew you were hiding there right then and needed to get out of there and hide?"

"It did seem a suspicious coincidence but I was rather out of choices."

"I do not work for that evil crone chasing you and your sister. She is all dark, not one spark of the light in her. And those men she keeps hiring are not all that much better." She frowned. "There is one whose only tether to her is fear but not for himself, for others." She shook her head. "Not that you can do anything about it." She lit a lamp sitting in the middle of the table. "Now, I have brought some salve for your bruises."

"I do not have many."

"I can see by the cautious way you move that you have a lot. Might need to remove your shirt."

Since he was no untried boy, Simeon had to wonder why her saying he should take his shirt off would make him blush. That thought left his head when she pressed a hand against his back and the pain of it stabbed through him. Grudgingly he took off his shirt and allowed her to tend to the scrapes and bruises he had collected while fighting his aunt's men. The moment she finished, he put his shirt back on, acknowledging that the salve helped, but only to himself.

"You were lucky to get away," she said as she pocketed the small pot of salve. "So stay here and I will let you know when it is safe for you to go to your uncle and his man."

Before he could ask how she knew so much she was gone and he was shut in. He did not even catch her name yet she knew all about the trouble he was in and whom he was trying to get to. Sitting down to eat the aromatic stew she had set out for him, he hoped she was just what she seemed to be. A young woman who saw things and acted upon them, one who would not just turn him over to his aunt. He had to keep surviving, not only for the sake of the name and title of which he was the last in line, but for his sister. They could not let Aunt Augusta win.

Chapter Ten

Bened was still uncertain about seeking help from his family even as he rode up to his cousin Sir Argus's new country house. Since the man had married the Duke of Sundunmoor's daughter he had become quite domesticated. If the number of children running about was any indication, the Duke was visiting, perhaps even others of his family had gathered. They might even know he was in trouble.

"Oh my, your cousin is having a house party," said Primrose, feeling uneasy about intruding.

His cousin's country home was massive, not at all what she had anticipated. There was money there and she began to wonder why Bened would think himself below her. One who came from such a group, had relations with such money, and even a duke as a cousin was not considered lesser gentry. His blood was probably a lot richer than hers no matter what his direct family did for a living.

Suddenly the hairs on her arm stood up and she frowned at them. "How odd."

Bened saw his cousin standing in the doorway of his manor looking every inch the powerful man he was. "Cousin Argus has that effect on a lot of people. He is a very powerful man but do not let him scare you."

"Would he try to?"

"Sometimes he does not even have to try." He saw a small woman with red-brown hair hurry out to stand next to Argus. "Ah, now I understand why there are so many of the young ones about. Penelope is here." He looked at Primrose. "Another cousin. She takes in any of the wee ones bred by some of the more roguish members of the clan. I fear most of them are tossed out by their mothers because of what they can do and despite the nice stipends given to them for the care of the child."

He laughed as she began to look confused. "Do not worry. The sheer number of them can be confusing but they are good people."

"And all gifted as you are?"

"With different gifts but I will not weigh you down with what they all are at this time. If any of them display one that alarms, you just let me know. I can explain most of them."

"Do you know if any here now have a gift that will tell me if my brother is alive and safe?"

"I believe there might be one."

Bened dismounted after they halted in front of the manor, handed his reins to a stable hand, and then helped Primrose down. He held her hand as he walked up and introduced her to Penelope and Argus. "Is someone in trouble?" he asked.

"According to the letter we got from Chloe that someone is you and your companion," said Argus.

"Penelope brought my boys up for a visit and the duke is here to see his grandchildren. He brought the brood," Argus said as they started into the house, "including the devil twins."

"Argus, do not speak so about my brothers," called out a pretty woman with dark red hair as she hurried up to them and was quickly introduced.

"I will say what I like when it was your father who stole our nanny away by making her a duchess. I know he did it because I took you and he had no one left who could keep those two from destroying the world." Argus looked back at Bened. "So how bad is this trouble you are in?"

Lady Lorelei sighed, grabbed her husband by the arm, and dragged him into a large front parlor. "At least let them have some drink and perhaps some light refreshments before you badger them."

Before Primrose could say anything the woman was rushing off to see to refreshments. She looked at the people whom Bened called cousins and with whom he obviously shared a comfortable intimacy. She prayed she did not embarrass him before these people he had such regard for and tried very hard to smother the nervousness that might cause her to stumble.

"Congratulations on your honors," said Argus. "Knighthood and a baronet as well. Very good. Heard that earl gave you a little piece of land."

"Aye, not far from Modred's castle."

"Pretty around there and good land."

"Glad to hear it. Have not yet seen the place for myself. It could be something impressive or just a cottage for some farmhand but the acreage is a good amount. I am certain I can think of something to do with it but it is not what troubles me at the moment. Just what did Chloe have to say about me and trouble?"

"Just that you were in trouble, evil follows, and that you were headed this way. If you stopped to ask for help, the cloud of doom hanging over you would ease."

It was the way Penelope began to giggle and Bened grinned that kept Primrose from being alarmed by the man's statement of doom and evil. As far as she could tell a lot of these people had gathered here because the woman named Chloe had told them to and to help Bened. Even with that touch of strangeness she began to think might be a deep-set part of the clan, this was the way family should be, she thought, and had the odd urge to cry.

"Chloe says it is you the woman truly wants to hurt," Penelope said to Primrose.

"Actually, she wants me dead and she wants my brother dead, too," Primrose said. "That way her husband, my uncle, will become the baron and she will be the lady of the manor." She looked at Argus. "Did she have anything to say about my brother?"

"Only that he is in danger. Bened being with you made what she saw concerning him more clear. She has no connection to your brother, although she thinks that will be changing. Something about one of us we have missed."

"Another surprise child?" asked Bened.

"I think she would have said so. She knows us all well enough not to be too shy of saying it bluntly." Argus shrugged and fixed his gaze on Bened. "You know we lost some of our connections when we had to destroy so many of our own records just to keep people out of the hands of the witch hunters or the church." Bened nodded. "Well, from time to time another pops up. Could be that is what it is. Another lost connection appearing."

Lorelei appeared with several maids who efficiently served everyone tea or coffee and set out all manner of little sandwiches and cakes to eat. She then sat down next to Argus whose harsh features softened into a manly beauty when he looked at her. Primrose suffered a pang of jealousy and worked to kill it.

"So one of us is already helping?" asked Penelope.

"Chloe said one of us would lead him to safety so that we should be ready for her. Said she has been alone too long which I take to mean that she has a gift she cannot really share with anyone or has trouble from those who see what she is. But all this trouble will, in the end, lead her to the rest of us."

"But whoever this is will lead Simeon, my brother, to safety?" Primrose asked, needing to be sure that good news was really what she had heard.

"That is what Chloe said and she has never failed us yet. Now, one cannot just sit back and think it will happen just like that. Chloe does not see everything that happens or everyone who is involved. She sees a possibility and might see one step that is very important for things to change. So, we respond as if someone has just delivered us some information and we act on it."

Primrose slowly nodded. "Which is probably what is already known and that is why she sees what she does. For you not to help would be out of character and thus change the fate she saw."

Argus glanced at Bened and grinned before nodding in agreement with Primrose. "Precisely. It does make life difficult, though. She sends out a warning and then you have to think carefully so that you know you are acting as you would normally and not as you think you ought to, which could change the whole. Our cousin Alethea sees things more precisely but also just small parts of the whole. Chloe implied that the one helping your brother is one of them but more. Not sure what that means."

"I sometimes think our Chloe likes to play at being mysterious," said Penelope.

"Could be," agreed Argus. "She can have a puckish sense of humor. But I believe what she does is try to be far too careful about putting her own interpretation on what she sees. We get a perfect description of what she saw. She doesn't want us to know what she thinks because it could change what she saw."

"So Simeon is still alive and will be safe," Primrose whispered.

"He obviously does not have people shooting at him from the roadside," said Bened.

"Why is your aunt trying so hard to see you dead?" asked Penelope. "You cannot inherit anything, can you?"

"No. But I think she realizes I might have guessed what she is up to and she will not allow that. Bened believes that, too. She will be rid of anyone who helped her or who she believes has guessed what game she played. I am still finding it difficult to understand how none of us saw this in her in all the years she has been lurking around."

"The closer it is the harder it can be to see," said Lorelei.

"I suppose." Primrose helped herself to one of the small cakes and immediately her puppy popped its head out of the basket she had carried in with her, causing both of the other women to gasp and then laugh.

"I am sorry. I did not even ask if it was permissible to bring her in. I have just gotten so used to carrying the basket with me everywhere. Is it allowed or do you have a place for dogs?"

"No, it is fine," said Lorelei, and she elbowed Argus when he muttered something. "A tiny dog like that will be no bother. What happened to its eye?"

"Does not have one. Born that way."

Lorelei moved closer and patted the dog. "Even with that mar it is quite a beautiful little dog."

"It is a man-eater," said Bened, and he grinned when Primrose protested.

"No, she is not. She was protecting me and went for the man's throat."

"She must have been feeling a bit peckish because she missed that and ate the man's ear."

"Stop it. If the fool had not yanked her off before she let go of him, she would not have taken a piece off."

"If one wished to, I suspect you could sew the piece back on," said Penelope.

Bened shook his head. "Dog ate it. That is what I am saying—a man-eater."

Primrose shook her head. "She is just a puppy.

Put anything in a puppy's mouth and it will try to eat it."

Penelope was laughing so hard she had to hold her stomach and Bened grinned at her. "Think that funny, Pen, you should have seen her expression when the puppy, fresh from her mangling of the man, licked her face." He nodded when Penelope laughed even harder.

"You will have to excuse our Pen," said Lorelei, even though she was grinning. "She has spent much of her life surrounded by young lads. Her humor sometimes reflects that influence."

"Poor puppy," Primrose said, scratching the dog's ears. "I need to give her a name. Cannot keep calling her Puppy."

"What were you thinking of? Anything in particular?"

"I was thinking of Boudicca or Hippolyta, Queen of the Amazons."

"Very impressive names."

"Bigger than the dog," murmured Bened.

"She tried to save my life. She deserves the name of a strong woman."

"Boudicca then," said Argus. "She hurled herself at a much larger foe and somehow came out of the fight the victor."

"Boudicca then. I had best take her for an airing and, if there is a place where I may do so, I would really like to wash off the road dust and the rock dust from the fall."

"What fall?" asked Argus.

Bened explained what happened and Primrose suddenly found both women escorting her off to a bedchamber. Sir Argus told his wife to put her and

Bened at the far end of the guest wing, which caused Lorelei to give him an odd look, but Primrose was quickly distracted by the chatter of the two women as they led her away. They gave her a thorough look-over, putting some healing cream on her scrapes and bruises, and showing the dog a tiny walled-in area where it could go outside. Boudicca rushed out, did her business, and raced back in to sit at Primrose's feet so fast both women laughed.

"She is very attached to you," said Lorelei.

"I suspect it is because I saved her from drowning." At their encouragement she told them the whole story and realized she had been a little reckless. "I suppose Bened calling her a man-eater is a bit better than having him continue to call her a rat."

Before Primrose knew it she was chatting freely with her new friends as they led her outside to meet some of the others. The first thing she noticed was that there were a lot of boys. One little girl with thick black curls and dark blue eyes took it all in her stride, doing as she pleased, and facing down any boy who tried to stop her.

It was overwhelming. She was so jealous she felt guilty. This is what she had always wanted. A huge, boisterous family one could always turn to for help, comfort, or a little bit of loving madness. When they returned to the house she excused herself and went back to the bedchamber they had said was hers. She needed to do something to smother these little bouts of jealousy before she said something to give herself away. Settling down on the bed, she welcomed Boudicca into her arms and soon fell asleep.

* * *

"Penelope, have you seen Primrose?" asked Bened.

"In the rooms we gave you. I have a feeling she is sleeping. After the adventure you had earlier and then the way we can so completely overwhelm someone, I suspect she was badly in need of a rest."

"Thank you. Any new blessings?" he asked, referring to the stray children the bachelors in the family produced at regular intervals.

"Three since I last saw you. No gifts that require announcement or investigation. Just the usual. Although Gawain, who is Cousin Morris's boy, can not only see and talk to ghosts but, if he touches you, can help you to see and hear them too."

"Ah, and therein lies the tale of why his mother left him to you."

"I fear so. Tell me, Bened, is this Primrose the one?"

"The one what?"

"The one you always said you would keep."

"I do not know. I am waiting for all this run-away, fight, hide, and run-away-some-more business to fade so we can look at it all in the normal light."

Penelope nodded. "That might be wise but watch closely, Bened. You might see at some point that it would be better to speak up or you could lose."

Bened felt the weight of those words as he slipped into the bedchamber they had taken Primrose to. It took only one glance around to see why Lorelei had given Argus an odd look. This was a suite of rooms meant for a married couple. There was another bed in an attached room here, which meant he could sleep with Primrose or he could sleep alone. On the other hand, they would still be together to talk, to see each other, to occasionally kiss, and to keep whatever was between them still growing. Crafty Argus, he thought as he went to sit on the bed next to Primrose, then to carefully stretch out on his side next to her.

Primrose stretched and felt her leg brush against something. Thinking it was Boudicca, she opened her eyes and had to swallow a screech of surprise. It was Bened lying right next to her and calmly watching her sleep.

"What are you doing in my bedchamber? Someone could see you."

"No need to worry about them seeing me, they know." He got up, walked to the door to the other bedchamber, and opened it, nodding when she gasped and blushed. "A suite for a married couple or, as in our case, ones who may or may not be lovers so they may have the need of an extra bed. A room with a choice."

"That is just a little embarrassing."

"Do not let it trouble you. All those children out there? Most of them are by-blows. But my family is very strict on the duty of any man who breeds a child. He will see to their care and make certain that child does not suffer for who he is or, in our case, what he can do. It was the mothers who tossed them into our Pen's lap and she was not much more than a child herself. There was a lot of trouble with her stepfamily but we sorted that out. She is very good at teaching them how to deal with their gifts and so she still takes them in when needed."

"But their fathers do not do it?"

"Most of them would make poor parents since

they are more gone than home and Penelope loves it," he said as he returned to the bed and took her into his arms. "She has all the support she needs and when the fathers can be with their children they come and stay."

"But she becomes the mother for them all."

"Exactly and they do need that. We are very fortunate that she found a man who, along with his own family, accepts that completely." He looked around for the dog and frowned. "Where is Boudicca?"

"Out in the little garden. The doors to it were left slightly open," she said even as the dog stuck its head inside, looked at her, and then went back out. "She keeps doing that as if she fears I will disappear but appears to enjoy the garden too much to give it up completely."

Primrose quickly forgot what she was talking about as he kissed her neck. He slid one big hand around to begin undoing her gown and even the thought of protesting that left her mind when he kissed her. She was faintly aware of how he was removing her gown as he kept her drugged with his kisses, but she did not care so long as he did keep kissing her, keep stirring up the thrilling desire he brought to life inside her.

"The doors to the garden are open," she said when he finally gave her a moment to breathe and clear some of passion's haze from her mind. "Someone could come in."

Bened got up and went to close the door. As he did so he removed his coat, then his neckcloth, and finally his shirt. Once the door was shut and latched he turned to come back to the bed only to pause. He cocked his head as if listening to something, reopened the door, and, with a heavy sigh, allowed Boudicca back into the room before latching the door again.

Primrose laughed softly as the dog went to curl up in her basket near the fireplace. She welcomed Bened back to bed with open arms, holding him close and enjoying the feel of his warm skin beneath her hands. The fact that, by giving them such a room for their stay, his family indicated they knew she and Bened were lovers troubled her but as Bened began to make love to her, she cared about that less and less. She would, she decided as he tugged off her shift and their flesh touched, worry about that later.

Bened felt her soften in his arms as he stroked her high, firm breasts, the hard nipples teasing his palms. He found it difficult to believe that such a delicate, pretty gentry lady was allowing him into her bed, into her body, with such a warm welcome. Too many had taken one look at him and thought he was just some farmer, too beneath their touch to be even considered as a choice to share their well-used beds. It was why he had kept his few lovers to the ranks of eager country girls and courtesans.

When he took her nipple deep into his mouth, her whole body shivered from pleasure and that only added to his soaring desire. Bened happily feasted on her breasts as he slid his hand down between her strong, slender thighs to find a warm, damp welcome. It was not until her small hands ran over his backside that his delight in simply giving her pleasure took an abrupt turn toward his own desires and what he needed.

Primrose was surprised by the groan that escaped

the big man in her arms when she stroked her hands over his taut backside. That her touch could move him so astonished her, she almost stopped what she was doing. She clung to the delightful knowledge that she could actively stir Bened's passion, adding to the desire he revealed for her. So involved was she in seeing which touches he responded best to she was shocked when the kisses he had been spreading over her stomach moved lower.

She gripped the sheets so tightly Primrose was astonished they did not rip. Shock warred with the passion roaring through her. Her body tightened until she thought she would break. Although what he was doing was still fueling her passion, it was also making her frantic to have him inside her.

"Bened. Now," she demanded.

Bened almost grinned. She sounded so forceful. He kissed his way up her lithe body and began to slowly join their bodies. He trembled as her tight heat slowly swallowed him up. When she lightly dragged her nails down his sides as she wrapped her beautiful legs around him, he knew he could no longer go slowly, gently.

When Primrose felt Bened begin to move harder and faster, she almost laughed, a tickle of joy joining with her rising passion. Bened was thrusting into her so forcefully, her body was sliding up the bed. Her clenching desire abruptly snapped and flooded her with delight. Bened thrust hard once, twice, and then his whole body tautened over her. She felt the warmth of his seed and then, with a faint tremor and a sigh, he settled over her, careful to keep his full weight off her.

He kissed her gently. "I was here to tell you that

dinner would be ready in an hour. There will be a bell rung."

He laughed when what sounded like a massive gong sounded through the house and Primrose bounded out of bed. As she hurried to get ready he stayed sprawled on top of the bed and enjoyed the glimpse of that small, slender yet womanly body he knew he could not get enough of. From her slim legs to her full round breasts he savored very inch of her, few that there were.

When she came back to the bed to frown down at him, he curled his arm around her waist and yanked her into his arms. She was just opening her mouth to complain when he kissed her. To his delight she quickly melted into his kiss, eagerly returning it. The moment the kiss ended, however, she wriggled free of his hold, got off the bed, and stepped out of his reach.

"No more of that. I am hungry," she said.

He thought about that for a minute, nodded, and got out of bed. It pleased him more than he could say when her gaze followed him as he walked into the privacy room to wash up. It was difficult not to strut like some vain peacock. Having the woman he desired like his looks as Primrose did, making no secret of her appreciation, was a feeling unlike any other he had ever enjoyed.

"Do you know if there is any help to be had here?" she asked as he dressed.

"Well, I believe we will leave here alone but we shall see," he replied. "We do not really need a guard. It would be nice but we can manage without it. We have thus far."

"I know and I did appreciate hearing what that woman Chloe had said."

"Chloe may be hard to understand at times and leave you wanting so much more, but she has never been wrong in what she has told us."

"I know. I did hear that when it was said. I just wanted someone to tell me that Simeon was fine. He is. That is more than worth the journey here."

He wrapped an arm around her shoulders and started to walk her out of the room. Before he could shut the door behind them, Boudicca raced through and stood by Primrose. "Will she stay away from the table?"

"She has so far, has she not? But I will ask Lorelei if she needs Boudicca set in another room or the like. I have eaten at homes where there are dogs right in the room, just well behaved. I am hoping that, to stay near me, Boudicca will remain well behaved despite all those children."

He laughed. "Good luck. That might be an empty wish for it rests on the ability of all of those children being well behaved." He kissed her on the cheek. "This could be a time of madness for you but just remember, you can ask anything you want if there is something you do not understand."

They walked into the big dining hall and it appeared as if chaos ruled. There was a massive dark wood table in the shape of a huge letter *U* that appeared to be already full, although Argus waved them over to two seats on his right. In the far left corner there was a small rectangular table where the women caring for the youngest members of the clan sat with those children. She quickly asked for and received Lorelei's assurances that Boudicca was welcome and her dog disappeared under the table. Primrose could feel the dog draped over her feet but soon some child tempted the puppy away by holding something under the table. A fast look around the table told her that Boudicca was being fed by nearly everyone at the table. All she could do was hope her dog did not end up being sick.

Conversation swirled around here. There was a lot of teasing and the talk revealed to her that there was much about the world that she did not know. The number of gifts the people had told her a lot about the close ties the family maintained. They needed one another if only for a source of people who understood what they could do and help one another through any learning that needed to be done. It was a wonderful thing to see, she decided, and sighed with a strong touch of envy.

"Is everything all right?" asked Bened.

"Yes, fine. I was just admiring your family." She patted his hand. "It is really quite miraculous, Bened. Mine was not bad—me, my father, and Simeon, I mean—but then there was the side that was my aunt and uncle. Yours is so close, so friendly with one another, so ready to help and that help being treated as the gift it is. As I said—you are a very lucky man."

He was touched and then thought that he was indeed lucky but it was not his family he was thinking of. Hoping no one was paying too much attention, he lifted her hand to his lips and brushed a kiss over her knuckles. "Yes, a very lucky man indeed," he murmured.

"Did she spill something on her hand?" asked

a beautiful little boy sitting on the other side of Bened.

Bened looked at the boy with his wild, deep red curls and huge green eyes. "And which one are you then, lad?"

"Morris's boy. My name is Gawain. I can see ghosts and, if you want, I can help you see them, too. My mother did not think it was fun," he added in a soft voice heavily weighted with sadness. "So, did she spill something on her hand?"

"Yes, I fear she did," Bened said, and patted Primrose's hand. "I hurried to lick it clean. I was happy to find that it was something I like this time."

"That is a good thing. You don't want to have to lick up something that is evil-tasting like sprouts."

"God save us all from such a fate."

Primrose knew Bened had made a face because the little boy giggled so hard he had to put down his spoon. And she realized, right at the moment she watched him take that sad look out of a little boy's eyes by being silly, that she was desperately in love with this man.

Chapter Eleven

Simeon woke at the sound of the door opening.
The knot of fear he had been unable to shake since
he had discovered he had been locked in began to
ease. He sat up on the narrow bed and watched the
young woman who, he hoped, had rescued him.
The doubt he now had was because of how she had
locked him inside and he wanted a good explanation for that before he even began to trust her.
There were several good reasons for her to do
that, such as an understandable fear for her own
life or fear of a robbery. Despite all her talk of
some sort of vision prompting her actions, she
did not know him.

Then he noticed she was walking like an old
woman, a slow shuffling step and bent over ever so
slightly. He quickly went to take the tray from her
hands and saw how pale she was. Her eyes were
dark with a pain she could not hide from anyone.

"What has happened to you?" he demanded,
setting the tray on the table before turning back
to her.

"Nothing for you to worry about," she answered, the firm annoyance in her voice weakened by its unsteadiness.

"Did I say I was worried? No. I worry about my sister, about being locked in here when I do not even know who you are, and I worry about that cursed murderous aunt of mine but I do not worry about this. This, whatever it is, is done and needs tending to. Did you bring that salve you used on me?"

"Yes. It is on the tray. I thought you might wish more of it. And, I am fine. 'Tis but fresh and the pain will soon pass."

"Then it will do so much faster with the salve. Sit down and undo your gown."

"I beg your pardon?"

He laughed softly as he went and pulled the wine shelf in place then shut the door before returning to her. "Sit and undo your gown. You will not shock me and you need to help those wounds on your back heal."

"How do you know I have any wounds upon my back?"

"Because she used to do the same to me, several times before I grew too big for her to easily do it and make me sit still for it. Is she still upstairs?" he asked as she undid her gown and, while holding it close in the front to try to maintain her modesty, tugged it down to her waist in the back.

Simeon winced. Augusta had not lost her touch. The marks of the caning were long, criss-crossing the woman's smooth, slender back from shoulder to waist.

"Nay," the woman whispered in reply. "She came looking for answers and I gave her none she wanted to hear. Somehow they knew that you had come into the alley and wanted to know if I had seen you. They did not trust my reply when I said I had not."

"Did you tell her any of the other things you can see or know about her?"

"Nay, I wanted to. I wanted to tell her she would never win, to describe the twisted evil inside her, and even how the one person she hates more than she hated your father will see to the ending of her but I knew better. She will leave none alive."

"I have guessed that myself. You are lucky she left you alive. And so am I for there was no way for me to escape from here without you and the key to the door." He caught the sound of her soft gasp as she looked over her shoulder. "I would have died in here, slowly, if anything had happened to you."

"I will not lock it again."

"Thank you. Just why are you still alive? You have become a witness to the fact that Augusta is not the genteel lady of the manor she pretends to be. No matter what you told her she may still think you have some knowledge, and that would mean you have to join the rolls of the dead she has left in her wake."

"She left her men to tend to the finishing of me. I scared them away."

Done treating the cane marks with the salve, Simeon moved to sit on the table facing her. "You scared them? How?"

"I told them how they would die."

"Then they will go and kill Augusta. That would only be a help to us."

"Nay, not yet. I did not tell them it was she who did the killing, although they believe she will in the end. She only orders it and then she will end the killer last. I did not tell them that. I only told them how they would die in great detail." She turned sideways to keep her modesty as she redid her gown. "It near to made me vomit to do it as their deaths could be bloody and vicious, but I did it. They ran."

"And I think that is what you should do. Run. As far and as fast as you can."

"That is my plan. We head to your uncle George's on the morrow before the sun fully rises. I just need to collect a few things."

"I truly appreciate what you have done for me, except for locking me in of course, but I can get to my uncle's on my own."

"Nay, we cannot change what I have seen. I saw me with you so be ready." She stood up and started to open the doors.

"I will try to be but I can promise nothing. There is so much to pack for the journey, you know."

"You are behaving very badly, my lord."

Simeon laughed. He waited to hear the locks turned but there was no sound and he breathed a sigh of relief. Then he sat at the table to eat the meal she had brought him and tried not to think too much on all the mistakes he had made concerning his aunt Augusta, mistakes that may have cost him his father.

Bened groaned his disappointment when he woke to find himself alone in the bed. After last night he had hoped to enjoy a romantic morning, to have some time to show Primrose that he could actually be romantic instead of just a rutting goat. Bened knew what others thought of him. Big and strong, a man of few words and little humor. He was the one they all called on when they needed someone to watch their backs, protect someone they loved, or help them hunt down the enemy. He was dependable, the protector, occasionally the hunter.

Lying on his back and lightly scratching his belly, Bened now wanted to be seen as a lover, as someone who knew how to laugh. He wanted people to see his strength but also his softer side. The trouble was he was not all that certain he had one. What he was sure of was that he wanted a touch of the courtier at the moment. He wanted to be able to woo Primrose with sweet words, the kind of words that touched a woman's heart.

"And is that not worth a hearty laugh or two," he muttered as he got out of bed and faced the day, the warm glow from the night's lovemaking fading quickly.

By the time he had finished his breakfast and called for their horses to be brought round, Bened decided it was past time to settle the matter of what help he might need and what he might be able to get from his family. He had seen Primrose briefly at breakfast and told her they had to keep moving so he knew she was getting ready. She understood the need for that as well as he did. The longer Augusta Wootten ran about free to create havoc, the more people died. It might be true that a lot of them deserved the fate they got, but anyone who thought they had the right to coldly take a life could not be allowed to run about free.

Argus walked out to wait for the horses with him. "I should go with you."

"You have guests," Bened said, "and I do not think I have need of an army to get to Elderwood."

"I would say we could watch your back but none of us can do that as well as you can. What I will do is set out a watch for her, try to stop her here. Best I may be able to do is slow her down, though."

"That would be most helpful. She has been a step or two behind us all along, close enough to send someone out to try to kill us on the road. The last time she tried that, she nearly succeeded in killing Primrose." He nodded when Argus cursed. "A day or two of travel without some dangerous confrontation with her hirelings would be a blessing."

Argus shook his head. "All this blood spilled for a barony. There must be a very fat purse that comes with it."

"I have no idea," confessed Bened. "Society is mostly a mystery to me and I'd never heard of the Woottens or the Baron of Willow Hill. They have land, a manor house, her father could afford to support himself and his children as well as his brother and the man's murderous wife, and both Primrose's horse and her attire are not those of a poor person. That is all. Never asked her if there was a lot of money for her aunt to get her bloody hands on."

"For that woman to go to all this trouble there has to be some money. Or, that woman knows how to use something the baron has to get a lot of money. I think I may look into that. Although it does you no good at the moment, it may be of use afterward. If the woman does not end up dead, she will need to be tended to by the courts."

"Oh, Aunt Augusta will never allow herself to be taken before some magistrate," said Primrose as she stepped up beside Bened. "The humiliation of being treated like some common criminal would be more than she could bear."

"So, what? Do you think she would end herself?" asked Bened.

"The more the possibility seems possible, the harder she will fight. And then she will wash the blood from her hands and become the foolish vain woman who fooled us for so long."

Bened cursed. "And some magistrate would never believe her capable of what she is being charged with. Nor, I suspect, would a jury of her peers."

"She is quite good at playing the vain lackwit whose only concern is the style of her gown and if she is going to get the right invites to the right events. And, sad to say, since that is what so many expect such a woman to be, they believe that is just what she is, who she is. That woman could never do the things we would be accusing her of. She lacks the intelligence and guile. Or so they would believe."

"What you are saying is that she must die before this can all truly be over with," said Argus.

Not hearing any condemnation or disgust in his words, simply acceptance of a fact, Primrose nodded. "I can see no other answer. It truly is her or us. I would feel worse about it except that she does have a lot of blood on her hands and some of it from people I cared about."

"Are you thinking there may have been others you might not even know about?"

"I am. If this is how she is rid of barriers to her dream of being an important person in society, then what did she do to anyone who blocked her from making that rise?"

Nodding, Bened frowned in thought. "It is also another thing that would be very hard to prove." He took her by the arm and escorted her to her horse. "We had best be on our way. Argus and the others are going to try to keep Augusta off our trail for a while."

"That would be lovely."

Primrose was still thinking of how nice it would be to travel for a while without having to fear her aunt was close on their heels when they gave everyone a final wave and rode off. It was a pleasant day for riding, cool yet with a bright sky and a lot of sun. Unfortunately, it meant it was a good day for her aunt to travel as well. If the woman caught scent of their trail, there would only be Bened's family and whatever interference they might be able to cause to slow Augusta down.

How had her aunt hidden this monster for so long? she wondered. Worse, how had she, her father and brother who were both very smart men, missed seeing it? There had to have been signs. No one could contain so much anger, envy, and murderous jealousy without there being some hint of it bubbling beneath the surface of their smile or hidden beneath their polite chatter.

The other thing that puzzled her was why her aunt had waited so long to act. They had all been so blissfully ignorant of who she really was, so why had the woman not taken advantage of that years ago and just killed them off one by one? She thought of her father and then her mother and shuddered. There was the strong chance the woman had been trying to, had just been far more cautious than she was now. Since the baron was dead and few in society had ever met her or her brother, Simeon, Primrose suspected the woman believed there would be no real outcry into their abrupt disappearance.

The fear and anger churning inside her suddenly began to ease and Primrose glanced over at Bened. His face was free of any real expression and his gaze was fixed too intently upon the ground in front of him. Primrose frowned as she thought about all the times he had been near her when she had grown calm, very reasonable fears or concerns fading away to just a thought.

"It is you!" she said, and pointed at him.

"What is me?" he asked, sensing her fear and anger were gone enough so that his gift backed away.

"You are doing something. When I start to get all tied up and twisted with a very reasonable fear or anger or even when a memory hurts so bad I wish it gone, you do something to soothe it all. How do you do that?"

He studied her closely and saw no fear or even anger over the fact that he might have actually done something. "I do not make it happen. There is something inside me that just does it. The moment I am around someone caught up in some strong, and bad, emotion like fear or anger or the like, it wakes up, reaches out, and calms the person, or people, down." He shrugged. "It can be helpful. It just does not allow me to ask the person if they actually want to calm down."

"Well, I certainly do not mind. Such emotions are very uncomfortable. Yet they do have their uses. Fear can be very useful when one is in actual danger."

"I know and I do fight to tamp it down but it is as if it has a mind of its own."

Primrose frowned. "You might wish to find a different way to explain that. It makes it sound a bit too much as if you have some creature inside you."

He laughed. "It can feel that way at times when it just starts to stir to life as if it was called."

"But it was. That emotion it was created to soothe called to it."

"I think I like that explanation a lot better than the ones I try to explain it with."

She laughed softly and looked around. "How long to get to your cousin's?"

"We go to your uncle George's first."

"Well, that is very near your cousin's so much the same time to get there. I was just curious as to how long your cousins had to try to divert Augusta. It will not be easily done."

"No, but even an hour will be a blessing. That would put her a farther distance back and she might miss finding us today."

He just grunted in reply and Primrose sighed. She did not have all that much hope either.

* * *

"We are being followed, m'lady. Watched."

Augusta looked up from her breakfast and frowned at Carl, a man she knew she should never turn her back on. He had cold, dead eyes. Since she had used him and his two men to kill one of her previous employees, the original intention having been to kill all of three of them and start anew, he had to know how she dispensed of any of the men she hired when they were no longer of use. It would not surprise her to find out he was watching for her to obtain her goal or draw near to doing so before he killed her. She would have to kill him first. For the first time since she had made use of the criminal class to claw her way into society, after looking into Carl's eyes, Augusta had doubts about her ability to come out the winner in a fight for power.

That added a little thrill to the game and she smiled. Out of the corner of her eyes, she watched Carl frown and step back. It pleased her that she could frighten any of the men who worked for her. That was what she craved. Power. The money she would gain would be nice but what she really wanted was power. She ached to hold the lives of the workers of Willow Hill in her hand. She wanted people in society to accept that she was their equal if not more.

No more would she be just Rufford's wife, his supplicant. Nor would she be relegated to just planning the dinner or making certain the maids did their work. A baroness was not very high in the ranks but high enough, far higher than the wife of a mere second son of a baron. It would be what she would make of it and she had plans to make it a power to be reckoned with.

Her first mistake had been to marry the wrong man. She had chosen the heir but before she could get him to the altar he had met that pale, skinny Miriam and married her. It was love, he had told her, and Augusta growled. So she had turned her attention on the younger son. Heirs did die on a regular basis, she had thought. The old baron had died before she had felt compelled to nudge him along but his heir had proven a very lucky man, or a very smart one, and her success had almost come too late to save herself from her husband's follies. Now she just had Miriam's brats to be rid of and she wondered yet again why she had not been more forthright in getting rid of them years ago.

"M'lady?"

Augusta glared at the man as if he had interrupted some important plan. "Who is watching us?"

"Those Wherlockes the big feller went to visit."

"Wherlockes?" said Jenson, who then fought to hide his alarm when both Carl and his mistress turned to stare at him.

"Do you know of them?" asked Augusta.

"They are often the subject of gossip. I have, in my years as a valet, met some of their valets and butlers. Fine men and usually had the odd name of Pugh or the very common one of Jones."

"Jenson, I realize the servants would be of interest to you but they are not to me. Who are the Wherlockes?"

"A very large family. Male children are the usual so some have actually made some very good marriages because of that. Lords needing to build their stock of heirs marry off a daughter to one of them if they can. Very closely bound, m'lady. Stand by and behind every single member of their family. I believe some of that may come from a past strewn with witch hunts and persecutions but also because there appears to be a tendency for parents to leave their children."

"I suspect a lot of people think on doing that but you say these Wherlockes actually do it?"

"They do not do it, the one they married does. Because they cannot abide what the Wherlockes are said to be and how that has come out in the child they bred."

"Jenson, just tell us. Be blunt, you old fool."

"It is believed by many that the Wherlockes and the other half of their family, the Vaughns, are cursed, witches, creatures of the devil, and other such nonsense. They appear to be gifted." Seeing how both Carl and Augusta were frowning at him, Jenson added, "Some can see the future, some can see ghosts, and such as that. Gifted."

"Nonsense." Augusta sipped her tea and studied Carl. "Is that why your men did not silence that girl we spoke with the other day. Was she *gifted?*"

"I was not here, m'lady. But the ones watching us do have some skill. I would not have even seen them if not for some drunken fool bellowing a greeting to one of them."

"They live near here; just because one has come into the village does not mean he is following us."

"It appears several families of them have come into the village, m'lady. Everywhere we turn, there is one of them. Not all adults, either. Last one I nearly tripped over as I walked away from where another stood was a little girl. She would not move and so I pushed her aside. Little brat fell down and started screeching so I ran."

"And just how did you get wet?"

"It rained."

"I noticed no rain and you are in the same village as I am."

"It rained on me, m'lady."

"Just on you."

"I know it sounds mad, but, aye, just on me."

"I see," she said in a tone that made it clear she thought him an idiot. "Well, go on with your story."

"When I moved on as quick as can be without actually running, a whole swarm of them gathered round her and some followed me. Went into the public house to tell my lads what to watch for and there were a few in there, sitting at the table right next to our men."

"Having an ale, no doubt. How very suspicious."

Carl shook his head. "M'lady, I been what you hired for a long time and I know right well when I'm being watched. That is what is happening here and they are nay even trying to hide it."

"If you insist, we will leave as soon as I finish my meal. Go on and tell the others."

After he was gone, Augusta watched Jenson. The man was becoming rebellious in that way upper servants did. All polite talk, the barbs so carefully hidden one did not always know what had been said to make the one who got slapped by the barb wince and back away. It might be time to remind him, yet again, of what the cost would be if he got too rebellious.

"Jenson, pack our things," she ordered. "We will be leaving soon. My niece shall pay dearly for causing me so much trouble," she muttered as, with Jenson's aid, she donned her traveling coats, hat, and gloves and left the room.

Jenson stared at the door for a minute. The woman intended to kill the baron's daughter. Just how much more did the bitch want to make an innocent girl pay for that? And what had the young master ever done to hurt his aunt? Nothing, as far as Jenson knew, unless one counted never having a word to say to the woman or his clever avoidance of all her matchmaking plans for him.

He sat down on the edge of the bed and put his face in his hands. He so badly wanted out of the mess he was in. Yet the fate of his brother and his family rested in his hands. His darling baby daughter, one he had begot upon a kitchen maid who died in birthing the child and whom he had never had the common decency to marry, was also at stake. Augusta had threatened to destroy everyone who mattered to him and he fully believed the woman was capable of it.

He rose and moved to look out the window. There were an impressive number of people wandering somewhat aimlessly around the inn. All handsome people, mostly male and with black hair. He suspected those were the Wherlockes. The fact that they were not even trying to be very secretive in watching Augusta must annoy her and that made him smile.

A little girl with thick black curls looked up at the window and he could see the blue of her eyes even from there. She waved and he cautiously waved back. She stood and scowled toward Augusta when the woman appeared to direct the packing of her carriage. When the woman went back inside the inn the little girl skipped after her and Jenson became concerned. He was about to go downstairs to make sure the child stayed away from the woman when a soft rap came at the door.

He opened the door cautiously and then looked down. Those blue eyes stared at him and then she smiled. A beguiling child, he thought, and looked around to make sure Augusta was not approaching.

"She is in the kitchens telling the people there precisely how to pack a basket of food for her to take on her journey," the little girl said. "You can tell me what you have to tell me now."

"Why do you think I have anything to say?"

"Because it is chewing its way right out of you so best to get it said quick before she comes."

"She is going to follow them."

"We know."

"And she knows where they are going. To their maternal uncle."

"We know that, too. Has she hired more men?" she asked after a moment of obvious thought.

"I fear she has. Some scum she found in the public house or, rather Carl found for her."

"Thank you, sir. You need to get away from her."

"I cannot. She will hurt my family."

"She is going to kill you. Best if you run. No need to worry about your family. She is done. We just want to"—she hesitated and frowned a little—"make certain she does not take the ones we need

to save down with her. There. That was all." She
shook a tiny finger at him. "Now do as you are told
and run then hide until you hear she is gone for all
time but not until the morrow."

"Why not until the morrow?"

"Because you have to help save our Bened."

"Me? You must be mistaken, child."

"No. Delmar told me to tell you that. He said it
would help give you some spine. He saw it so it is
true, too. You best be believing it. Save Bened then
run and hide."

Before he could ask any more she was gone. He
listened carefully but could not even hear the
patter of her feet as she ran down the stairs. It was
odd that the Wherlockes would send a child with
such a warning although, if he judged right, she did
very well at recalling any specific message she was
to give. And, now that he considered it, who would
notice a child or care what she had to say to anyone?

A tiny spark of hope flickered to weak life in his
heart. Perhaps, for once, Augusta had chosen the
wrong people to anger. And it appeared there
might be some truth about the rumors concerning
the Wherlockes. He took a deep breath and returned to preparations for the never-ending journey they appeared to be on.

It would help give him some spine, a child had
said. It did not matter that she had just been repeat-
ing someone's message, which was undoubtedly
just from another child. He had seen the judgment of his cowardice in her startlingly beautiful
eyes and that was enough. That stung and he
could almost feel his back straighten. He would do

it. If his fate was headed his way, he would greet it like a man and just, maybe, ruin Augusta's grand plans for her glorious future of reigning like a queen over society. Even better, he would be the one who saved a good man who was only trying to do what was right.

Chapter Twelve

Pacing around the campsite was not helping anyone, Primrose scolded herself. She turned to go back to her bedding on the ground, careful to avoid Boudicca who had been pacing right along beside her. Sitting down on the blankets, she welcomed the puppy onto her lap and lightly scratched the dog's soft ears.

Bened had been gone for too long. Although they had traveled for a long time to reach this spot, and with as few stops as possible along the way, there had been no sign of her aunt or any of her hired men. Primrose had begun to believe the Wherlockes had done as promised and delayed the woman. It had been wonderful to relax but now Bened was missing. What could Bened have found that was keeping him away from her for so long? Just how far had he gone to seek out anyone who might be following them?

Something was wrong. Primrose was certain of it. She had fought to ignore a growing feeling of unease but had failed miserably. Unlike the Wherlockes and their ilk, she had no *gifts,* but she was inclined to have very trustworthy instincts. Right now those instincts were telling her that Bened needed help.

Setting Boudicca aside, she stood up and checked her pistol before the light faded any more. Primrose hesitated and then put Boudicca in her basket. If she was just allowing the fear of waiting alone in the dark direct her, she would quietly accept the lecture she was certain Bened would burn her ears with, but she could not risk dismissing the overwhelming feeling that something had gone wrong. Everything inside of her, heart, mind, and gut, was telling her that this time it was Bened who needed help and protection.

Having watched Bened closely as he followed a trail and listened to the answers he had calmly given her every question, Primrose tried to see the signs of which way he had gone. His big horse made it easier than she suspected it would have been if Bened had walked away but Primrose doubted she could follow the trail for long. If Bened had tried to hide it, she was doomed.

She came upon another small clearing and frowned. Something had stirred up the ground but she knew she had no chance of reading it as well as Bened could have. Then she heard the jingle of a harness and looked up to see two tall, dark men sitting at the edge of the clearing, watching her. A soft growl of warning came from deep inside the little basket she still carried Boudicca in. One of the two men grinned and, even as she pointed her pistol at them, she began to believe she was facing some of Bened's family. The Wherlockes and Vaughns did share a certain look and the one grinning at her looked a lot like Bened except with the softer handsomeness so many women sought.

"We are not the enemy, m'lady," said the one who smiled.

"Well, since you have not yet thought to tell me who you are, I cannot be certain of that, can I?"

"I am Morris Wherlocke and this is Bened's brother Bevan. We got to Argus shortly after you and Bened rode away. Argus sent us out to watch the woman and her men. We watched them follow you and so decided we had best come along as well."

Primrose sighed as her heart clenched with fear even as she looked back down at the disturbed ground and saw the sparkle caused by the sunlight touching a drop of blood. "They have him."

"Now, we cannot be certain of that yet," said Bevan as he dismounted and crouched down near the spot where the ground was most disturbed.

She watched him study it and waited patiently for his opinion. "Someone took Bened," she said again as her patience swiftly ran out. "I have been watching and studying how Bened reads the ground. I know it is his gift."

"Oh, it is. Bened could look at tracks like this and tell you how many were here, their height and weight, male or female, and probably even what they had to eat for their morning meal. All I can see is that someone tussled here."

"And bled." Primrose pointed to the blood splattered on the leaves. "And if I recall my lessons correctly . . ."

"Bened was teaching you?"

"Explaining. I kept asking how he could know

what he did and he would try to explain. I have a very precise memory"—she frowned—"except for a few short spaces from my childhood, and recall all he said. I also know Mercury's print. They took him away on the back of Mercury."

"Show me," Bevan said, and ignored Morris when the man walked up to crouch down beside him. "Come and show me. With what I know and what you say, we might find the answers we need."

Primrose carefully set her basket down on unmarked grass and crouched next to Bened's brother. "We agree some men came here where Bened was or had been. Correct?"

"Yes, and I would say three or four men."

"Four. The hoofprints are clearer outside this area and it shows four horses entering this clearing from the road and only one coming from the direction of our camp. All five horses, when they went off, were carrying a man's weight, one just a bit more awkwardly than the others. I think they tossed Bened over Mercury's back and the way so much of Bened would be dangling and moving around made the horse's gait far more awkward. But they hurt Bened." She shifted and looked at it from another direction. "One of the men came up behind him."

"That is impossible. No one can come up on my brother from behind. That is also part of his gift. He can feel the enemy, feel them and know where they are and how many there are."

"I cannot explain how his gift failed him this time but it did. These prints say that someone came up behind Bened even as he faced off with the other men. It could be that he simply was too busy fighting off one threat to face the one he knew snuck up behind him."

Bevan sighed. "I can see it now." He carefully stood up and walked until he located a clear trail of the horses leaving the clearing. "They have made no attempt to hide their trail so we should be able to track them down."

"Just allow me to collect my horse," Primrose said.

"Wait!" Morris called, and she halted to look at him. "This could be dangerous. I do not think you should go with us."

"I see. So you think it better if I, a woman with only a tiny dog, sit here in the wood, in the dark, and hope no one comes along to cause me trouble? That is better."

"Oh, very good, m'lady," Morris grumbled. "Go get your horse."

As Primrose left she heard Bevan say, "What?! Are you mad? Why did you agree to that?"

"And what would you say? Everything she said was right. There are no choices. She goes with us, which could be dangerous, or stays here, which could also be dangerous. So she goes with us and at least we can set her someplace safe while we help your brother."

"Set me someplace safe, is it?" Primrose grumbled as she collected her things and packed them on her horse. "Men, Smudge. They can be such a nuisance. You are lucky to be surrounded by geldings." She mounted and hurried back to join the men.

"That was quick," said Morris.

"You sound so surprised," she said.

"I am. Women . . ." His words ended on a loud

oof as Bevan swung his arm into the man's stomach. "What did you do that for?"

"To stop you from digging a grave for yourself. We will follow the trail now, m'lady," said Bevan.

It took all her willpower to smother a laugh despite the fear for Bened eating at her. It was evident that Morris and Bevan had known each other for a while or, like a very fortunate few, had become lasting friends within moments of meeting. They would work well together and that could only be good for Bened.

The sun was just beginning to rise over the horizon when they paused on a small hill overlooking a very small village. It was so small that Primrose was able to see Augusta's carriage for it sat behind the inn. It was obviously too large to fit into the stables and there was no appropriate carriage house for it. A river already busy with barges shone under the rising sun. What Primrose did not see in any abundance was sheep, or cattle, or crops despite many open fields.

"There is something odd about this town," she said.

"Smugglers' town," said Morris.

"But it is on the river."

"Not all goods are smuggled only by sea and, if a deal has been made, the smugglers will get their goods wherever they are being asked and paid for. Taken from a ship and put on a barge."

"How very industrious. So, do you think she has Bened in that inn? That would seem risky."

"Not if this town is what I am thinking it is."

"You mean a town full of men my aunt would like to hire."

Bevan chuckled. "More or less. I suspect she would

not be trusted or would even want to approach many of these men."

"So what do we do now? I cannot get near the inn as she and her men, if she still has the three I saw, will recognize me."

"One thing we need to do is wait until it is dark again. This is not something to do in broad daylight when one will stand out as a stranger in town anyway. There is a chance she is not even at the inn."

"Her carriage is there."

"I think it is because that is the only place that could house the horses as she wanted. I will have a look, though."

"Now we find a place to camp."

"Good plan, if we can find one where we will not be discovered."

Bevan found a perfect spot within the hour. His only warning was to stay out of sight of the river as much as possible. No going down to the river's edge unless the waterway was completely empty of boats. Primrose had only just gotten settled when Bevan disappeared. He returned two hours later and then Morris disappeared. It went on like that until the sun started to go down and she wondered when one of them might think to tell her what they had been up to.

"You have been very busy spying out the town and, I suspect, the inn. Perhaps even the little homes scattered just outside the village as well. I would have looked at them, too. Have you seen my aunt or caught sight of Bened?" she finally asked when Morris finished sharing out the food he had bought at the inn.

"We have. You aunt does not know us and spying

on people is something I am very good at," said
Bevan.

"He is that," said Morris. "No idea how he does
it, but people can walk right by him and not see
him and yet, I know he does not disappear or anything strange like that. 'Tis a wonder."

"Do you become part of what you hide near?"
she asked. "Like one of those chameleons?"

"Something like that." Bevan smiled at her. "You
are not only not troubled by it all but you try to
understand."

"A gift from my father, I think. Curiosity and the
need to know. He said one must learn and learning
sometimes meant you have to face things you fear
or do not truly want to know. The fact that your
son," she said, looking at Morris, "sees the dead and
could let me see them if I wanted is fascinating even
as something inside shies away from it. Papa said
never listen to that voice unless it is a matter of
life and death, your good health, or your safety."
She shrugged. "I try to follow that lesson. I rather
like to learn things. It helps that I recall most everything I read and, to some extent, everything I hear
although I have recently discovered some rather
large holes in my memory from when I was a child.
But, I will sort that out when we get Bened free and
make certain my brother is safe."

"And, I hate to say this so bluntly, but we need
to be rid of your aunt."

"No need to apologize, sir. That I know. Since I
am almost certain she is the one who killed my
father and quite possibly my mother years ago,
I have no difficulty accepting that this will end with

her dead. After all, she means to see me and my only brother dead."

"Good that you can see that clearly. She has Bened in a cottage behind the village. It is at the end of a tiny lane between the dressmaker's and the apothecary."

"He is still alive?" she asked, unable to fully hide her fear and not surprised when Bevan patted her hand. They were both worried about his brother.

"Yes, he is. Last I looked he was just rousing from the blow on the head." Bevan frowned. "I do not know what is planned for him but I am certain it is not good." A slight color touched his face. "He is naked and tied to a chair."

"Good heavens." Primrose frowned and thought on all the books on battles and wars she had read and felt her blood actually chill in her veins. "Torture," she said. "I have read too many books on battles, wars, and such as that, perhaps, but I think they want some information and mean to torture it out of him."

"It is what I thought, as well, so we need to get him out of there before that happens. He is still unconscious so that is a good thing. It has kept him safe from any harm while we came to get him. She has half a dozen men lurking about if you include the one they all refer to as her servant. I listened to them laughing about it as they say she needed the fool to press her gowns."

"Sad to say that is probably exactly right. Did they mention a name?"

"Johnson? Nay, it was Jenson." Bevan looked at her in surprise when she gave a short laugh.

"She has taken Uncle Rufford's valet with her."

"Do you think he is also her guard? Someone we need to worry about if we get to her?"

"No. He is a valet. Fussy, not too brave, needs everything clean, and such as that. I am not certain he could even use a pistol or want to. In many ways, he is a nice man. No, Jenson will not fight anyone." Primrose sipped the cider Morris had bought and served them all. "I wonder what she has threatened him with to get him to go along with her, to leave my uncle."

"She would have to threaten him to do that?" asked Bevan.

"Yes. He hates travel and knows my uncle would never let him go. I wonder if she had more than one reason to take him. He is probably the only reason she never killed her husband. Jenson fussed over my uncle. But, then there is the fact that she needs my uncle alive to become the baron if she is to be the lady of the manor."

"But he might not live long to celebrate that moment for long."

"That is what I think, Morris." She frowned. "Is that all of your name? No sir before it or anything?"

"Actually, I am Lord Morris Wherlocke. A viscount. Will step up when, and pray it is not soon, my father dies."

"Oh, I am sorry then, m'lord."

"No need to be. The Wherlockes actually have more than their fair share of titles. When we are together we tend to toss them aside or we would be m'lording ourselves to death."

"Is there a plan to get Bened back?"

The silence that greeted her question made Primrose uneasy. It would be six against three—if they counted her and she suspected she would need to force them to do so. Not good odds. Not unless they could come up with a way to winnow that down until it was at least even.

"We were going to plot it out as we ate," said Bevan, and Morris nodded slowly.

"Then we had best get started," she said, and ignored the look they exchanged. When neither of them did just that, she offered, "The only thing I could think of is that we need a plan to knock down the six men to at least three. Much more favorable odds."

Bevan nodded. "You have a good grasp of strategy. I am just not sure how we can do it without bringing too much attention to ourselves or causing your aunt to act against my brother too quickly."

"Then we have to do it as stealthily as possible."

It was a challenge and they quickly took it up. In some ways it was all done to keep her from joining in the rescue of Bened. She knew they wished her to stay right where she was alone, in the dark, safe. That was not something she intended to do and so she intended to hear all of their plan. If she could participate in any way, she would, and, if not, she would find another way to do so. Bened had helped her and she intended to repay that in the best way she could. He did not deserve to suffer at the hands of her mad aunt.

She smiled when Boudicca rushed over to sit on her lap and both men frowned at the dog. Men did not much like tiny dogs and poor Boudicca was going to be tinier than most. The dog looked at Morris, curled her lip, and snarled in a deep tone. Morris looked startled and Bevan laughed heartily.

"Ferocious little thing," Morris said.

"I suspect she will always do her best to protect me since I saved her from drowning." She patted the dog's head and gave it a piece of her roasted chicken. "We need to make some decisions quickly as he cannot sleep much longer. They will wake him if he does."

"Then we best make our plans. I do not suppose we can convince you to just wait here."

"No, so best come up with something I can do. I know how to use a pistol."

"First, we get rid of as many of her men as we can. Then, we need to try to get into the room where Bened is from as many ways as we can. There is a window and one door so the choices are few. To the house there are two doors and a window in each room."

"I can get in the window," said Bevan.

Primrose listened to the plans and soon thought they had a chance. If they had a few more people, they would have an even better one but she would take a nice gift of luck if she had to. While they tried to make a plan that would give her something to do yet not be in too much danger, she tried to think of where she could keep her dog.

Simeon was pleased to see the woman moving with her previous grace when they slipped out of the house to get their horses. "I realized we have not introduced ourselves. I am Lord Simeon Wootten of Willow Hill. And you?"

"Lilybet Wherlocke of here." She glanced back at the building they had just left. "My parents bought this and were doing well. Too well. It stirred jealousy. It cost them their lives. If I had not been so young, it might have cost me my life as well but a cousin of my father's arrived and took over. Since then I have been no more than a maid. So, I found my mother's birth name and took that for myself. I had no wish to be a Foddam."

"Ah. Relatives can be a curse. It is my aunt and uncle who are causing me and my sister such grief. I think a lot of that stems from jealousy as well. That and greed." Seeing how she continued to stare sadly at her home, he said quietly, "But you still need to leave. My aunt will not leave you alive. Those men could return at any time."

"I intend to leave but I am uncertain of where to go."

"Find your mother's people?"

"It is a thought. Let us get you to your uncle first."

He nodded and mounted his horse. They were a few miles away by the time the sun came up and he relaxed. Not only was he back on the road to his uncle's but he had gotten his rescuer away as well. If he could just find his aunt and make her pay for the things she had done, he would be a happy man.

By midday he could see that she needed to rest and began to search out a place for them to stop. He took one look at the village below the hill they sat on and frowned. The village was too quiet and he was certain that was his aunt's carriage in the inn yard near the stables. Simeon signaled to Lilybet and drew her back down the hill on the side away from the village.

"There is a bad feeling to that place," Lilybet said.

"I think it has been taken over by crooks and smugglers. River pirates and all that. Not that well read on the criminal class but what there is out here in the country are the sort holding that town. I am certain of it. We will find a little clearing to take a rest in."

Wondering why a man would think he could learn about criminals just by reading about them, Lilybet said, "Aye, we must and there is one just through those trees." She abruptly grinned at him. "Come along."

Since she looked so pleased, he did not complain but followed her into the trees. He had followed her for only a few minutes before he heard a voice he knew as well as his own. A glance at Lilybet told him she had known Primrose was close. Simeon's pleasure suddenly faded as he feared Lilybet would now go off on her own and she was not safe, any more than he was, while Augusta was still alive.

"Nay, I will not leave yet. Being with you is what will lead me to my mother's family."

"Well, always happy to be a useful fellow."

Lilybet laughed. "I suspect many find you very useful for a lot of things. Let us go meet your sister. She has been searching for you."

"I need to find someplace to put my dog so she is safe while we do this," said Primrose.

"Safest place would be with you, sister dear," said a deep voice from the edge of the clearing.

Primrose's heart leapt so hard and fast she had to put her hand over it as she spun around and looked at the two riders at the edge of the clearing. Simeon looked far less elegant than he usually did and rather tired. The pretty black-haired woman next to him looked as if she badly needed to rest. Primrose set the basket down and ran to her brother's side even as he dismounted. She immediately noticed his wince when she hugged him, however, and stood back a little to look him over.

"You are hurt," she said. "Did they get hold of you?"

"For a short while but I escaped and this kind woman hid me from them," said Simeon as he held out his hand and assisted Lilybet in dismounting. "This is Lilybet Wherlocke. She paid dearly for her kindness to a desperate man for they came after her as well. Aunt has her cane rods with her."

"A Wherlocke?" asked Morris, studying Lilybet closely. "Yes, I can see it now."

"My mother said we shared a certain look about us," said Lilybet. "We can discuss that later, if you would be so kind, but you must get that man out of there. That woman seeks information on her niece and she will use any means she can to get him to give it to her."

"Bened would never . . ." began Primrose, and ignored the sharp look her brother gave her over her familiar use of the man's name.

"Nay, he would not and that is why you must get him out of there quickly. She will see that she needs more than her cursed rod and get her man who is so good with a knife."

"You need to rest," Simeon said. "I think you could use some salve on your wounds as well."

"I have some and mayhap you can help me put some on when you return." Lilybet slowly seated herself beneath a tree.

"Of course I will." Primrose set the basket with her dog next to the woman, worried about how pale she looked. "Could you watch my dog for me?"

"I would be happy to. Now, go and get him away from that woman who is nothing but a curse for your family."

Chapter Thirteen

A sharp pain stabbed repeatedly in the back of Bened's head as the darkness faded from his mind. Then he cursed. The dryness in his mouth and throat told him he had been unconscious for a long time. Someone had gotten behind him and he had not realized it until too late. He knew why he had missed the warning as well. He had been so concerned about the enemy getting to Primrose that they had managed to get to him. It was a bad time to find out that his gift had a weak spot.

As he surveyed the room he was trapped in, his next clear thought was that Primrose was alone in the wood in the dark and he would not be there to ease her fear. From what he could see out the window he was not in the small inn, he was in one of the cottages. He could see the backs of the village buildings through the window. He hoped the people who had allowed Augusta to use their home were still alive and, if so, were getting as far away as they could.

The next thing he noticed was that he was naked,

wrist and ankles tied to a chair. Being naked did not trouble him much. Having been a soldier for a few years, he had lost all modesty a long time ago. Being naked and tied so firmly to a chair was something worth worrying about. He did not think a man could be much more vulnerable. There were a few reasons someone would keep a captive in such a condition and none of them were good ones.

Bened gritted his teeth and tested the strength of his bonds. He hissed at the sting when the rope cut into his flesh but now he could move a few fingers just enough to pluck at the knots. If he could just get one hand loose, he could untie himself quickly, perhaps even quickly enough to flee before his captors returned.

That small hope was crushed when the door opened and Augusta Wootten walked in. Behind her was a taller, thin man with a narrow face and a head full of silver hair. The man's eyes widened as he stared in shock when he saw Bened.

"M'lady, this man is naked!"

"I am quite aware of that, Jenson," said Augusta. "Please move that chair over here and set it in front of him."

"But . . ."

"Jenson! Do as I say. Sweet mercy, you old fool, I have been married for many years. And there are sound reasons for forcing a prisoner to remain naked. Humiliating him is but one of those."

"Ah, well," Bened said as Jenson set out a far more comfortable chair for Augusta than he was tied to at the moment and she took her seat as if she was ready to be served tea. "I was a soldier for a

few years. Lose all sense of modesty in that work.
'Tis a luxury a soldier cannot afford."

"Listen, Vaughn . . ."

"Sir," Bened said. "'Tis Sir Vaughn, ma'am. I
earned that knighthood and the baronetcy and
I would appreciate it if you used the right address."

"Would you, now? Well, *Sir*, where is my niece?"

He shrugged and then kept his face as free of expression as he could when Augusta held her hand
out and Jenson paced a thick cane rod in it. There
was reluctance in every move the man made. Bened
just wished the man's reluctance had caused him to
refuse to help the woman.

She slowly stood up, lightly caressing the length
of the rod, and, before he could fully prepare himself, lashed out. The force of the blow across his
shoulders made him grunt softly but he knew the
true pain of it would come later. Bened suddenly
wondered if the woman had caned Primrose that
way. When she struck again he held back even the
grunt of pain as she caned him three times right
across the chest. The woman had surprising
strength behind her blows.

"As I thought, you are made of hardier stock
than most," Augusta said.

"Hardier than whom?"

"Than that foolish girl in the last village for one.
But, I suspected you would be in need of a heavier
hand than I, a mere woman, could ever apply. I
believe that Carl and his knives are needed."

Watching her leave, Bened shook his head and,
as soon as the door shut behind her, said to Jenson,
"That is a woman who should have been chained in
Bedlam years ago."

"I think I would have preferred her to be shot," said Jenson. "She could have escaped Bedlam."

Seeing how pale Jenson was made Bened want to ask just what Carl could do with his knives, but he bit back the question. "True. She trusts you to not let me go, does she?"

"She does. I could not go against her before because it would put at risk everyone I care about but a young girl recently told me that I must, so I am to find my spine and just do it. I must save you." The man hurried behind Bened, crouched down, and began to untie the ropes around his ankles.

"Stay calm," said Bened when he could feel the trembling of the man's fingers.

Jenson moved to untie his wrist from the arm of the chair. "She threatened my brother and his whole family. Then she threatened my precious little girl. I sinned, you see, and she was born but her mother died. My brother and his wife care for her while I work. I never thought that wretched evil woman would even notice such things."

"She is working on a long plan, Jenson. An old one and has the patience and tenacity to keep at it." Once his arm was free, Bened untied his other wrist by himself and happily accepted his clothes from a pale Jenson. "She has been working on it since the day the baron married another woman and not her. She took the second son but has always planned to be the baroness, to have the manor and all that comes with it."

"Her ladyship and the babe she carried . . ."

Bened nodded, wincing as he donned his shirt. "And she may have killed the baron as well. Hello,

Bevan," he said as his brother climbed in through the window.

"Almost shot that bitch, but she stopped before I could bring myself to kill a woman," said Bevan.

The sound of shots being fired made Bened start for the door but Bevan grabbed him by the arm. "Best to give them some time."

"And who are *them*?"

"Your lady, Morris . . ."

"Primrose is shooting people?!"

Bevan hurried after Bened as he stormed out the door. "I do not believe she is out there killing anyone. We just planned to keep the men busy while I got you out of here and I do not think charging out the front where the shooting is is the best way to go."

"There must be a back door."

Even as they started to the back of the house they heard someone rush in through the front door. They ducked back inside the room Bened had just been released from and waited. It annoyed Bened to hide but he was wise enough to know an unarmed man did not stride out into the middle of a lot of people shooting at one another. He had to wait until things quieted down and pray that Primrose came out of it all unharmed.

Primrose did not need any more urging, nodded in complete agreement with Lilybet's words, patted Boudicca on the head for luck, and followed her brother and the other men. Bevan had slipped away earlier to go around to the window of the room Augusta had put Bened in while she, Morris, and Simeon now sneaked up on the men who were proving to be very lax in their guard on the house, laughing and drinking ale as they lounged in the shade. Perhaps they thought there was no threat to worry about now that Augusta had Bened but she was pleased to be a part of proving them wrong. Just as they had discussed on the way, they spread themselves out in the trees in the hope of making the men think there were more attackers than there actually were.

Primrose took a deep breath and fired the first shot, hitting one man in the shoulder. She loaded her pistol as Morris shot another. As Morris reloaded, Simeon fired. Her aunt's men fired wildly back and Primrose could feel her heart pounding with fear so hard and fast she was surprised she could catch her breath as she fired again and got a man in the leg. With four men wounded, the others decided leaving was the best plan but then Augusta suddenly walked out of the house. Primrose could see her brother take aim at the woman but Augusta was no fool. She heard the gunfire, saw her wounded men running away, and raced back inside the house just as Simeon fired. His shot hit the side of the door just as her skirts cleared it.

Seeing that her aunt's men were completely intent on getting themselves away, Primrose raced for the house. Shots echoed behind her and she hoped none of her people had been hurt as she struggled to find her aunt inside the warren of a house. The slam of a door drew her gaze to the far back of the house, and she ran that way as fast as she could only to look out the door and see the figure of her aunt disappearing down the lane toward the inn.

Deciding she would never catch up, Primrose went looking for Bened and found Morris and Simeon instead. "She escaped out the back, Simeon, and I last saw her going for her carriage."

"Then her men were right to run or she would leave them behind," said Simeon.

"And we are very lucky that they did not find what she was offering worth fighting hard for, not when half their number got wounded so quickly. Fine shooting, Primrose," said Morris.

"Thank you but I think I would rather not recall it right now. Have never shot a man. Never even shot an animal." She looked around the surprisingly large house. "I need to find Bened now."

"Then you are in luck for there he is."

Primrose saw Bened striding toward her with Bevan right behind him and a man she recognized as Jenson hurrying to keep up. She ran toward him and he caught her up in his arms. Despite her joy over his apparent good health she felt him wince a little and stepped back, holding his arms as she looked him over.

"They hurt you," she said, "but I cannot see where."

"A few slaps with a cane and an aching head from the blow that took me down. I will be fine."

"Well, I will be sure to look over both things if only to put some salve on those cane wounds."

She hugged him again, careful to do so gently. Bened held her close and looked over her head at the others. A man with guinea gold hair and strikingly blue eyes glared at him and Bened sighed. It appeared Simeon had been found. Although Bened was pleased for her and very pleased he had been rescued himself, he was sorely disappointed at the fact that there would be no more long, sweet nights of lovemaking.

Primrose finished tending the cane marks on Lilybet's back and sat on her heels to clean off her hands. "She did a nasty job on you. You must have made her very angry."

"I did. Had no intention of telling her what she wanted to know. Did find that I can lie beautifully when inspired, though." Lilybet exchanged a grin with Primrose. "She is a very angry, selfish woman, you know. She will not stop until someone stops her permanently."

"I know." Primrose sighed. "How did you find Simeon? I swear I have been over half this country looking for him."

"He was in the alley at the side of my house. I see things, you know."

Primrose nodded. "Like the woman Chloe the Wherlockes told me about."

"Well, I do not know of this Chloe but suspect she is much like me. I saw your brother and that he needed help, even where to find him. I also saw that I had to go along with him on the rest of the journey and that would help me find my mother's family." She glanced at Morris. "I have."

"He is but one of many. And I mean many." She was not surprised to see Lilybet's eyes brighten with hope and pleasure. The woman had been alone for a long time and, she did not know it yet, but that would never be the way of it again.

"It will be good to know people who can understand what I am."

"Do you have any plans other than that?"

"None. I will solve the problem of what to do to live when I know where that will be." Lilybet smiled. "I am not worried."

"Because you would know if there was trouble ahead."

"Not always when it concerns myself. I only see things that change what steps I take when I am involved in another's problems. Such as happened this time. I have been wanting to meet others of my mother's family for years but the sight I had concerning your brother was the first time I was shown a way to do that."

"Well, that seems mightily unfair." She smiled when Lilybet laughed. "Just let me know when you wish a little more salve. Those cane marks may not be open wounds but they are painful and badly hurt the skin."

"I will be sure to let you know. Although it pains me to admit it, your salve is much better than mine as it heals faster and eases that pain better. You might ask your brother if he wants some. He took a battering before and as he escaped that woman."

"If you wish it, I can write the receipt for the salve so you can make your own."

"I would like that. Thank you. And, if you could ask Lord Morris to come and tell me something of the Wherlockes, that would be wonderful."

Primrose sent Morris over to Lilybet and noticed her brother frowned when he saw the two of them talking so easily, Morris sitting next to Lilybet. Then she took Boudicca for a walk. She was just turning around to return to their camp when Bened appeared. She smiled in greeting but discovered she suddenly felt cautious. He had been paying her very little attention since they had rescued him and she was not sure why.

"You have finally found your brother, so what are your plans now?" he asked as he slowly backed her up against a tree.

"We go to my uncle's. Now it will be more for advice than for protection, though."

"Your aunt is still out there. Her plans are still in her head and heart. Do you not think she is a danger now?"

"She will always be a danger. Even if she decides she cannot win the game she will turn her mind to making us pay for that. In her eyes it will be all our fault. Yes, she is still a danger and I think even Simeon understands that. She is forcing us to see her dead."

"I would not fret over that too much. It truly is a matter of her or you and Simeon, and she already has a lot of blood on her hands."

"That is true. I also know I do not share in her shame. I did not make her do this. It is her own greed that pushes her. Yet, she is family and by being such, she shames us all."

"No, how you deal with her is where the shame could be but I know you will stop her."

He bent down and kissed her, savoring the sweet taste of her on his mouth. Primrose wrapped herself around his as best she could and let the desire he could stir with his kiss sweep over her.

She wanted him and knew some of that fierce
need had been bred by her deep fear of losing
him to her aunt's murderous plans. When he
ended the kiss she gave him what she prayed was a
smile of invitation. If the way his eyes narrowed
were any indication, it had worked.

"This could be risky," he murmured as he undid
the back of her gown and tugged the top down far
enough to give him access to her beautiful breasts.

"How odd. That actually made me want it more."

"Naughty, Rose." He bent his head to kiss and
suckle at her breasts, enjoying her soft cries of
delight as he did.

"I am feeling a bit naughty." She slid her hands
down his back and caressed his backside, loving the
way that made him rub up against her.

Bened began to tug up her skirts until he could
slide his hand between her legs. They both murmured with pleasure when he found what he was
seeking. To his delight, Primrose slid one of her
hands around to the front of his breeches and
undid them. When she slid her small soft hand
inside and wrapped her long fingers around him,
he knew he would not be able to enjoy this play for
long. He was too hungry for her.

Primrose gasped in surprise when Bened picked
her up and urged her to wrap her legs around his
waist. Then she felt the hard length of him rub
against her and sighed. She might not be certain
how this was going to work but she was more than
eager for it to do so. Then he kissed her and slowly
began to join their bodies. At first they moved together in a slow, almost lazy enjoyment but then
passion began to drive them and the lovemaking

grew fierce. Primrose hung on to him tightly as he drove them both to completion and continued to hang on after they ceased trembling from the force of their releases. She idly wondered if she had yelled and alerted the ones in camp to what she and Bened were doing. She suspected she would probably worry about that later but, right now, joined with Bened, wrapped tightly in his arms, she did not care.

Reluctantly, Bened eased free of her body and began to tidy their clothing. They had only shared a bed twice but he already missed that time of just holding each other with ease and no need to quickly dress and then act innocent. He had to wonder why some people found such things exciting. He was far more excited by the thought of not having to leave her side.

And then he knew. He was well and truly caught. When a man wanted to wake to the same woman's face every morning, to spend a lot of nights holding her close, he might as well buy the ring. All he needed now was some confidence that what she felt for him was more than friendship, gratitude, and desire. Nice as those were, and he welcomed them, they were not what one could build a happy future on.

Once they were fully dressed, he helped her tidy her hair, plucking out a few pieces of bark. A soft yip drew his eyes down and he realized they had both forgotten the dog. He picked the little puppy up and handed her to Primrose.

"It is a good thing she is too attached to you to go exploring on her own," he said.

"True but she is a dog and something could have

caught her attention. I need to get a leash for her. She is so tiny even a hawk might mistake her for dinner." She rubbed her cheek against Boudicca's soft fur and glanced up at Bened. "You know this area better than I do; how much longer before we reach Uncle George's?"

"Two days. Unless the weather turns on us, it is an easy pleasant ride." He hooked his arm through hers and started to lead them back to camp. "I was happy that you had found Simeon, but not happy, if you understand what I mean."

"I do." She grinned at him. "Simeon is usually a very playful, fun man but he appears to have become very somber and responsible all of a sudden."

"I may not have a sister but I understand what troubles him. He is now the head of your house. You are his responsibility and I am not making it easy for him to deal with it."

"I am not some young girl preparing for a debut. I am three and twenty, nearly four and twenty and many consider me a spinster. He needs to understand he cannot rule my life."

Deciding the faintly militant look she wore was perfect to return to the others with, Bened did not argue. Such facts would not mean much to a young man who suddenly found himself the head of a household with an unmarried sister. It was a heavy burden but he had no intention of easing it for the man by staying away from Primrose. After the truth he had just faced, he knew that would be impossible.

* * *

When Simeon saw Bened follow after Primrose, who had taken her ridiculously tiny dog for a walk in the woods, he started to get to his feet only to be yanked back down by Bevan. "That is my sister he is sniffing about."

"And he is my brother and I know him well. You need not worry."

"No? Do you think he has gone out there to pick up after that silly dog?"

"Bened is one of the most serious, responsible men I know. Everyone in the family calls on him when they need someone to protect a person or find someone or help them track their enemies. He has made his fortune, and a fortune it is, protecting the idiot sons of the gentry and investing his pay smartly. He is not some courtier out to make a quick conquest and then walk away. Leave it be so whatever is building there can be finished."

"So I am just to sit back, smile, and let him ruin my sister?"

"I do not see her being ruined, but, yes. Sit back and stay out of it. This is an easily upset process we are watching here, you know."

"No, I actually have no idea of what you are talking about."

"The slow uniting of two people who are perfect for each other."

"Exactly," said Lilybet as she sat down on the other side of Simeon.

"Have you seen the future for them?" asked Simeon.

"Not so clear I hear wedding bells but I have seen this dance before and if you, as her much-beloved brother, go barging in and yank them apart, you could prove a large blockade to what is a very natural mating dance." She smiled when Bevan nodded. "Come, look me in the eye, and try to tell me honestly that, if you met the one you wanted to spend your life with, you would feel no strong desire." When he just glared at her she laughed. "Exactly. The moment I saw the two of them together, I may not have seen anything but I certainly felt the rightness of it. She is not some young miss, either, m'lord."

Simeon sighed. "But she was a sheltered, innocent, and well-bred woman."

"Let it go, m'lord. I will be blunt then. You do something to make Bened walk off now and you risk losing your sister. Oh, she may still live in your house but she will have stepped away from you, for as each lonely day passes she will think on the reason why she is lonely."

"Well, damn."

"That says it much better than what I was spewing," said Bevan.

"I have seen it all before. The woman meets the man she is meant to be with but bows to the wishes of her family and marries their choice. What she ends up with is pure misery. She is not lying with the man she truly wants, not having the babes she dreamt of, not living in the home she had imagined having, and all through that, if she is particularly unfortunate, she will see the one she walked away from go on with his life, giving his heart to another, as well as that house and those babes."

"That is a horrible fate." Simeon frowned. "Wonder

if something similar is what has left my aunt such an evil twisted mess of a woman?"

"It certainly did not help but she had that evil seed inside her from the beginning. From what I heard, she did not love your father, she loved his title. No, she is a bad example of what I was talking about. She is just one who was born wrong, in heart and mind."

Simeon was still thinking about what Bevan and Lilybet had said when he watched Bened escort Primrose back to the camp. He studied them and realized there was some truth in what the others had said. He could see a match there. In their eyes he could see the softness of affection as well as the heat of desire. His sister had never had a season and there had been few dances or beaux.

To many men in society she would be a plum ripe for the plucking and not necessarily for the sake of marriage. There was not one thing about Sir Bened Vaughn that made one think of a heartless rogue who seduced women just for the pleasure of it. Simeon suspected the man had seduced very few women in his time. He was just what he appeared to be, a big strong man with the sort of special gifts that allowed him to help people, something he did readily. If he was going to be fully honest with himself, Simeon would admit that he would have heartily approved of such a man for his sister. Of course, if he had had control over the courting time, they would not be slipping off into the wood to do the sort of things he did not care to think of his sister doing.

He looked at Bevan who just winked and decided he even approved of the family his sister might soon be joining. It was not going to be easy but he decided he would just leave it be. Bened would probably wonder at his apparent acquiescence but Simeon promised himself he would not interrupt what Lilybet called a mating dance. His sister deserved her chance at happiness.

Chapter Fourteen

"There is my Uncle George's." Simeon looked at the tidy stone manor house surrounded by luxurious gardens and smiled at Lilybet who rode beside him. "You are looking better. I mean, healthier."

"I feel a great deal better. Your sister has been tending my back and, I hate to admit it, but her salve works far better than mine does in healing the wounds and, just as important, dimming the pain."

"Primrose is extraordinarily clever when it comes to healing plants and herbs. Papa built her whatever she needed for her work. I envy her for that. She has something that pleases her and which creates things to help people."

"You have found nothing like that?"

"Not yet. I can talk you to death about philosophy, in several languages, and I have been trying to invent things. I keep playing about at it but have not yet succeeded."

"You will, and cease glaring at Sir Bened."

"I know what you said and I actually agree with most of it, but does he truly think I do not know what he and my sister are about with all their late-night walks? Must think I am an idiot."

Lilybet sighed. "I doubt he thinks much about you at all. M'lord, she is a grown woman, a spinster by many people's reckoning, and he is a very good man. I thought you had made up your mind on that."

"I had but he should ask to marry her instead of just continuing on as her lover."

"Best if they decide that all on their own if they are suited enough in all ways to actually marry."

"Have you seen anything about their future?"

"I have and it will not start out smoothly but that is all you need to know. Just stay out of the way."

Simeon sighed and glanced back at Primrose who was, as always, riding beside Bened. Primrose certainly looked happy and Bened had not once shown her anything but the greatest respect, courtesy, and, he had to admit, affection. Simeon just felt as if he was failing her in some way.

His uncle hailed them from the front step of his home and Simeon waved at the man. Right behind him was Frederick, a huge bear of a man who loved cooking. The beautiful garden with its massive number of roses in bloom was all George's work and Simeon was not surprised to see Primrose already off her mount and walking through it toward the house, pausing to inspect any plant she found beautiful or just interesting.

"Oh, Uncle George," Primrose said when she finally reached the man, "you have outdone yourself this year. It is all so very beautiful."

"Thank you, sweetheart." He kissed her on the cheek and then took her into his arms and hugged her tightly. "And I was so sorry to hear about your father. He was a good, good man and my sister loved him dearly."

The sound of the burr in his voice, one she could recall from her mother all those many years ago, warmed her heart. "Well, he is with her again and I like to think they are both happy."

"I am sure they are." He cupped her face in his hands. "You do look so much like her." He glanced at Bened who had moved to stand beside her.

"This is Sir Bened Vaughn. Bened, my uncle, the Honorable George Haigh." After her uncle shook Bened's hand she introduced Frederick even as she hugged the man who smelled deliciously of cinnamon. "Have you been cooking, Freddie?" she teased.

"With company riding our way? But of course. I even made the cinnamon buns you so like."

"You are an angel."

"A Vaughn, are you?" said George as they all headed into the house. "Related to the man in the castle?"

"He is the head of the family, aye. Vaughns and Wherlockes," Bened said, and nodded at Lilybet and Morris.

"Rumor has it there is a Vaughn who now owns the old manor on the other side of the castle."

"I would be that Vaughn." Bened succinctly explained how he had come into possession of the place. "I was hoping to visit Modred and have a quick look at the place before we have to leave."

"The young couple tending it for you have everything well in hand. Repairs and all are moving along at a good pace. We could not resist having a look when we heard it might be lived in once again."

"A good sturdy building," said Frederick as he stood up from the seat he had taken next to Simeon in the parlor. "Now I need to get us some food and drink and prepare something for the children."

"Children?" Primrose asked her uncle.

"Yes, we adopted two orphans. It was a battle but since no one else would take them in and we had signed intent allowing us to do it from their parents, they are now ours. A boy and a girl. Their parents worked for us and tragically died while fishing. One of those horrible storms that appears to pop up for the sole purpose of killing someone."

"How wonderful for you yet how sad it came about because of such a tragedy. Where are they?"

"They should be returning from their tutor soon."

"You are having the girl tutored as well?"

"Of course. Had to fight over that as well but found a good lad just back from Oxford who was more than happy to take them both. I made it clear he is not to temper what he teaches the girl and he appears to be of a like mind. Idelle and Gerwin Craddock, now Haigh. We are very proud about how far they have come in just this year, especially after all they went through after their parents died. Too many refusing to help them and the officials refusing to honor the wishes of their parents." He shook his head.

"I am happy for you that it all worked out in the end."

"We had a duke on our side. Hard for pompous officials to argue with a duke."

"Modred helped you?" asked Bened, and smiled when the man nodded. "Sounds like our cousin."

"Strode in on the day we truly felt all was lost and told the men they were breaking the law. The will was fully legal and they were trying to thwart the last will and testament of the ones who had died. If they did this, they weakened that law, which meant their own wills could be contested. Even said he might consider it himself since some of the lands they would bequest in their wills abut his. He then pointed out that since no one else was offering to take the children they would be put on the parish and that meant a regular cost to them. Hard. Cold, precise, and very effective."

"The smartest approach. That is our Modred," said Bevan.

"We could never thank him enough but I did send him a few rose cuttings which Dob prettily thanked me for and Frederick sent him some of his very fine cakes."

"A perfect choice."

"To be quite honest the roses were more for Dob," confessed George. "His Grace told us that he had had one more arrow in his quiver if they had still balked. He had been given permission to use Dob, to point out that these were the same men who had, without hesitation or question, handed his care over to Dob and they had known all about her."

"Actually, he could have just threatened them with sending her down to argue your cause and they would have quailed in their boots." Bened laughed softly. "Dob is a force to be reckoned with." He took one of the tiny lemon cakes Frederick offered and, after one bite, closed his eyes and hummed his appreciation.

"Frederick cooks like a god," said Primrose as she savored one of her favorite cinnamon buns.

"So, Sir Vaughn . . ." began George.

"Bened will do."

"Thank you. So, Bened, when do you become our neighbor?"

"Not long now. Had to help Rose with her troubles and all. Been sending off instructions and funds when needed but do need to go have a quick look. The couple handling it all for me appears to be very good at it. Hard-working and responsible and, even more important, careful with the funds I send."

"They are good people. Pughs. Your family seems fond of them."

"When I saw the name of the caretakers, I did find it comforting."

"It used to belong to Vaughns many years ago, did it not?"

"It did. Modred and Dob were quick to send me all sorts of information. I shall have to do a more thorough study when I settle in as I think it may be why that earl handed it over."

Primrose listened to her uncle and Bened discuss his new lands and wondered if she would ever see them. Before she could fret over the future Frederick caught her attention and he rose to his feet and hurried out of the room. A moment later she could hear two childish voices with only the occasional interruption of Frederick's deeper one. He walked in holding the hands of a boy and a girl, both with bright red curls and wide brown eyes.

The children patiently allowed all the introductions and then sat politely while Frederick made them each a plate of treats.

"They were born to a poor couple who had no learning but we could see the spark," said George in a quiet voice as the children talked to Frederick. "We want grand things for them and Frederick insists that means learning such skills as good manners as well."

"Very wise. They are lovely children and seem quite content despite the tragedy they suffered."

"Thank you for saying so, sweetheart."

It was later that afternoon that Bened asked Primrose to join him, Bevan, Lilybet, and Morris in going to see his cousin the duke. Since she was not family she protested that she would be intruding. Then she worried that Simeon would feel left out if not invited only to find out he had been and had declined for he wanted to spend time with his uncle. Uncertain, Primrose finally joined the others. It was not until they were almost there that she noticed she was not the only one who was feeling intimidated.

"Lilybet, you did not have to come if you did not wish to," she told the pale-faced woman riding next to her.

"I came on this journey to meet with my mother's kin," Lilybet said. "I will do that." She grimaced. "I just had not realized one of those kin would be a duke in a castle. I was hunting for Wherlockes and he is a Vaughn. But, as Morris said, the Vaughns and Wherlockes are just branches off the same tree, their roots all having started at the same place and time."

"Do you know what the duke's gift is?"

"He can hear what you think."

"I find that rather frightening and yet have not been at all troubled by anything else. Not even how Bevan can almost disappear in an open field."

Lilybet laughed and her color improved. "Your brother's face when he did that was funny."

"I was not all that easy with it myself. Fascinating though it is. A puzzle, too, as he swears he cannot go invisible or change colors. I am thinking it is some trick he can play on our minds and he may not even know how he does it."

"That makes a great deal of sense. It is not him who disappears but our eyes that do not see him because our minds tell us he is not there."

"I just do not see how he can do that, either, but it is the only answer I could come up with."

"Well, I like it. It feels right." She frowned. "Do you get the feeling we are about to be put to some test?"

Primrose stared at Lilybet in surprise. "Yes. I thought I was being foolish but wondered why I was being brought along when it is clearly intended to be a family visit, the cousins coming to pay their respects to the head of the family and all that."

"They are certainly doing that and bringing me to meet the head of the family so he can acknowledge me as family, I suspect. There just seems to be a little secret the three of them are sharing. Nothing huge, or really worrisome, just a little something."

When they halted in the courtyard and let the stableboys take their horses, Primrose stared up at the huge castle. This family was old. She got the deep, sure feeling that they went back centuries, maybe even to the far distant time when there were many kings and not just one. She also noticed that the rose cuttings her uncle had sent were growing beautifully in a tidy little garden near the massive front doors.

She nudged Lilybet and nodded at the roses. "I must not forget to tell him about that."

"I will be certain to remind you if it looks like you might have," Lilybet said.

The man who came to the door was no servant and Primrose was shocked to realize that it was the duke himself. He was so handsome, he was almost pretty. He also looked far too young to be the head of such a huge powerful family. Then Bened grabbed her by the hand and pulled her forward. She looked into the duke's beautiful sea-green eyes and thought he seemed almost ethereal.

"This is the Honorable Primrose Wootten, Your Grace," he said. "Primrose, this is His Grace, the Duke of Elderwood, Modred of the half dozen names."

The young Duke frowned at Bened and said, "Are you certain it is only a half dozen? It often feels like more." He then took off his glove and reached out to take Primrose's hand, a gesture so unusual she was shocked speechless. "I am very pleased to meet you, Miss Wootten."

"Primrose will do, Your Grace."

"And I shall tell you to call me Modred but I have a feeling it may take you a while to do so."

"We also have another surprise." Morris tugged Lilybet closer. "This is Lilybet Wherlocke. She has come looking for her family and we thought she might as well start from the top. One of the ones we have lost touch with, Modred."

"That is wonderful news." He shook her hand as well and smiled. "And even better now." He turned and yelled down the hall. "Aunt Dob! You must come meet the new guests."

"Must you bellow some like some fishmonger?" came a woman's voice, moving closer with each word. "Who are the ladies? I recognize everyone else."

Modred took both Lilybet and Primrose by the hands and tugged them forward. He introduced them with utmost courtesy to his aunt Dob despite the fact that he was holding hands with two women who had only just been introduced to him. The way the woman's eyes widened as she saw that made Primrose expect a lecture but the woman just smiled so brightly it had to be hurting her cheeks.

"High walls?" she asked Modred.

"High, wide, and very strong," he replied.

Bened looked so pleased that Primrose began to think she had been right to think she had been brought to face some kind of test. Obviously she had passed and so had Lilybet. Then, when Bened took her hand from the duke's she recalled the man's gift again. The necessity for such a test came to her so quickly, the reason so clear, she almost gasped. She glanced at Lilybet who was frowning at Morris. They had wanted to see if the duke could read their thoughts. Primrose would have been angrier if she had failed.

"You did not tell them," said Dob, and slapped both Bened and Morris upside the head. "I would get my spoon and do that except that I am in too good a mood right now. A newfound Wherlocke who can come and go here as freely as she pleases and a new friend who can do the same. You brought us two treasures so you are forgiven. By me. Might take a little longer to be forgiven by the ones you tricked."

"You did not smack Bevan," said Bened as he rubbed at his abused ear.

"He is just too adorable and I am sure was just following your directions. Now, into the parlor all of you and I will bring some food and drink."

The moment the woman left and Primrose found herself seated next to Bened in a lavish front parlor, she scowled at him. "You could have warned us."

"Nay, because then you may then have worked to build walls and that is never a true judgment," answered Bened.

"You mean you can actually make it so he cannot see inside?"

"Yes, although it is hard work. You and Lilybet are what is best, ones he can actually befriend, even come round for a visit without a long warning. You just do it, without thought or effort. It is a natural part of you."

"And obviously with you, Morris, and Bevan."

"With most of the family, of the blood. It does appear as if the high strong walls to the mind come hand in hand with the other things. It requires a strong emotion to put a crack in them and then he is assaulted by a little of what is there."

"You are right. That is more a curse than a gift," she said softly, watching the duke prompting Lilybet to tell him everything she knew about her mother and her mother's family.

"It is and I am sorry I did not warn you but I could not. It had to be as normal a meeting as possible to know for sure."

"Apology accepted and now I am going to go find his aunt Dob and see if she needs any help in the kitchens."

Bened gave her the directions and Primrose walked away, allowing herself to inspect everything she passed. When she stepped into the kitchens, Dob turned to face her, holding a bloody butcher knife. On the board covering the counter behind her were a lump of brown fur and the innards of the butchered rabbit corpse she could see on the stovetop. But that scene rapidly blended into another as horror, grief, and fear surged up into Primrose so fast she could not stop it. She heard herself scream as Dob became Augusta and the mangled fur and blood became Constantine.

Modred suddenly jerked and leapt to his feet. "Where is your lady, Bened?"

"The kitchens. Why?"

"We need to get to her now."

Then the screams echoed along the hallway and Bened was running for the kitchens, faintly aware of everyone else running right behind him. He entered the kitchen to find Primrose shaking, her hands over her face and hoarse little screams escaping her. Dob was frantically cleaning up the remains of a rabbit she had obviously readied for the pot, all the time trying to soothe Primrose with words. He went to Primrose and rubbed her back, saying empty useless words that did nothing to calm her as she quieted to a whispered repetition of "Constantine. She has killed my Constantine."

He was pushed aside by Lilybet who whispered an apology and then slapped Primrose, hard. Bened grabbed Primrose when she staggered back but swallowed his angry words for Lilybet when he saw Primrose's eyes clear then darken with annoyance as she glared at the other woman. Acting as if she did not even know she had been a babbling mass of hysterical woman but a moment ago.

"What the bloody hell did you do that for?" she demanded.

"You were hysterical. A good hard slap is one of the cures for it. Bened rubbing your back and saying 'there, there' was doing no good," Lilybet replied.

"I did not say, 'there, there,'" Bened protested even though he could not be all that sure he had not.

"Near enough."

Modred stepped over and took both of Primrose's hands in his. He was still pale but he no longer looked as if he was about to collapse, and Bened had to assume that Primrose had her shields back in place for he showed no sign of hearing anything.

"I fear you were hysterical, Miss Primrose," he said, "but not without reason. Do you recall what set you off?"

"I recall coming into the kitchen and Dob moved and then I saw . . . I saw . . ." She took a deep breath and the duke squeezed her hands.

"I know what you saw and it was vicious, cruel, evil. I think you have a very good mind, clever and able to retain all kinds of things you read, hear, or see, but it is also strong enough to slam up a wall and hide what it feels will hurt you too much. You just recalled one of those things, did you not?"

"Days ago I recalled why I was so desperately afraid of the dark, especially if I am out in the woods alone."

"And you just recalled another thing. This was not caused by that memory. You have adjusted to that."

"Constantine," she whispered, and felt tears run down her cheeks. "I remembered my dog. I was twelve and he disappeared. All I could recall was that he disappeared and we looked for a few days. No more than that. I thought it strange. But I just recalled what happened to him, didn't I?"

"Yes, I fear you did. And your clever mind knew that, at that tender age, it could break you so it did what it felt it must to protect itself. It walled it all in so you could not remember." He smiled faintly. "Even though I suspect you could give me all of Act Three of *Othello* word for word." He nodded when she blushed and then let go of her hands.

"She butchered him." When the duke stepped aside so Bened could put his arm around her, she leaned into Bened, welcoming his warmth and strength. "She showed me his coat of fur and said she was going to make mittens of them for me.

I think that is when I swooned. When I woke up all I knew was that my dog, my constant companion, was gone and so we looked for him. I just don't understand why my mind hid that away. It could have made us see Augusta for the sick, evil woman she is so much sooner."

"It would have broken you," said the duke.

"I would like to think myself stronger than that."

"You were a young, sensitive girl on the cusp of womanhood."

"A very sensitive time for a girl, a time of high emotion and easily broken hearts," said Dob as she handed Primrose a cup of hot sweet tea. "Drink that down."

"I suspect all your love and affection, things the woman in that house never returned, went into that dog." The duke reached out and patted her on the arm. "You must rid yourself of this woman. She will never stop and her actions will simply grow worse and worse."

"It makes me sad to think I had the knowledge of just how ill she is and it was hidden away. It could have saved my father."

"I think if your mind had not hidden it away and it had broken you, whatever you had the ability to say would not have been listened to."

"Ah, of course, for everyone would have seen me as the one who was ill."

"The wound has been mended now, though. Whatever trouble that walled-in memory caused will pass away now."

She nodded and let Bened lead her back into

the parlor. After she finished the tea, she joined Dob and Lilybet out in the gardens, thinking they nearly rivaled her uncle George's. When she said as much to Dob, the woman blushed with pleasure.

"This is made for Modred mostly, for it can calm his poor mind after a bad day, although I discovered I loved doing the gardening."

"You do a great deal for the duke, I think."

"He needed me at a time when I needed to be needed. We healed each other. We have servants, you know. 'Tis just that they all have this afternoon off for a wedding of one of their family. That is the problem with taking one's servants all from just two families." She laughed. "There are times when we wonder how we manage but we do. I know the Pughs will have work at the place Bened is going to. There is a couple already there with a fine home in the gatehouse."

"Bened was pleased to hear how well they are working for him."

"So when are you going to marry that boy?"

"One needs to be asked first."

"One could nudge a bit."

"I want to be asked when he knows for certain it is what he wants."

"Reasonable, but kill that bitch of an aunt of yours first. Best not to be marrying and bringing new ones into the world while someone like that is still running about free."

"Agreed. I am going to tell Simeon all I have recalled."

"Get him to tell you about his beatings and a few

other things," Lilybet said. "He is suffering a lot of guilt and it is because he knew things and never said. He also wonders if he could have saved his father just by telling what he knew. Guilt. Both of you have it and neither deserve it."

"How do you know? Did he tell you?" asked Primrose, wondering if there was something about Lilybet and her brother that she had missed.

"Did not have to. I can sense emotions."

"I thought you saw things, the future and all."

"I also can feel the emotions of a lot of people. One occasionally leads to the other."

"Oh. That must be unpleasant at times. Not everyone is experiencing pleasant emotions all the time."

Dob studied Lilybet. "I could teach you how to close the door on that now and then."

"I just might want you to when I get more settled."

"Well, time to get back inside, for dinner will be served soon." Dob patted Primrose on the back and added, "And it is not rabbit."

Primrose laughed and knew she would recover from the shock of this last memory just fine.

Simeon stared at his sister in open-mouthed shock. "She did what?"

"Please do not make me repeat that. 'Tis bad enough knowing the memory has now been freed inside my head and could be pulled forth at any time. Yet, I feel horrible. Modred says it was just my mind protecting me but by hiding the truth it

put us all in danger for we did not see just how truly
evil she is."

Simeon hugged her. "If it had crushed you,
crippled your mind, no one would have paid any
attention to what you had to say."

"That is what Modred says."

"Modred, is it? You now call a duke by his proper
name?"

"Once you meet him it becomes harder and harder
to think of him as The Duke. He is so young."

"And he can read minds?"

"Something like that. He was so happy to meet
more people with high walls, as he called them,
that one would have felt very rude asking him
specifics about his gift. But when I got so upset,
no, hysterical, he knew it even before I screamed.
He also knew what I had seen. It was all right at
that time because he was being comforting and
helping me. But when I thought on it later, I realized that he is a rather scary young man. Oh, and
thanked my puny mind for having big strong
walls."

"I wonder if I have walls?"

"It may well be something that runs through a
family. He says he can read none of his own, none
he has met, anyway. I thought that was interesting.
And, you could see that he was thoroughly enjoying having company that he could not read, to
just be a normal young man having a normal conversation and telling silly jokes. I think he is alone
too much."

"That is sad. A young man with his title and
money should be out learning how to be as bad as

he can without actually breaking any laws or losing his place in society."

"I am certain that is what all young men aspire to."

"So what do we do now?"

"What everyone says we must do. Find our aunt and end her."

Chapter Fifteen

"I think it might be best if you started back home," said Lilybet as she walked into the dining room the next day.

"Good morning to you, too, Lily," said Simeon as he put some ham on his plate.

"I mean it," she said as she got a plate and began to fill it with some of Frederick's excellent cooking

"I know you do but do you perhaps have some explanation for saying it? We lesser mortals arrived here to break our fast after a pleasant night of dreaming of our favorite things such as food, especially lemon cakes, water, boats, fluffy clouds. We do not have"—he waited until she sat down and took the seat across from her—"the peek inside the planning room for our futures that you do."

"She is angry. She means to destroy all you love and need."

"That would be idiotic since she, whom I must assume is Augusta, is after getting her filthy hands on all I love and need."

"Anger does not always make a person make sense.

She needs to strike out. I think the manor and all that are safe as she does covet them very deeply and spends a lot of time dreaming on how much she would change to meet her horrific tastes in decorating."

"How do you know they are horrific?"

"Ah, a good question."

"Which would be an even better one if you would answer it."

"I think when she had hold of me and was beating me, she and I, well, became connected in some odd way. I have been seeing her, a lot, doing things that rarely appear in my usual seeings. Such as her dreams of the crimes she would commit in making the manor more to her taste. If you can call that taste," she muttered. "Maybe I bled on her a little or something."

"Lily, you do see that I am trying to have my morning feast, do you not?"

She laughed. "It is no pleasure for me to have that witch in my head so much."

"No, I can fully understand that. Is it ruining your ability to do what you usually do?"

When she did not answer, Simeon looked up from his food and saw that she was sitting very still, her eyes unfocused, and a little chill went over him. "Where is Frederick?" she asked, in that tone of voice that Simeon was learning to absolutely loathe, a flat tone utterly devoid of all the warmth and life that was Lilybet.

"He is walking the children to the tutor's house," answered George as he strolled in and went toward the food. "He does it every morning that they go there and then he is off every afternoon and walks them home. He would have done it yesterday but he wanted so badly to cook that he had one of the Pugh boys do it for him."

"We have to go and walk him home," Lilybet said as she drank down her cider and stood up.

"Why?" demanded George as he watched Simeon hastily fill his mouth with the last of his ham and stand up.

"We must do it now. Simeon!"

"Coming. I will explain later, Uncle George, as soon as she explains it all to me," Simeon said, gave the man a quick pat on the back, and hurried after Lilybet.

Bened saw them rushing out the door and followed. "What is wrong?"

"Hell if I know," said Simeon. "Lily says we have to walk Frederick home from the tutor's house so we are off to do that."

"I will join you."

"Oh, that would be good," Lilybet said, and smiled at Bened.

"Hey!" Simeon glared at her. "I am no weakling, you know."

"I do but you have to admit Bened looks far more intimidating."

Glancing at Bened, Simeon had to agree. Although he was having a little trouble catching his breath as they nearly ran along the path to the road, he asked Lilybet, "And we will be in need of someone intimidating?"

"Yes. I fear it is your aunt again."

"She followed us here?"

"She knew you were coming here. She then thought on how much you care for your uncle."

"Frederick is not my uncle."

"But he is your uncle's best friend, his love. It will crush him if something happens to Frederick."

"Damn. Well, maybe we can end her here."

Lilybet shook her head. "She is not here. She sent some hirelings. She is headed for Willow Hill."

"Right at this moment, I am beginning to not care so much about what she is planning to do or has done. I want to shoot her down just for being such a nuisance."

If Bened had not been so concerned for the amiable Frederick, he knew he would have smiled. He wondered if the two had yet noticed what was stirring between them. Then he saw the tutor's house and Frederick walking out of the door. Just up the road from him were three men. He did not need any special gift to tell him they were the ones they were here to stop.

Lilybet ran straight for Frederick while Bened and Simeon went for the three men. Seeing the glint of a blade in one man's hand, Bened called out to Simeon, "Knife!"

Bened got in front of Simeon and kicked the man in the face. He howled and clutched at his nose, which allowed Bened to disarm him. He then swung the man around to use him as a shield against a second knife-wielding man. Out of the corner of his eyes he saw Frederick move Lilybet out of his way, grab the arm of the man trying to cut him, snap it, and then punch the screaming man three times in the face before letting the body drop to the ground. Frederick, he thought, could probably have taken care of himself.

"Nicely done," he said as he walked up to the man and looked down at the one Frederick had punched.

"It certainly was." Simeon frowned at Lilybet. "Makes me wonder why I had to interrupt my morning feast."

"I did not know he could fight like that," said Lilybet. "And it was three against one."

Frederick huffed. "Three men who think they are big and bad because they have a knife. I have faced worse. Ten years in the infantry."

"You did not even see them until we arrived."

"So they may have been able to wound me but I would have managed."

Simeon saw Lilybet's eyes narrow and said quickly, "I am sure you would have, Frederick."

"While bleeding and fighting the other two while weakened by that and risking another wound," said Lilybet, and then she nodded her head toward the tutor's house, where they saw two terrified children standing in the doorway. "Right in front of your children,"

"Da?" said the little girl, and Frederick hurried up the steps to soothe the children while talking in a low voice to the tutor.

"I think we offended his manliness," said Simeon.

"Men are idiots," said Lilybet. "Do not give me that look. You can be. One against three. Three armed men against one unarmed man. That makes it perfectly reasonable for me to see what I saw as a warning that he might need help."

Frederick sent the children back inside with

the tutor and walked back down to stand in front of Lilybet. "You are right. Seeing three men against one with killing in the mind of the three is a warning. I do thank you for rushing here to help me. You were also right to say I would have gotten bloody and poor little Idelle was terrified enough without having had to see that. The tutor sent someone off to fetch the magistrate's men." He looked up the street and smiled. "And here they come. We will soon be able to go home."

When they finally arrived back at the house, George looked up from the book he was reading at the table and Primrose cast them a worried look as George asked, "Everything all right?"

"That woman sent three thugs after me. We dealt with it."

Bened moved to the sideboard and filled a plate with food even as a yawning Morris and a sleepy-eyed Bevan entered the room. He moved to sit next to Primrose, trying to forget how much he missed her lithe body curled up in his arms all night long. It was odd to see George smiling faintly when he had just been told that Frederick had been attacked.

"Do not get your feathers ruffled, Frederick," George said. "They have never seen you fight."

"True and she"—he nodded at Lilybet who was back in her seat enjoying some fruit—"was right to see it as a dangerous threat. She was also right to point out that I would have ended up wounded in some way even if I took all three down, as I would have, and the children seeing me hurt like that would have been very upset. They came at me from behind so I would have had to endure at least one pinprick."

Bened noticed how George went a little pale at the news that three men had come at Frederick from behind but the man said nothing, just stared down at his book for a moment until his coloring returned to normal. "Do you think this was part of her temper tantrum?" he asked Lilybet.

"Oh, yes." She looked at George. "Mind if I ask who you are leaving all your worldly goods to?"

"The children will get most of it such as the land and house, but we have set aside a large fund for Simeon and Primrose as they were my sister's children and she and her husband helped us get this place."

"Oh, Uncle, you should set that aside for the children as well," said Primrose.

"No, it is the exact amount your father lent us and he would not take payment. So we told him what we would do and he accepted that. It siw quietly in a safe funds account and there it will stay."

She recognized his do-not-argue tone of voice so let it go but asked Lilybet, "Do you think this was just a lashing out then?"

"It was but I suspect she knows where every ha'penny of your money is and thought this would gain her two things. Hurt you in a personal way and add more money to the pile she thinks she will soon get her hands on." Lilybet looked at Simeon. "Do you know if there is anyone else who would be leaving you something she might covet?"

"Only Cousin Geoffrey. He has land near Willow Hill that used to be my father's but refused to be gifted with it so he leases. She would not bother with that arrangement, I think, as it produces money enough just as it is. Well, unless she felt she could lease it for more or sell it for a nice sum of money. Hell, I guess I better send a warning to Cousin Geoffrey."

"That might be best since the woman is headed that way now."

"Then I guess we had better plan to go back to Willow Hill and be ready for her."

"We could start out today or leave on the morrow," said Bened.

"The morrow will do. It has been nice to just be off the back of a horse for hours on end," said Simeon. "At least this time we will be following her."

Lilybet shook her head and then sipped at her tea. "She will be at Willow Hill before you no matter when you leave here so best to be prepared for that. She has plans. I just do not know what yet."

"You seem to be getting a lot of information about her," said Bened, curious as to what gifts this woman had and how they worked.

"The evil wretch is stuck in my head. I do not know how or why, but she is there. I wish I could scrub her out for it is wearying to deal with so much anger and evil, especially when it is not your own."

"I could not bear it," said Primrose.

"That is why I am staying close to you, because I need to be there to make sure she is ended. Harsh though it is to say that, she has earned hanging several times over by now."

Everyone nodded their agreement and turned their attention to finishing their meal. Primrose was just heading to her bedchamber when Bened caught her by the arm and led her outside. She had to admit it was a beautiful day. Such sunny days were rare and meant to be enjoyed. She rather hoped it would raise her spirits, which had been low since she had recovered another horrible memory and made such a scene at Elderwood.

"I am sorry for causing such trouble at your cousin's," she said.

"You have nothing to apologize for," Bened said firmly, and kissed her on the cheek. "One thing my family understands, in far too many ways, is the cruelty adults can inflict upon children. Modred has his share of bad memories from his childhood and probably has wished that he could forget them from time to time."

"You do not have any, do you?"

"Nay, but I was one of the fortunate ones in that my mother accepted all that my father was and what gifts her sons ended up with." He smiled. "Bevan's was the only one she complained about."

"Oh, yes, I can see that. A child who can hide so well would be a sore trial to a mother." She grimaced. "I obviously also know how to hide but not in a particularly good way. Now I worry about what else has been hidden inside my memories."

"I just find what Modred said about your own mind protecting you fascinating. It shut it in a box and sealed it."

"That is what he thinks and in a strange way it makes some sense. Something I did not have much to do with hid those memories from me. It troubled me when I thought on what I could not recall because

I recall so much so easily. Then I even thought it might be when I hit my head after my first horse tossed me down. That suited, was a sensible explanation, so I let it stand even though now I realized the times do not match."

"It is a good thing that you did not hurt anything when you hit your head. That sort of wound can cause all manner of troubles."

"It did destroy my eyesight, which had been perfect up until then."

"It did?"

"Yes. When I woke up everything was a blur. At first we thought it would ease and return to normal as the wound healed but it did not so the physician decided something had been broken and I have worn glasses ever since."

"Did you know we have healers in our family?"

"Truly? That is wondrous and, I suspect, very convenient."

"What I am trying to say is that, perhaps, one of them could do something. If the matter is a natural weakness, they cannot fix it, but you seem to have suffered an injury and many of those they can fix."

Hope stirred to life in her chest but she beat it down. "It is a pretty old injury, Bened. I could not have been more than ten or eleven years of age when it happened and am now three and twenty."

"And scars may have formed over the injury. I know. That, too, would mean it could not be fixed. But what is the harm in having one of them at least see what they can see?"

"None, really, save for the pain of disappointment when they cannot do anything. Yet, I lived through that many times before with physician after physician coming to look at me. I can live through it again."

"As soon as matters are back to normal, I shall ask around amongst the healers in the family. Each can be just a little different, you see."

Primrose had to think about it for a moment and then sternly told herself not to be a coward. If there was even the smallest of chances one of the family healers could fix the problem with her eyes, she would have a whole new life. It would not only be cowardly to refuse such a chance but stupid.

"If you find one who thinks it worth a look, I believe I can do it."

"Just think of it as a trial but one with no big consequences if it fails. An experiment, if you will, one in which our healers can test the reach of their gifts. Nothing will have changed or grown worse."

"True and that is just how I will think of it." She looked around and realized they were walking to the edge of the hill, to the side that would give a beautiful view of Modred's castle. "This is not one of those walks like we took in the woods, is it, because I see no shelter here."

"Nay. Sad to say there is none. I just wished to get out and walk before we face hours in the saddle starting on the morrow. And look at the family seat from this point. It is a fine place."

"It is very grand and yet, once inside, it just feels like any home. Well, any home of someone with money for some of the finer things."

"That is Dob's doing. She looked at what Modred's parents had created and decided it would not do. So exact, so much about showing off one's power and wealth, and so pristine. Modred needed a nest, she said, someplace where he could relax and not worry. The way his parents had done it, you dared not even curtsey as protocol demanded without fear of breaking something more valuable than you could ever afford to replace. He was still very young when she walked in to take care of him. Dob's opinion was that consequence would not save his mind and made the castle far more suitable for a boy than some king."

"She said they healed each other."

"They did. We all only have one worry about him now and that is that Dob is not a young woman. We need Modred to find himself someone to care for who loves him for him despite the gift that makes so many uneasy, and to find her and win her before Dob's time comes."

"That certainly sounds like a good thing to pray for."

"Your uncle needs some trees," he muttered as he looked around at the barren hill, sheep grazing in every direction.

Primrose laughed. "Yes, a little copse of them here and there, ones offering people taking in the view from here a little shade and shelter, the kind you can slip into for a bit of privacy, and which everyone knows why people would go there and what you are doing if you stay within the shelter of them for very long."

"Unfortunately, that would be the truth of it. I suspect even the villagers would see them being made and say to themselves, 'Why is George putting in so many trysting spots?'"

"I should probably go and check on Smudge, make certain he is ready for a long journey."

He followed her as she headed for the stables. The horses were content in their stalls but Bened looked Mercury over anyway. He appeared to have taken no harm from the long ride to Uncle George's and Bened was confident the animal would not suffer for the ride back to Willow Hill, either. It was why he had chosen the animal. Even when Mercury had been a colt he had seen the promise of stamina and strength. The speed the animal had revealed had been a beautiful added blessing.

He crossed his arms on the wall of Mercury's stall and looked over it to watch as Primrose brushed down her horse. She was very good to any animals under her care and he respected that. In truth there was a great deal about Primrose that he respected.

As soon as she started to leave the stables he fell into step beside her. He could see Simeon standing on the steps in front of the house with Lilybet obviously giving him her opinion on something. The look on his face told Bened that the man was hearing something he did not like if only because his clever mind told him it was reasonable and he should agree.

Bened leaned over to whisper in Primrose's ear. "Be sure to leave your bedchamber doors unlocked tonight."

"You cannot come creeping into my room at night."

"I can actually and I intend to."

"If you get caught . . ."

"Nay, I will not be caught."

She watched him stride away and thought he was a little too confident in himself. The only ones who thought it acceptable that he was her lover were her and him. That left six other adults, all sleeping on the same floor, who could catch him and suffer shock, outrage, or—she glanced at Simeon—anger. Shaking her head, she decided to go find her uncle George and talk to him about gardening.

Primrose settled into bed with a book on gardening her uncle had given her to read. She glanced at her bedchamber door and sighed. She had left it unlocked but if Bened was actually going to be cautious, she doubted she would see him. That gave her such a sense of disappointment she cursed and went back to her reading.

Just as she was about to doze off over a particularly dry treatise on the good and bad of planting flowering vines, a soft sound caught her attention. She looked at the door and saw the latch slowly lifting. Then, so abruptly it startled her into nearly dropping her book, the door opened, Bened slid inside, and then he silently closed and latched the door. He turned and grinned at her like a naughty boy. It was a look that should have been ridiculous on a man of his size but she found it charming.

"Are you certain you were not seen?" she asked quietly as he walked toward the bed shedding his clothing with each step.

"Very certain." He yanked off his boots and underdrawers and stood there proudly naked. "Gardening? I would have thought you did not need to read such a book."

"There are always new things to learn, although this is clearly written for beginners. Yet, despite that, I have found several interesting tips to make use of. Odd for my uncle to have spent coin on it as he is no beginner, either." She glanced at the proud proof of his intentions jutting out from his body and then rolled her eyes. "You have no modesty at all, do you?"

"Not a drop," he said cheerfully as he climbed into bed beside her, turned on his side, and studied her nightdress. "You, however, may have too much."

Before she could protest that assessment, Bened was removing her nightdress. Primrose had barely a minute to be embarrassed by her nudity and then he pulled her into his arms. The moment their flesh touched, she no longer cared about having no clothes on, did in truth revel in the lack of them.

"Mmmm. I have missed this," Bened murmured before kissing her with a fierce passion that quickly heated her blood.

"We have not shared a bed that often."

"I know," he said as he caressed her breasts and nibbled at the side of her neck. "And that is a pure shame."

Primrose quickly lost all ability to think clearly. Bened had obviously told the truth when he said he had missed what they shared for his greed, for her was clear to feel in every kiss and stroke of his hand. He turned her onto her stomach and just as she was about to ask what he was doing, he was sliding into her. She gasped, the way he could fill her feeling much more enhanced in this position. When her release came, she smothered her cries by burying her face in the pillow and soon he was doing the same.

Collapsing beneath him, Primrose had the thought

that there must be a lot of ways to join two willing bodies but bit her tongue against asking. She was sure it was something no proper lady should show any curiosity about. The way he spread kisses over her spine sparked a little interest in her sated body and she almost laughed. It was obviously not just Bened who was feeling greedy.

Chapter Sixteen

Rising passion burned the last dregs of sleep from Primrose's mind. Big, lightly calloused hands stroked her breasts while long fingers teased the tips that ached for his kiss. Then she woke enough to realize Bened was kissing her and just where. For only a heartbeat, shock pushed aside the haze of desire his lovemaking had stirred and she put her hands on his head intending to push him away, to put an end to such a shocking act. Then he stroked her with his tongue and desire rushed back to rule her again. Instead of pushing him away, she buried her fingers in his thick hair and held him close.

Tighter and tighter her need wound itself until her pleasure grew close to painful. Primrose tugged on his hair. To her relief, he responded to the silent demand and began kissing his way back up her body. Finally, he was kissing her on the mouth and she wrapped her arms around him, then her legs around his waist as he began to ease their bodies together.

He began to move, thrusting in and out of her with a slow rhythm as if he had all the time in the world to savor the way it felt to be joined with her. Primrose growled softly, reached down and grabbed his buttocks. Bened yelped, but kept his voice as subdued as she had, when her nails dug into his taut flesh and then he laughed. He began to move faster and with more force, bringing her passion to its peak and ending the aching need that had possessed her. She held on tightly, letting the pleasure flood her while he grew even fiercer in his movements until he found his own pleasure.

It was several minutes before Bened could move. Despite the blinding strength of his release he was pleased to see that he had retained enough of his wits to collapse just to the side of her, keeping the bulk of his weight off her slender body. It would be very rude to crush one's lover, he thought, and smiled faintly before kissing her and then rising to get a wet cloth to bathe them with.

Primrose watched him. He had a body she enjoyed gazing at as he moved; seeing all that sleek muscle beneath that taut skin was a pure delight. When he started back toward the bed she noted that he was a goodly sized man in every way. It amazed her that they fit together so well but, in her studies about illnesses and the workings of the body in order to help her decide what medicines to mix, she had learned that the body was a rather amazing thing.

Still a little embarrassed by the ritual after their lovemaking, she closed her eyes as he cleaned her off. Listening to him move, she was ready when he climbed back into bed and she curled up in his arms even as he reached for her.

"There is nothing as good as sharing a loving in the morning," Bened said, enjoying how relaxed and replete he felt.

"In the morning, Bened? Is that normal?"

"I believe it is," he replied in a very solemn voice, then ruined it by chuckling.

Then Primrose realized the full implications of what he had just said. It was morning. People would be rising soon. They could be caught. Clutching the covers to cover her chest, she sat up and saw the sunlight that streamed into the room through a small space between the curtains.

"Oh no! We were not supposed to go to sleep!"

"You exhausted me," he said as he reached for her, and then frowned when she scrambled out of his reach.

Primrose leapt out of bed and tugged on her nightdress then scowled at Bened who still sprawled in the bed, arms crossed beneath his head as he watched her. "You have to go now!" she said, and hurried around to his side of the bed, picked up his scattered clothing, and tossed it on top of him.

"I hope you do not expect me to climb out a window or something," he said as he got out of bed and began to dress.

"Just do not let Simeon see you."

"Rose, do you really think he does not know what is going on between us?"

"Knowing it and being brazenly confronted by it are not the same things."

Bened thought that over as he finished dressing and then nodded. "Nay, you are right, they are not. I can slip out and creep down the hall to my room."

"Without anyone seeing you? You are not exactly small, Bened."

"Pleased you noticed." He gave an exaggerated wince when she slapped his arm. "No one but us is awake."

"No? Are you certain about that?"

"Very certain." He took her into his arms and kissed her. "I am glad you found your brother, safe and unharmed, but I do wish he would go away now."

Primrose had to bite her lip to keep from laughing as she pushed him toward the door. She admired how quiet and cautious he was as he left, and then waited for some sound to tell her he had been seen. The tension caused by a fear of discovery and an uncomfortable confrontation with Simeon began to fade as minutes ticked by and there was no sound, not even of him going back into his own bedchamber. She crawled back to bed, pulled the pillow he had rested his head on into her arms, and fell asleep surrounded by the tempting scent of him.

"I love my horse," Primrose said as she stood by Smudge, her belongings neatly secured on the saddle.

"That is nice," said Lilybet, looking at her in a way that told Primrose the woman was confused and a little bit concerned about her.

"I just do not particularly wish to ride her today. Yet she looks eager to get going."

"As do the men," Lilybet said as she swung up into her saddle.

"Very well."

Primrose mounted and did her best to hide a wince. She was still rather new to lovemaking and her body was making it very clear that she had been too greedy last night. In truth, Bened had been very greedy and she had had no inclination to say no. Now even her thighs ached, she thought, and waved farewell to her uncle and Frederick.

Sleeping would have been wise as well, she thought as she clapped a hand over her mouth to hide a huge yawn. Bened had not allowed her to get much of that but he did not look as if he had suffered from not sleeping. Then again he had been a soldier and they could ride all night. She chuckled as she considered that thought and saw the humor of it. Shaking her head, she decided she was losing her mind.

By the time they stopped near midday to rest their horses and have a meal, Primrose was wondering if she could just tie herself to her horse and let someone lead Smudge along as she slept. The only thing keeping her awake at the moment was the mere thought of having something to eat. She was starving.

Bened frowned as he went to lift Primrose down from the back of Smudge. She was a little pale and looked exhausted. There had been a few times he had seen her shifting in her saddle and wincing a little. He felt guilty for keeping her awake most of the night but did not regret even one of the many hours he had spent making love to her. Once her desire burned away her shyness, Primrose was a passionate, eager, occasionally demanding lover.

"Are you all right?" he asked as she swayed against him, resting her forehead on his chest.

"Just tired." She roused enough to straighten up and look around. "And hungry."

"Bevan is already preparing the campsite and we will eat soon. Frederick packed us a feast."

"Oh, lovely." She slowly walked toward where Morris already had a fire going.

He had to nudge her awake to eat. Even though she seemed not to be tasting the food at all, she did eat with a steady speed and efficiency. What she needed was a full night of sleep, he decided, fighting the urge to take her to the inn in the village and tuck her up in bed. He scolded himself for being a rutting dog but he suspected he would just have to hear the words *Primrose* and *bed* in the same conversation and his desire for her would leap to life in hope.

The moment she set her plate down, her eyes closed, and Bened put his arm around her to keep her from falling over. He frowned and put his hand on her forehead just to make sure this was only exhaustion. It did not surprise him when Simeon rushed over to crouch in front of her but the angry look the man sent him did.

"Is she ill?" Simeon demanded.

Reminding himself yet again that the man was her brother and was well aware of the danger she was in, Bened answered pleasantly. "No, I think she is just tired. Riding about the countryside looking for you has not been easy for her," he could not resist adding.

"No, it would not have been," Simeon agreed softly and sighed. "I should have sent word to her about what I knew, or believed I knew, and where I was."

"And have it fall straight into Augusta's hands."

"There is that. Maybe we should make it a short day of travel."

"Or I could carry her up with me on Mercury." He struggled to keep his expression one of pleasant blankness.

"If she does not wake up when we are all ready to leave, it might be a thought. But, I should do it."

"If you wish, but Mercury is a bigger mount than yours, and built for some added weight. He can carry two more easily."

Simeon looked at Mercury. "He is a big beast, like a plow horse."

"Only half a plow horse and one of an old, honored breed. A very brave stallion about the size of your gelding romanced his mother. She let him live." He almost laughed at the shock on Simeon's face. "I named him Mercury for a reason as well so if anyone sets after us, my plow horse will leave them in the dust."

"Truly?"

"No doubt in my mind. My father has begun breeding more like him although it can be a dangerous business. Mercury has a lot of admirers."

"But you gelded him."

"Had to but he bred a few before I took him and

trained him. You do not really want a full stallion of that size for a riding mount, not with a stallion's temperament."

"Oh no, of course not. Fine then. If she is really exhausted, she will not even wake when you pick her up so then you take her up with you. If she does wake, she can ride on her own."

An hour later, Bened mounted his horse and Bevan handed a limp Primrose up to him. He set her in front of her, almost grinning when she snuggled up against him and he got a hard glare from Simeon. It was not kind to pinch at the man who had to know what was between Bened and his sister, but Bened could not resist and the badly smothered laughter from his brother who rode at his side revealed that that sort of humor was clearly a family trait.

They rode as fast as they could without wearing down the horses. Bened understood the need to cover as much ground as possible while the weather favored them. Augusta was still out there and they all suspected that she was riding back to Willow Hill. The less time they gave her to destroy something or set up a trap the better. They also had to try to stop her efforts to be rid of anyone or anything that could be used against her. For a woman who had to be insane she was proving to be a formidable opponent.

Jenson watched his brother and his family, along with his child, ride away to stay with his wife's brother and sighed. Now he had to warn the other servants and find a place to hide himself. But first, he thought, he was going to try to find something to help the Wootten siblings bring the woman down. He owed it to Sir Bened and Miss Primrose, who had not punished him for being with Augusta, but kindly set him free of the woman.

To his dismay his idiot employer, Rufford, found him before he could begin the search. "Jenson! Where the bloody hell have you been? I have been struggling with one of the pages here and it has been a dismal fortnight."

Jenson winced as he looked at what the man was wearing. "Your wife demanded my services."

"What use would that cow have for a valet?"

Jenson shrugged. "To tend her wardrobe."

Rufford swore viciously and got himself a large snifter full of brandy, gulping some of it down as if it was cheap ale. "She too often forgets who is the man in this family. I will have a word or two about that when she returns."

"She is returning?"

"Just got a letter from her saying she should be here in a day or two. She could not find my nephew. No idea why she went haring off to find him as she never much liked the lad. Hated that girl."

"Miss Primrose?"

"What other girl lived here, fool? Yes, Miss Primrose. Looks like her mother." He gulped some more brandy and gave a drunken sigh. "Lovely woman. Sweet and kind. My brother was a lucky man. My good friend Sir Edgar is heartbroken about how the girl ran away rather than wed him."

The thought of the kind, sweet Primrose in the hands of Sir Edgar Benton made Jenson feel ill. The man might have good blood, been to all the right schools, and have a lot of money but he was scum. He shook aside that distaste and started to plot a way to get free of this man so that he could be far away when Augusta returned.

"I need something to wear to Edgar's for tonight, Jenson. See to it."

Gritting his teeth, Jenson set about preparing to send the fool off to his friend's house. He worked as fast as he could, cajoling the man into his bath and ignoring his suggestions of what he thought would look best. By the time Rufford staggered off to lose more money he did not have, Jenson was in a cold sweat but decided to hold to his plan to at least look for something the Wootten siblings could use to bring the woman down.

Jenson was pulled out of his intense study of the family ledgers when he heard a voice that made his blood run cold.

"Where is my husband?" Augusta's sharp voice cut through the air.

As he heard some mumbled reply made by a terrified servant Jenson hurried over where he knew there was a small room behind a door hidden by the bookshelves. His heart pounded with fear as he waited for the door to slowly open but then he ducked inside and it closed behind him. Collapsing in a chair some past resident had put in so he could steal a smoke, Jenson fought to calm himself, to find that spine the girl said he needed. To his dismay the woman came into the ledger room.

"Has someone been in here?"

"Not that I am aware of, m'lady."

Jenson recognized the voice of the housekeeper, Mrs. Jakes, and sighed when he heard the fear in the woman's voice. Augusta terrified all of them. He held his breath to see if he could hear what answer Augusta accepted, Mrs. Jakes, or one of her own.

"Then it was probably my fool husband who does not have the sense to even hide his intrusion here. Get me some tea and a few cakes."

"As you wish, ma'am."

"M'lady. I will be called m'lady. Remember that."

Jenson held back the snort of disgust he felt ready to give. That woman was not entitled to the honors of the barony but clearly planned to usurp them. The only way to do that would be to wipe out the whole family. It was diabolical but he was not truly surprised. The woman had been talking as if that was her plan for as long as he had been trapped with her.

"Oh, and Mrs. Jakes, fetch my man of business."

Jenson sat down near the door so he could be sure to hear as much of what was about to be said as possible. Augusta was evidently so certain of victory that she was already taking over the entire household. He did not think that fool Rufford knew the extent of his wife's thefts or her intention to grab that title for him. That meant he did not know how near he was to being killed. Augusta would not allow him to throw away the money she saw as hers.

The wait was long, however, and he began to feel very tired.

The sound of a door shutting and Augusta's sharp voice jerked Jenson out of a nap. He rubbed his eyes and settled in to see if she meant to pull poor Mister Sutton into her plots through guile or threat. Could even be through bribery, he thought, although the man would have to be a fool to think he would ever see any of the money promised.

"Mister Sutton, I have some business that needs tending to."

"Such as what, ma'am? Do you wish some advice on investments?"

"No, I need to deal with some of the business of Willow Hill."

"That business is the sole province of the new baron, or in a few cases, Miss Primrose. You have no authority."

"Here is my authority. You can see right there that both Simeon and Primrose have signed allowing me to deal with matters while they are gone."

"But, they have not even heard the will read. This is most unusual."

"They are not certain when they can return and do not wish to leave things untended. Can you think of anything in the will that would prohibit any normal sort of business?"

It was quiet for a few minutes and Jenson decided Mister Sutton was pulling the will out of his bag and quickly reading it through. "Ah, here is one thing that severely changes how business is done here. Courtyard Manor. It goes to Master Geoffrey and thus there will be no more payments."

"Peter gave it to Geoffrey?"

"Every inch of it. All that is asked is that he agree to continue to be one of the regular suppliers to Willow Hill. I suppose that is because the baron saw the quality of the man's goods."

"That loss could cost Willow Hill dearly."

"There is still ample income, ma'am."

"Ample, perhaps, but that is still a large bite out of the purse. Do you think Geoffrey will sell it to us?"

"No, he is quite happy there and had done well enough that he never failed or even struggled to pay the lease. There is also a list of things to be done with Miss Primrose's dowry, the lands and the money. It is not too long now before she is five and twenty, which would be when she would be handed it all to do with as she pleases."

"What does she get?"

Jenson listened as Sutton listed several nice little properties and an enviable purse. That was not going to please Augusta at all.

"That is ridiculous. She is the daughter of a baron, not some princess. Willow Hill cannot afford to lose so much property or such a heavy purse."

"This is what the baron wanted for her and he was well able to afford it. So is Willow Hill."

"This kind of thing could bankrupt the estate."

"Nonsense. I researched it carefully and he could see that, although when it is first handed out money will be a little less for a year or two, Willow Hill will fully recover."

"And these things cannot be argued."

"No, ma'am, and I see no reason for it to be.

There is no case for what you claim, that it will bankrupt this estate."

"I must think on this, Mister Sutton, but we will be sure to discuss it again. Now I need some funds to deal with the cottages."

"What is wrong with the cottages?"

"They need new paint and roofs."

"I just rode past them and their roofs looked fine."

"I believe the word of the people living in them should count for more than the opinion of a man who just rode by and looked at one or two."

Jenson could almost feel Augusta's fury and he was certain Sutton could. It did not surprise him to hear her thank him in only a few minutes and then send him on his way, asking him to tell Mrs. Jakes to send in Jim Petty. He was just wondering what he should do when she left when he heard the door open again. This time he could actually hear a booted tread cross the floor and he knew it was another of Augusta's hirelings. He had never met a Jim Petty, though.

"I need you to take this to a man named Geoffrey and tell him he must sign it or he and his family will pay very dearly. If he still objects, come find me. I will probably be in here struggling to find a way to keep that little bitch from taking such a big bite out of Willow Hill."

"You want that threat vague or very, very clear?"

"I want it to make him shake in his muck-covered boots."

The moment the door shut, she cursed, fluently and profanely. "This cannot be allowed. That fool

Peter wrote a will that was going to beggar me," she complained as she paced. *I cannot and will not allow it*, she decided. Geoffrey would be crushed and when that was done, she would see to making Sutton pay for standing in her way with all his papers and laws. She knew he disliked her, did not respect her, and looked down his long nose at her all the time. When she ran Willow Hill, he would have to find himself a new position, or, even more to her liking, a grave.

Jenson waited and waited. Even had another little nap. Then, just as he gained the courage to see if she was gone and get himself out of the smoking room, out of Willow Hill, and even out of the parish, a soft rap came at the door. He hesitated, terrified she had figured out where he was.

"Jenson, I know you are in there. You probably have about a half hour to get away from here so you better move."

He quickly stepped out and stared at Mrs. Jakes. "I need to warn Sutton that he is stirring up the wrong woman."

"He knows. That boy needs to get here and take his place. He is the only one with the power and right to get the magistrate after her."

"That boy has been running for his life as has Miss Primrose. If Augusta gets her, she will either kill the poor girl or marry her off to Sir Edgar Benton." Jenson nodded when Mrs. Jakes looked at him in horror. "Payment for gambling debts. Augusta has blood on her hands. Lady Wootten and her babe and the baron. She killed them both."

Mrs. Jakes sat down heavily in a small chair near the desk. "Are you certain?"

"I am and so are Miss Primrose and Lord Simeon. There's just no hard proof to get her to the hangman. She has been chasing them all over the countryside and kills anyone who knows what she is up to when she has no more need of them. I only got free of her with my life because of Miss Primrose and some man helping her, a Sir Bened Vaughn. Now, before I run and hide as I was strongly advised to, I am trying to find something, just one little thing that will help them in their fight against her."

"Not her husband, I suppose."

"If he is not the complete ass he acts, then he is in this with her, so no. Not him. I cannot take the ledgers away for that would be noticed." He looked over what little there was strewn on the desk. "And she did not leave behind the papers she claimed Miss Primrose and Lord Simeon signed giving her the power to do Willow Hill business. And, no, they did not sign anything. That was a lie."

"I have no idea what to do, Jenson."

"Do not make her angry. Want to know why I was with her? Because she threatened the lives of my brother and his family and my daughter. She has just sent a man off to do the same to Master Geoffrey because the baron left Courtyard Manor to him and she will lose the lease money. That is how she works. And she has done something somewhere that makes them believe it, or her hirelings do for they are all violent men."

"I might have something they can use," Mrs.

Jakes said as she stood up and started out of the room.

Jenson hurried after her. She went down into the wine cellar and he frowned. As far as he knew neither Augusta nor her useless husband had ever been down here for they expected, always, to be served. Then Mrs. Jakes tugged a little book out from between two bottles, the reddish-brown leather cover elaborately carved with a butterfly.

"It is Lady Wootten's journal. She wrote in it all the time. I had just learned to read when she died and thought it would be lovely to read her words, that it might help me deal with the grief I was struggling with. She suspected Augusta of crimes, small ones at first but then larger and increasingly evil. It began slowly, with a few writings about hurt and disappointment concerning a woman she considered a sister to her. Near the end there was fear and on the last page she had decided to tell the baron."

"At which time she conveniently dies in a fall," Jenson murmured as he took the book from her hands. "Thank you, Mrs. Jakes. I will get this book to them. Even if, in the end, it is little help, it is something I think Miss Primrose would treasure. Now, be very careful and do nothing to anger the woman."

"I will be careful. Just do your best to get that to one of the baroness's children so they can end their mother's killer. Now that she is back and searching every part of the house for something, perhaps more evidence of something valuable she can steal or sell, I fear she will find it."

Jenson slipped out of the manor and into the

woods. He knew of a shepherd's shack on the hills where he could hide for a while. Being up on the hill would also give him a very good view of the road. For now he would just do his best to remain hidden but the moment he caught sight of any of the people riding with Miss Primrose, he would do all he could to get this book to her. Augusta was drunk on her own power and it was past time someone sobered her up.

Chapter Seventeen

Willow Hill Manor appeared in view as they crested a small rise. Primrose looked at it with relief for it signaled an end of a very long ride. She wondered if it would ever feel like home again now that her father was gone. It occurred to her that her brother was going to have a difficult time putting his own mark on the property for their father's was so strong, so intertwined with all that was Willow Hill.

"It is not the same," said Simeon as he reined in beside her. "It looks the same, I know, but it does not feel the same." He shook his head. "And I am making absolutely no sense."

"I know what you mean. The heart of it is gone." She frowned a little. "Something else troubled me and I believe I now know what. None of us have been here and yet there are no signs that that has mattered. It has been run and cared for so efficiently, it appears it does not even need us. That is very unsettling. It is not a welcoming feel when I look at it, but it's almost as if the house is shrugging and saying, 'Well, come in if you must, but if you track mud from your boots on my carpets, I will crush you.'"

"Oh well," he stuttered out, and then scowled at the house. "That was very fanciful and somewhat unsettling. It has been cared for correctly is all and, at some point, one of us would be needed. It is just that Papa hired good people."

"Yet allowed two adders, one of them extremely poisonous, to freely slither about the place?"

Simeon sighed. "I did no better."

"Nor I but I keep reminding myself that we were only children. Children are very good at believing everything is their fault, especially if some adult says it is, nor do they wish to give a parent any news that will cause discord. Penelope said a few things about the children she takes in, every one of them tossed out by their mothers. They all come to her thinking it is all their fault, that they are evil or whatever cruel thing they were told. Augusta was always telling me what a bad child I was. Why would I wish to tell Papa about that? I think I was terrified he would agree and not love me anymore. Then there is all that trouble I had with forgetting the truly horrible things she did to me."

"It is why I never told him about the beatings. Then there were the times she told me that he was the one who had ordered my punishment and how sorry she was to have to do it."

Primrose muttered a curse, causing Simeon to laugh. "That was particularly cruel of her, the bitch. We were not only too trusting, but, I think, we live in our own heads too much. It was easy for her to fool us, smart though we are. And we are. But we just never learned enough about people to see the signs of her sickness."

Simon nodded. "We are. Papa was. You could become lost in studying your plants and herbs. Papa and I could be lost as we tried to sort out some invention or thought through some problem. We should have looked around now and then. Should have learned how to deal with and understand people." He straightened up. "Best to go down there. Our companions must wonder why we linger here so long."

"I was wondering why you were taking so long to move," said Lilybet as she rode up next to Simeon. "'Tis a very fine view but I assumed you had seen it before."

Primrose bit back a grin as she watched her brother scowl at the woman. Lilybet appeared to delight in irritating a man well known for his calm, amiable nature. The woman played the game so very well, too, Primrose thought. Simeon never failed to snap at the bait. For such a brilliant man, he was being especially obtuse in his dealings with Lilybet.

"We were just about to go down," Simeon said.

Simeon nudged his horse onto the path that led them out of the hills. Men were coming out of the stables before he even reached the flat area that led up to the doors of the manor. Primrose shook her head. Her father had made the house efficient; hiring people who did their jobs well and never wavered in their work. Except that bills needed to be paid, stock and crops sold, and papers needed to be signed, but her father had also made sure that he and his family were little troubled by the simple routines of the running of the estate. It had been smart, making life pleasant, but it had also made the perfect hunting ground for a predator like Augusta. It had opened the door to her thievery as well.

Bened studied Willow Hill carefully and sighed. A tasteful elegance could be seen in every inch of the building. Lawns and gardens were beautiful, lush, and as close to perfect as any he had ever seen. He had the sinking feeling that the inside of the manor would be equally as perfect.

The men from the stables greeted the Woottens with quiet respect and all of their belongings were swiftly collected by the servants from the house, all of them dressed in pristine blue and white uniforms appropriate to their positions in the household. Mixed in with the proper greetings and introductions, he could hear both Simeon and Primrose asking various servants about some health problem or a family member, revealing that they knew the people who worked for them very well.

He had his hereditary title, his knighthood, and his big manor house with several acres of good land but it would all look like a ruin if compared to Willow Hill. Despite the money he had put into the house, he doubted Primrose would see more than the hulk of a stone building it was. He had not brought his manor back to its former state but even that would never match the beauty of Willow Hill. It had none of this quiet elegance or softness.

Seeing the inside only depressed him more as an aging butler took his coat. The place was so clean it shone. Wealth was evident in the paintings and furniture but nothing was too ostentatious. In truth, the care taken to not appear too proud of one's history and wealth, to not be ostentatious and vain in the display of what one had or could have, was just a little too obvious to Bened, nearly ruining the attempt.

He felt someone move up beside him and looked down into Lilybet's face. The awed yet uneasy look she wore probably mirrored his own, he thought. One could almost feel the weight of a long history and smell the wealth. It did not intimidate but it did impress. It also made Bened painfully aware of his place in such a world. That place was certainly not standing next to Primrose.

Bevan came up on his other side and slapped him on the back. "It is all so very precise, is it not?"

It was, but Bened frowned at the hint of criticism in Bevan's tone. "*You* think that is bad?" he asked in a quiet voice, not wanting any of the servants to hear what could sound like a complaint, and knowing that his brother had a similar need for such precision and cleanliness, but not so much that he could not be comfortable in the chaos that was real life.

"Odd, mostly. I got the impression from stories told by Simeon and Primrose that the baron was intelligent, affable, and even a little silly at times. The house does not match the man unless he learned at a young age to have his servants keep it so while he did as he pleased."

"That could be the way of it but, aye, it is difficult to see the man they spoke of living here."

He looked around as the butler ushered them all into the parlor. Here were a few hints of the possibility that someone actually lived here. A few books on a table, a coat over the back of a chair, and an empty teacup, all of which a visibly flustered butler collected up and took away. Bened wondered if it had been a few of the upper servants taking advantage of their employers' absence to enjoy a lovely sit-down in a comfortable room who had left the items behind.

Several maids appeared with refreshments for them but it was nearly an hour before Primrose and Simeon joined them. Neither looked happy and Simeon looked furious, an expression that sat oddly on his almost-pretty face. Perhaps Paradise was not as perfect as it looked. He waited as Primrose ordered the tea and food freshened. She then came and sat down next to him, and Boudicca hurled herself up onto the settee to nudge her way in between them.

"She has been here. Stayed here for two days, claimed a power to do as she wanted or we ordered, and even showed papers with our signatures on them to give her that power," Primrose said.

"Do you think she has now turned her attention to just stealing from you?" Bened asked.

"We will have to go over all the ledgers and speak to our man of business to know that but I will not be surprised to discover she has helped herself to some funds."

"According to Mrs. Jakes, the housekeeper, Augusta has ended Geoffrey's lease and ordered him out of the house and off the land," snapped Simeon as he waved aside Lilybet's offer to pour him a cup of tea. "It seems Jenson made it here safely and was looking for something to help us prove what we believe Augusta is up to. She called our man of business in but he did not give her anything she wanted until she produced those papers. All she got was some funds to fix roofs."

"Well, I am pleased to hear Jenson came back. One must hope he got his family out of her reach," said Primrose.

"Jenson told Mrs. Jakes to warn Sutton not to push Augusta too hard and I said that would be a good idea. Jenson's family has left and she has no idea of where Jenson is except that he would be hiding and watching for us."

"I believe he has just found us," said Bened as he helped himself to a little lemon cake and fondly wished it was one of Frederick's.

Jenson entered the room warily. He did not look quite so stiff and prim as he had the last time Bened had seen him. Hiding from a woman with a growing love of killing obviously wore the man down. He shook aside that unkind thought. People born into service did not think like one who had lived independent if not rich and spent a lot of time as a soldier. Jenson was not guilty of anything except not knowing how to face down the ones he had been raised to obey and serve. He watched as the man approached Simeon, bowed slightly, and handed him a little leather book.

"Mrs. Jakes had it," Jenson said. "It was your mother's and although I do not believe it will help you capture Augusta, it will give you another's word on what she has done to your family if you need it. She has men at Master Geoffrey's home. He greeted her at the door with a rifle but one of her men already had his oldest boy so he quickly backed down. Augusta left shortly after they had all gone into the house."

"Damn," said Simeon. "She is playing her usual trick. Do as I want or I will kill your family. She discovered that will make the bravest of men bow and will just keep doing it to anyone in the way of what she wants if she is not stopped, and soon."

"So we approach Geoffrey's home as cautiously as we did the place where she held Bened," said Bevan.

"Aye." He set down the cup of strong tea he had been enjoying. "I can tell you where the enemy is. Once we know where they are, it will be easier to know what to do, how to remove them."

"What of Augusta?" asked Jenson.

"If she is there she will be *removed* as well. She has shown us time and time again that she has every intention of killing us. Time to think of her not just as our aunt or a woman, and call her the killer she is." He rubbed his hand over the soft leather cover of the book. "I actually ache to read this but Geoffrey needs our help now." He handed it to Mrs. Jakes. "You kept it safe for years. Please keep it safe for just a little while longer."

Primrose tried to still the trembling that had seized her at the thought of being able to read her mother's words. She wanted to rush over and snatch the book from Simeon's hands. Try as she would, she could not keep her attention on the talk of helping Geoffrey. The journal held all of her attention and she waited to see what would be done with it.

"I will, m'lord." Mrs. Jakes grabbed Jenson by

the arm. "Come along, Jenson. You need food and clean clothes. If that woman comes back here, there is always the wine cellar to hide you in."

Careful not to draw any attention to herself, Primrose slipped out of the room after Mrs. Jakes and Jenson. Guilt tried to turn her back for she really felt she should also be doing what she could to help Geoffrey. Then she thought on the long, complicated argument there would be before any of the men would allow her to join them in what was sure to be a battle and the guilt eased. They would leave quicker if they thought they were slipping away without her.

It was a long time, one that required a great deal of sneaking around, before Mrs. Jakes put the journal in the place the baron had built for Primrose to work on her plants and all her medicines and lotions. Primrose waited silently in the shadows as the two servants talked quietly and, to her surprise, gently kissed before Mrs. Jakes led Jenson away. Then, after assuring herself that they were gone, Primrose hurried over to get the journal.

"Huh." Simeon scratched his chin. "I did not know that Mrs. Jakes liked Jenson. Valets tend to keep themselves above other servants."

"Oh, she likes him just fine," said Lilybet, refilling her cup with hot tea and then putting in a lot of sugar. "If the fool would just look about a bit he would not spend his declining years alone."

"Servants are not usually allowed to marry." He winced at the look Lilybet gave him. "Did not say

I agreed with that, just that it is a custom. Those who make such rules think it interferes with their ability to do their jobs. Did once say to a man that I could not see how that would be true and had anyone done a study to be certain. He gave me a look just like yours, Lily."

"I think it is a rule made to make certain the servants have no life *but* serving the ones who pay them a pittance," she said, and poured a lot of cream into her tea.

"Can you actually taste the tea?" asked Morris as he watched her drink some of it.

"A little. It flavors the sugar and cream very nicely." She grinned and had another drink. "So, are we going to go rescue this Geoffrey person and his family?"

"We?" Simeon asked. "We will be me, Bened, Bevan, and Morris. Perhaps a few of the male servants. You will stay here."

"Nay, I think not."

All the men opened their mouths to argue, looked hard at her, and shut them. Lilybet nodded and then they all began to plan how they would help Geoffrey and his family not become yet more victims of Augusta's greed. The man had three children and not one of them doubted that Augusta would have them killed as well.

Bened was not surprised to find himself unofficially made leader of their rescue party. He had been a soldier once and people who had never been soldiers always assumed one who had would be better in such situations, would somehow know every move to make and how to lead. Someone needed to tell them that a lot of the ones who had been soldiers, especially men like him, were little more than cannon fodder.

"Where is Primrose?" Bened asked when he suddenly realized she had left the room.

Simeon looked around the room and cursed softly. "Went after that journal, I suspect. But, at least we do not have to argue with her about going to help Geoffrey. She will be set on that journal for quite a while."

"I thought she liked this Geoffrey fellow," said Bevan.

"She does as well as she likes his wife but this journal holds her mother's words, a mother she lost years ago and which we have had little to truly remember her by."

Bened nodded, thinking it could work out for the best. Not only did he have to spend time needed to rescue Geoffrey making her understand this was not a fight she should be joining, but it would also allow him to ride away afterward without causing a large confrontation far too many people would undoubtedly observe. He knew it was cowardly but he was feeling cowardly. Bened did not care so much about an emotional farewell, not as much as he feared she could all too easily convince him to stay with her when he knew he should not.

The sound of something crashing to the floor yanked Primrose free of the spell of reading her mother's words, of hearing that beloved voice from the past in every written word. She tucked the journal beneath a cushion on the settee she had been sitting in and crept toward the door. Listening carefully, she could not hear any voices and she reached to open the door just as it was flung open from the other side.

Primrose turned to run but was grabbed from behind by her skirts. Seizing one of the pots close at hand, she swung around and broke it against the face of the man hanging on to her skirts. He let go of her to clutch at his bleeding head with one hand and she read her murder in the furious gaze he fixed on her.

She was yanking her skirts free of his grasp when Jenson stumbled into the room, so pale that she feared he was about to swoon. Right behind him stood Mrs. Jakes who looked as angry as she did afraid and Primrose's heart sank. It did not surprise her when Mrs. Jakes was shoved into the room and Augusta appeared behind her, a pistol pressed hard up against Mrs. Jakes's back.

"You, m'dear, have been a very great nuisance," said Augusta.

"I do so beg your pardon for that, Aunt, but I cannot but wish to avoid your plans for me as they appear to be very unpleasant ones."

"Carl, stop moaning and get her." Augusta looked at Primrose. "You really do not wish me to shoot Mrs. Jakes, do you, dear? So, be a good child and come quietly."

Mrs. Jakes let out a soft moan and dropped, her whole body going limp and tumbling to the floor with surprising grace. Primrose almost laughed at the way Augusta nearly fell on top of the woman. Mrs. Jakes was not small and had almost succeeded in taking Augusta down with her. Primrose rushed toward the back door that led out into the gardens, frantically wondering where everyone was for they had to have heard all the noise. Right behind her she could hear the man chasing her down. She yanked open the door and caught a brief glimpse of everyone riding off toward Courtyard Manor and Geoffrey before she was wrenched back against the man called Carl.

He wrapped one arm around her neck and slammed the door shut. Primrose did her best to fight free of his hold, her flailing feet connecting several times with his legs. Then pain exploded in her head and she fell into a black emptiness.

"You better not have hurt her too badly," snapped Augusta as she watched Carl drag an unconscious Primrose back toward her. "I need to be able to talk to her and she needs to be able to make sense."

"She will wake. I did not hit her that hard. Where do you want her?"

Augusta looked around the room and pointed to a sturdy chair set by a worktable covered in pots and small gardening tools. "We need to get her to the church. Secure her and then help me get these two old fools locked up with the other servants."

Chapter Eighteen

As they left Willow Hill, Lilybet looked back toward the house and thought she saw Primrose attempt to run out of a side door to join them. Then she was gone and Lilybet frowned even as several visions ran through her mind. She looked at Bened, opened her mouth, and then shut it. Instinct was screaming at her not to say anything to him about the danger Primrose was in. She wanted to tell that voice to shut up but she had come to trust it too much. Shaking her head, she decided it was Geoffrey and his family that they needed to save first and then she would warn them all about the trouble Primrose was in.

Once near enough to the manor to finish the trip on foot, Bened led everyone right up to the house. He signaled Bevan whose gift would come in very handy at the moment. "Need to see inside this room. The enemy is in there. We need to know if the family is as well." While Bevan did what he was so good at and looked into the room, Bened moved closer to Lilybet who stood quietly and scowled down at the ground. "There is one man in the kitchens keeping the servants from escaping. I wish I could tell you how many servants but I cannot feel them as I can someone who is a threat."

She nodded. "The gifts all have something like that, something you wish they would do but never do. Sometimes they also do things you wish they would not especially if they make you follow what path they want you to and not the one you think you should. Do you want me to go help them?"

Deciding that now was not a good time to ask her what she meant, Bened nodded. "As soon as Bevan is done and we know who is in this room I want you to head toward the kitchens. Once we strike out, if we can, the servants may need help but it is certain the enemy you must seek out will do one of two things."

"Turn on the servants or run for his miserable, stinking life."

"Exactly." She did, he realized, have a somewhat military mind and that made this all that much easier. "We do not want him to do either. Do you think you can judge which way he will turn at the right moment?"

"Aye. Close to the kitchen as I will be, the fear of whoever he has trapped there will give me enough of a connection I may well see what to do or what I am supposed to do."

"Good. Just do not put yourself in any serious danger." Because Simeon would want to kill me, Bened thought to himself, but kept silent.

"I have no intention of doing so."

He shook his head as she slipped away. Lilybet Wherlocke would fit very well into her newfound family. Creeping back to the house, he suddenly saw Bevan crouched beneath the window drawing a square in the dirt. It took Bened a moment to realize his brother was marking out the positions of everyone in the room. Just seeing the five figures huddled near the fireplace made his heart ache. He did not even try to understand how Geoffrey must feel as he sat there and knew that he, the woman he loved, and all of his children were facing death. It was a horror too large for Bened to want to even imagine.

"Bevan, what we need is for you to slide in through the door to this room. Then go after the man closest to you and disarm him or hit him or whatever takes your fancy and allows you the most time to then hurl yourself to the ground. The confusion that will cause will allow us to get in through the window and deal with the others." He looked at Simeon. "Is Geoffrey the sort of man who will have the wits left to do what is needed to best protect his family when we do this?"

"Without a doubt," Simeon replied. "Man was a soldier for a while so he will recognize an attack on the enemy and probably guess that they could try to take some of his with them. He will do whatever he can to cover his family even if it is with just his own body."

"Let us hope he finds a better alternative. Look carefully at the drawing Bevan made so you know what you are headed into. I will go through the window first and take down as many as I can as you come in through the door. The faster we get this done, the less chance any of the family getting hurt."

Bened watched closely for his brother's man to

fall, guessing that he would take the one right inside the doors. Quick, easy enough, and would surely pull the attention of the others his way. They would see that they had just lost the man watching their backs. The fact that they would not see how it was done would, he hoped, make them afraid enough that they would not be quick to see the more tangible threat coming at them through the window and door, or react to it in time to save themselves.

The man's head snapped back and he yelled in shock, twisting this way and another to try to see who had struck him in the face. He yelled even louder when his pistol and knife were snatched from his hands, leaving him defenseless against something he could not see. His friends started to yell as well for they could see that their friend was being hit but could make out nothing but the pistol moving by itself, the butt connecting hard with the man's head at least three times before he started to fold and sink to the floor.

Bened slipped into the room as the men searched for what had knocked the fourth man down. He hoped they could not hear Bevan's heavy breathing as easily as he could, then briefly caught Geoffrey's eye. Something in the way the man looked at him told Bened Geoffrey could be trusted to get his family out of the dangerous situation breaking out all around them.

One by one they took down the four men. It had not been as easy as he had hoped. Bened and each of the others in his crew were bruised and battered, but they were soon tying up the enemy. Augusta had chosen truly hardened men this time, and ones with the kind of skills that hinted their training came from some of the king's own officers. He walked over to where Geoffrey was settling his still-trembling wife and three children in seats near the fire, noting that at some point in the battle he had scraped his knuckles against someone's face.

Geoffrey glanced at his knuckles and smiled, a hint of satisfaction in the look. "One decided he should end us. Less to worry about as he fought whatever the bloody hell took the first man down."

"That would be my brother," said Bened as he looked toward where he could see Bevan sitting in a chair and dabbing at a cut lip with a handkerchief. "Odd that bloody lip did not give him away," he muttered.

"I did not see him," said Geoffrey. "How could he have just walked in and taken down that man and I not see him? It looked as if the pistol was slapping the man senseless all on its own."

"Because he did not want to be seen so he was not." Bened shrugged at the man's confused look. "Have no way to explain it clearly."

"Not sure you could even if you had time to do so."

"There is that to consider. Are any of you hurt?"

"No, just a few bruises. This is because of Augusta, is it not? She obviously did not want to wait to see if she could just evict me."

"She wanted to but the Wootten man of business said she could not."

"I threatened her with going to him and to the magistrate. Feared I put her in the position to do this. 'Tis a bit of a comfort to know I was not the only one telling her that, although I suspect Sanders was less blunt, more gentlemanly and evasive."

"Probably. I need to go see how our compatriot is doing in the kitchen. Lilybet may need some help."

"You sent a woman in there?"

"Not my first choice but Lilybet is no timid lass. Did Augusta come in with her men? Did she speak to you?"

"Just for a moment to make certain we knew what was to happen to us and why." He sighed. "I had thought my too-ready mouth had just cost me my whole family."

Bened slapped the man on the arm. "Not you, Geoffrey, but Augusta's greed."

After assuring himself that the family was fine, if still somewhat terrified and upset, Bened headed for the kitchens. He was not surprised when Bevan fell into step beside him. The split lip had probably come from one of the man's fists as he had flailed around trying to fight off what he could not see.

"Geoffrey does not seem particularly concerned about how you did that without being seen," he said.

"Good. 'Tis best that few people give it much thought. While having his family saved might make him more acceptable, it does seem as if most people do not like to think someone can play such tricks on their eyes and even their mind."

"I can understand that."

Once near the kitchen door Bened started to move as silently as he could. Bevan did as well, and Bened was pleased that his brother had learned their father's lessons well. He could not hear anything in the kitchen and that made him fear he had sent Lilybet into a danger she could not overcome.

Cautiously opening the door, he peered into the

kitchen and sighed. Lilybet was seated at the table, a battered unconscious man tied to the chair next to her, as she ate what looked to be some very nice little cakes a beaming cook set in front of her. He stepped in, ignoring the fear the servants showed, and looked across the wide table at Lilybet.

"You did not think we might like to know that you managed to accomplish this?"

"Was not sure you were finished and thought I would just wait here until I was certain it was safe out there," she replied.

"It is safe. Geoffrey and his family are well and he has sent for the magistrate. So, I believe I am done here."

"Are you now."

"Aye, Lilybet, and I believe you saw why."

She shook her head. "And I think you are just being a man, an idiot man who thinks he knows what everyone else wants when he cannot even make up his own mind about what he wants." She smiled at the cook who handed her a tankard of cool cider. "Thank you, Mrs. Jasper."

"How did you do it?" asked Bevan.

"Peered in all the windows until Mrs. Jasper caught sight of me. Then I made some noise at the door. He hurried over to see what it was and Mrs. Jasper grabbed the fry pan and swatted him on the back of the head. Brought the man to his knees but he was still trying to aim that fool pistol at me, so I rushed in and told her to do it again. Then we all worked to tie him to that chair."

"That was embarrassingly simple." Bened shook his head. "Well done. Before I leave I wish to suggest that you go to Elderwood, spend some time there to get as much information about your family as you can, and have Dob teach you a few things."

"I just might do that. Want to know what I think you should do?"

"Nay," he said, and walked out.

Lilybet looked at Bevan. "Are you not going to tell him not to be such an idiot?"

"Nay," Bevan replied, and grinned at her look of annoyance. "He has made up his mind. Best thing is for him to see his mistake for himself."

"I was hoping he would see it right now for then he could be the hero that rides to Primrose's rescue."

"Primrose needs to be rescued?"

"She does."

"You saw this?"

"Just before we got here."

"Why did you say nothing?"

"Because it was meant for us to come here where a whole family was being threatened."

Bevan grimaced. "I should go tell Bened."

"No, because then he will not have made a decision about this leaving idiocy. He will go rescue her and then leave. You are right to say he needs to know his own mind and come back because he knows he has to, for her, not just to ride to the rescue." She finished off her cider and stood up. "But we best get everyone else back to Willow Hill. And see if your cowardly brother even stopped to tell the others what happened here in the kitchen."

When Lilybet reached the room where the others were, she found Bened saying a few final words to the magistrate and his men. With Bevan at her side she moved to stand with the others. There was an anxiousness building inside her and she knew they would have to take care of Primrose's problems soon.

Simeon looked her over. "You look hale and that pleases me."

"Something I strive to make sure of every day." She looked at Simeon. "While you men were all here congratulating yourselves, I dealt with the fool in the kitchen. There was a moment where I thought I might get shot but"—she looked at Geoffrey—"your cook swings a frying pan like a true champion. Not sure you will be getting any answers from that one for quite a while, if ever. Think I heard something crack."

"Are you saying you just walked into the kitchen to face down an armed man? A man quite ready to kill a group of innocents for a madwoman?" Simeon asked, his last word almost a shout.

Lilybet stared at him for a moment and then blinked slowly as she replied, "Aye, I believe that is what happened. And it worked."

"Lilybet, cease," Bened ordered quietly, seeing by the expression on Simeon's face that it was not a good time for her to goad him and certainly not in the way she was doing.

He did not flinch when she stared at him and almost laughed when she finally looked away and moved toward the woman and children to see if they needed anything. It pleased him that neither she nor Bevan said a word about his plans to leave for he wished to tell the others himself. For a moment all he could think of was that day when he had stared down Primrose's silly little dog and carefully explained to her how he was making himself head of the pack. Bened looked around and decided his pack needed to get back to Willow Hills and lick their wounds, small though those were.

At that moment he knew with utmost certainty, one that had hardened even in the short walk from the kitchen to where he stood now, he could not go back there. He could not see Primrose there in the place that so clearly marked how above his touch she was. It might be cowardly but he also prayed the quick, clean cut would be better for her. He stepped over to Bevan.

"I will be riding out for my lands now," he said, ignoring the puzzled look on Bevan's face. "I might stop by at the parents' if you care to ride with me."

"But . . ."

"There is no but. I am the son of a farmer, a man who was given his rewards because an idiot's father gave them to him for taking a bullet for the fool. No history, no great battle, and, I doubt, no fortune to even closely match what she has. Doing this quick and clean."

"Lilybet is right. You are an idiot."

"Been thinking it through for several days now. You will see it, too, given time."

Bevan shook his head. "You are the one who has to see whatever needs to be seen. Go on then. I intend to stick with this right through until the end. There is still that murderess to be rid of."

"Primrose is here, well guarded, and Augusta is close. I believe Simeon and you and any of the others are capable of catching her or just shooting the bitch as she tries to run away again. Take care. Our mother might be a bit grieved if you got hurt even though we all know I am her favorite."

He smiled as he left, his brother's arguments to his last statement echoing behind him.

"Where did Bened go?" asked Simeon as they left Courtyard Manor.

"He is headed off to his lands," replied Bevan. "Says the battle is near done and we are capable of dealing with it."

"Men are such idiots," said Lilybet as she rode up between them. "Thought he might actually have the wit to see more clearly by now, that he was still lurking about after leaving the kitchens because he had regained his senses, but it appears I was wrong."

"You knew he was going to leave now?" asked Simeon.

"I did."

"You should have told us."

"No, because then you may have acted in a way that would change everything and that would be very bad."

"Why? What happens if someone does act in such a way?"

"I have no idea but something always tells me where one just has to let it roll on by to get to the destination it has to. If I am shown someone losing his life, it is usually because I am supposed to do something. Bened's being a big dumb male is one of those things where all the feelings that come with seeing what he will do, tell me to stay right out of his way."

Bevan cursed. "Do not like it but it is best that

way. If the fool turns back of his own free will, it will be for the best. And will he? Turn back?"

"He will and will be doing so very soon."

They had not even reached the door of Willow Hill when the servants arrived and told them of how Augusta had come and taken Primrose. Bevan stared at Lilybet. "Did you not see this coming?"

"Not precisely but I did see Bened coming back this way and facing that evil witch Augusta. Just not why he would be doing so. Also thought I saw Primrose trying to come out a door at the side of the house, the one leading from the garden to her little workshop, but it was too quick a look to be sure and I was being nudged to Courtyard Manor."

"Gifts such as yours can be bloody frustrating."

"Aye, I am well aware of that."

"Was there anything you saw that told you she survives this?" asked Simeon.

"Oh, aye, there was. This was Bened's story I saw, you know," Lilybet said, and both men nodded. "It ended with him very happy."

"And?" pressed Simeon when she said nothing else.

"Why does there need to be any more? It ended with him happy. He would not be if harm had come to Primrose, now would he."

Bened rode along, making no effort to get anywhere fast. He knew he should have just ridden away at a faster pace but he was faltering. He did not want to go. He thought about Willow Hill and grimaced. He could not match that elegance, and doubted he would be able to match what Primrose had as a dowry. With each length the horse went, the less he cared.

He was making up Primrose's mind for her. He had not even given her the courtesy of asking her what she wanted. The reason for that, he admitted, was pure cowardice. He suspected that was the cause of the looks the others had given him when he had said his hasty farewells. They were disappointed in him because he did not have the backbone to face Primrose, say what he wanted, and wait for her to decide on him.

Realizing he had come to a halt in the middle of the road, he sighed and shook his head. This was wrong. Primrose was a well-bred lady, an innocent who had allowed him to become her lover. He owed her more than slipping out of her life like a thief in the night. The more he thought of how she had been with him, the less he felt inclined to run away.

He frowned and slowly turned his horse around, staring off in the direction of Willow Hill. There was no arguing that she had better than he could offer her yet she had given him a lot. She had given him her innocence, her warmth and laughter, her trust, and even her acceptance of him and his family. There was a chance that she would give him even more, that she would have not one single objection to becoming his wife and bearing his children in a too-large stone block of a house in the wilds of Wales. All he had to do was gain the courage to take that chance.

Chapter Nineteen

Primrose woke to a pain that engulfed her head. It took her several minutes to wade through it to find the source and she started to reach up to touch the back of her head only to discover her wrists were tied to a chair. She took several deep breaths, letting them out slowly, to push back the fear that surged through her at the discovery.

Then memory of what had happened returned and she cursed. A brief struggle against her bonds was all she needed to know she would not be breaking free of them easily. Her only hope of escaping what Augusta had planned for her was that Simeon would return in time and come looking for her.

She looked around the room and frowned. It looked very like the schoolroom at the parish but that made no sense. Why would Augusta risk so much by imprisoning her so close to Willow Hill and in a building that was rarely empty?

Realization struck her like a blow to the stomach and Primrose gasped. She was here because Augusta planned to go through with the marriage plans she had made, the ones that would clear away all of Rufford's debts, and the same ones Primrose had run away from. For a moment she saw a glimmer of hope because the pastor was a good man and would never agree to perform a forced marriage. Then good sense returned and she cursed. Augusta would issue threats to him or his family to make him comply and it would work. The pastor had never been known for his bravery.

The door opened and a very smug Augusta walked in. "Awake at last. Thought I might have to throw some water in your face. I was actually looking forward to that."

"Augusta, you cannot possibly believe you can get away with this," Primrose said, even though she suspected there would be no reasoning with the woman.

"Of course I can. The pastor loves his wife and child, you know. Deeply. It is quite touching."

"Just as Geoffrey loves his but you will fail there as well."

"Oh, has dear Simeon run to their rescue? Just as I knew he would?"

"He is no longer the sweet little boy you used to beat."

"Who he has become does not matter when one man runs blindly toward three armed men."

She did not know about the allies Simeon had with him, Primrose realized, and her fear for Simeon faded a little. He had Bened, Morris, Bevan, and several servants as well as Lilybet. Simeon was also too smart to run blindly into the house when he knew Augusta was behind Geoffrey's troubles. They had seen how fond the woman was of having her hirelings ready to do her killing for her.

"You do know you are quite mad, do you not, Auntie dear?"

"Mad? I have almost succeeded and *will* succeed in getting all I want, all I have wanted for a very long time. How is that mad? That is intelligence, you silly girl. That is cunning and skill."

"It is madness when one leaves behind her a trail of the dead. It is madness when you think you have some right to what was never yours or could be yours, not by birth or blood. That is just base thievery."

"A trail of the dead? You exaggerate."

"Oh, I do not think so. But you have failed to rid yourself of all witnesses and that will help to bring your murderous games to an end."

"I have not failed. Not yet. There is still time. I will even find Jenson. If he proves elusive, I have a way to draw him back into my grasp."

"And just what would that be?"

"His brother and his family plus the little bastard he bred on my maid."

"Ah, yes, your favorite threat. Do as I need you to or I shall kill your family. Do not defy me or I will cut your baby's throat." Primrose thought about Jenson (a man who had been called Saint Jenson by the other servants and not always in a flattering way), the maid, and the baby. "You set your maid on him." She had to wonder if the woman ever stopped plotting.

"I did. It worked very well for I always knew what

Rufford was doing and was able to stop the fool most of the time. Ending his many idiotic plans all too often took time away from my own or this would have been finished years ago."

"When I realized what a murderous bitch you were, I was surprised you had let him live."

"He has to be named the baron first."

"Ah, of course. How silly of me to forget. He is still useful to you. And, yet, you see no madness behind all of this." Primrose shook her head.

"You will not stir me to attack you. I have worked for years to get even this close to what I seek. I will not allow you to push me into doing something foolish now."

"And killing off an entire family is not *foolish*. What a mealy-mouthed word. It is evil, Augusta. It is depraved. You killed my mother and the child she carried. You killed my father who had only ever helped you and his idiot of a brother. You even killed my dog! Now you intend to kill me and my brother."

"I do not intend to kill you. I am giving you a husband."

"You *are* killing me. That depraved man, a man banned from society, which is overflowing with depraved and sinful people, because even they consider him too nasty to share a ballroom with, has the pox. From what I can see he is riddled with it and very close to madness and death. So, yes, Augusta, you are trying to kill me and make certain I never bear a child who might one day have the power to take back all you have stolen."

"Do not be so ridiculous. Edgar does not have the pox."

Primrose noted not only the familiarity her aunt used in speaking of Sir Edgar Benton but also that the woman had gone a little pale. "When did you bed down with him?"

"He does not have the pox!"

"If it was a long time ago, you might be safe. If he used a sheath, then you are safe. You would also be showing signs of the disease by now just as he does. Of course, this mad, bloody quest you are on could very well be a sign in itself."

"You will cease talking about that. Edgar does not have the pox."

Primrose shrugged. "I am the one who deals in potions and salves, if you recall. To do that well you need to understand about injuries and diseases. The man does have the pox. And, even if I am wrong, which I am not, it is still killing me for he will eventually beat me to death as he did his other wives."

"That is just evil gossip."

"I cannot believe someone like you managed to kill my mother and father and no one caught you."

"Your mother's death was an accident."

"That is what Edgar said about both of his wives."

Augusta ignored her. "Your mother goaded me and I lost my temper. The next thing I knew she was lying at the bottom of the stairs and everyone was yelling for your father."

"My mother goaded you? The woman everyone who ever met her called sweet, shy, and quiet, goes from being a 'gentle soul' as people were fond of calling her to suddenly becoming a woman who goads you, or anyone, into a murderous temper? No, Augusta, your temper was already on the rise when you confronted her, afraid she might be breeding the all-important spare. More obstacles, more time to spend in slithering up the path to be called by a title you never earned."

The slap came so quickly, Primrose had no time to avoid it in even the smallest way. Pain seared the entire side of her face and the back of her head slammed into the hard wooden back of the chair. For just a moment she thought she would lose consciousness. Her vision wavered and she closed her eyes to fight back a wave of nausea. She wanted to give in to the blackness trying to flow over her mind but fought it. She knew it would not be safe to be unconscious before Augusta.

"And what did you or Simeon do to earn it? What did your father ever do to earn it? Nothing! I am at least working toward my goal. The rest of you only had to come squalling out of the right womb, sired by the right man."

"Yes, and I am certain that leaving that trail of blood behind you clearly shows everyone how very hard you are working."

"I have not left a trail of blood! I have not killed anyone."

"I find it a little hard to believe that you have not killed anyone. But you must know that just because you did not use your own hands, you are not innocent of the crime. But you did use your own hands a few times, did you not, Aunt? On my father, my mother, my bloody dog!"

"Enough of this. 'Tis time to prepare you for your marriage."

"Untie me and I will strangle you."

It did not surprise Primrose to watch her aunt take a hasty step back. The murderous tone to her words had even surprised Primrose. The fury she felt toward this woman who had destroyed her family astonished her even though she doubted anyone would question the righteousness of it.

There was nothing she could do to halt her aunt's meager attempts to tidy her up. When the man untied her, she tried to wrest free but he was too strong. Then she tried to drag her feet as she was taken up to where the altar was. It was hard to believe that the kindly pastor she had known for years would officiate over such a marriage.

It took only one look at the pastor's face to tell her that the man would officiate and that he was too terrified not to. Augusta had become very proficient in threatening even good men into doing as she ordered them to, to go against their own beliefs and rules. Seeing the pale, shaking Pastor Robbins standing near the altar broke her heart and not simply because he was about to marry her to a man who made her skin crawl.

She looked at Sir Edgar, as the man named Carl dragged her over to stand next to her groom. His wrinkled face was well decorated in patches that had gone out of fashion a long time ago. "They do not fool anyone, you know," she said.

"What are you speaking about?" Sir Edgar asked.

The look he gave Primrose told her he did not like women much at all even if he did keep marrying them.

"Those silly patches. They do not fool anyone. All know you but try to hide the sores caused by the pox that is eating you alive."

His age-spotted hands clenched into fists and she was sure he was going to strike her but Augusta stepped closer. Primrose knew it was not to save her niece from a blow but to keep Sir Edgar from giving the pastor any reason to speak out later. How the woman could ever have bedded the nasty little man, Primrose did not know but she doubted whatever reward Augusta got for the act was really worth it.

"Now, Edgar, my dear, soothe your temper. She is a very disobedient child who speaks as if she has some right to tell everyone what is on her mind. Her father's fault, of course."

Sir Edgar took a deep breath and let the air out slowly. It was a very foul air. Even Augusta winced. Primrose heard the man holding her in place curse softly and had to agree with the obscene sentiment. Sir Edgar was a walking dead man. His breath was so foul, she knew he had to be rotting away inside.

Clearing his throat, the parson sent Primrose a look that screamed for forgiveness and, with one curt nod, she gave it. Sir Edgar reached out for her hand as the pastor cleared his throat and opened his prayer book. Primrose actually leaned farther against her captor. The fact that the man did not just smack her and shove her back in position told her that he found the man pretty disgusting as well.

Just as Primrose was wondering how she could get out of this mess, the door to the chapel was thrown open and in strode Bened followed by the others who swiftly spread through the church. Primrose grinned, and that's when Edgar hit her hard on the side of the head with his closed fist. As she fell to the floor she was certain she heard a gunshot.

Willow Hill was in chaos when Bened rode up and he felt a growing alarm tighten its bands around his heart. He dismounted quickly and tossed his reins to a nearby stable hand. The fact that none of the horses had yet been led off to the stables troubled Bened as did the wide open doors of the manor. He raced into the house and followed the sound of a lot of loud voices all trying to talk at once. He found them all gathered around the open door to Primrose's garden room where she grew and worked with her many plants and herbs.

After only a moment of listening to shouted questions that gained no coherent replies only to have the questions shouted at someone else, he yelled, "Hush! All of you cease this loud babble at once!"

The silence was immediate and everyone turned to stare at him. He studied them all and then fixed his attention on Mrs. Jakes and Jenson who appeared to have had some confrontation recently. "What has happened? Were you attacked?"

"We were, sir," said Jenson. "Augusta came here

shortly after you left to help save Geoffrey. We tried to stop them but I was shoved along while Mrs. Jakes was grabbed by Mrs. Augusta and had a pistol shoved in her back. She and one of her men dragged us in there and she confronted Lady Primrose."

"Her ladyship was very brave but no match for the man and he was a scurvy sort of fellow. She almost got free and ran for the other door. It leads into the garden, sir, and she was so close to escape but the man caught her and pulled her back inside," said Mrs. Jakes.

"And they took her?"

"They did soon after that."

"Did they say where they were taking her?"

"To the church." Mrs. Jakes wrung her plump, work-worn hands. "That horrible little man has come after her and that woman means to give her to him."

"The pastor would perform a marriage she so clearly does not want?"

"I suspect he would, Bened," said Simeon, "if Augusta played her usual game. The man has a pretty little wife and a few children. Young ones. One born only a few months ago. And, if I might ask, what made you come back?"

"Because I intend to ask your sister to marry me. So, I suppose we better hurry and get her back so that she is not forced to marry anyone else."

"Since I am now the baron, should you not be asking me my permission to ask for her hand?"

"I just did," said Bened as he started back to the front of the house.

"No, you told me." Simeon ignored Lilybet who was yanking on his coat sleeve. "Not the same thing at all."

"I do not intend to marry you so why ask you. Just told you my intentions. Now I will see if she has any urge to say yes."

"But . . ."

"Simeon," snapped Lilybet. "How old is Primrose?"

"Oh, so just because she is on the shelf, I should accept this fellow's arrogance?"

"On the shelf?" Bened shook his head. "Gentry. You are all mad. Lady Primrose is young, healthy, and pretty but because she is at a certain age she suddenly becomes on the shelf like some china bowl one has forgotten to dust?"

Simeon glared at Bened's back as the man swung up into his saddle. He quickly mounted his horse as the others did theirs. Without another word they all headed for the small stone church at the far edge of the town.

Just out of sight of the church, Bened signaled everyone to tether their horses and approach the building as quietly as possible. His heart was tight with concern for Primrose. She had fled her home to get away from this man and yet Augusta had found a way to get her to the altar. With Bevan's assistance he quickly silenced two men guarding the doors to the church. Quietly he and the others began to slip inside. Seeing Primrose being held in front of the altar by a tall, thin, yet obviously strong man, Bened frowned, aching to make the man pay dearly for handling her so roughly.

Then he had a good look at the man Augusta

wanted Primrose to marry and shuddered. The man was short, spindly, covered in age spots and, if he guessed the reason for the beauty spots stuck on his sunken cheeks, sores caused by the end time of the pox. Augusta had chosen a particularly nasty way to make sure her niece died. And because of the banishment from society the man had suffered, there would be no finding someone to help her after she became Sir Edgar's wife. She would also find herself utterly ostracized.

Bened and the others were just creeping down the aisle when the man punched Primrose right on the side of the head. She was just falling to the floor when someone shot the man but Bened paid no heed to that. He went straight to her side. In his opinion, whoever had shot Sir Edgar, that someone had been doing the world a service, as well as saving Sir Edgar the pain of dying of a particularly nasty disease.

Lilybet beat Bened to Primrose's prone body by a heartbeat. She checked over her friend, then fought to hide the startling knowledge that came to her. Lilybet met Primrose's gaze and knew her friend was aware of her condition but was keeping it silent so she just nodded. A glance at the dead man sprawled far too close to Primrose made Lilybet a little ill. She breathed a sigh of relief when the men hastily removed it.

Primrose groaned. She began to sit up but hands held her down. For a moment she struggled thinking it was her aunt's men or Sir Edgar, a man she did not wish touching her no matter how injured and unsteady she might be. Then she saw that it was her friends and Simeon leaning over her.

As she let Lilybet help her sit up, she put her head in her hands in the vain hope of easing the ache there. Out of the corner of her eye, she caught a movement. Augusta was trying to do something without being seen.

"Will someone please get that woman before she escapes to plague us another day?" she asked, and struggled to move when her aunt lunged toward her with a long knife appearing in her hand.

Several people moved at once and Primrose winced as she heard another gunshot. She did not need to look again to see who had fallen to that shot. She could see her aunt's arm stretched out beside her. Slumping back against Lilybet, she was both relieved and pleased that the threat her aunt had presented for so long was finally gone.

All she felt was tired. There was no grief, which did not surprise her. There was just emptiness. The woman had destroyed her family all for greed. She watched as her aunt's body was taken away, surprised to hear her uncle yelling and demanding answers as he chased the cart with the bodies of his friend and his wife inside. Primrose wondered if she would eventually feel some sympathy for the man but doubted it. She would leave the problem of what to do about their uncle to Bened.

"Come along, Primrose," said Bened as he swung her up into his arms. "The pastor has already gone to fetch the magistrates."

"Is where we are going now free of all of Auntie's men?"

"Actually, I thought we would stay here for just a bit and have the good pastor marry us," Bened said, watching her closely.

Primrose stared up at him but saw no attempt to make a jest. "You wish to marry me?"

"Yes."

"Why?"

"Perhaps we could have that talk after the ceremony."

"No, I think not. How about you set me down in one of the pews and we can talk quietly. All these people can go stand about outside for a few minutes."

She almost smiled as she watched Lilybet herd the others outside, even the preacher. Despite her aching head, she was eager to hear what Bened had to say. She was also eager to marry him but she would not do so if all he spoke of was honor.

"I was going to leave," he began. "I saw all you have, all you've known and knew I could not match it so I was going to be honorable and just ride away," he said. "I could not do it. Obviously I don't have that much honor. I decided I would come here and ask you at least. Instead of assuming I knew what you want and need, I would offer you all I have and leave it to you."

The man looked like he was in pain, she thought, and tried not to let sympathy force her to put a halt to what he was saying. "What is this *all* you are offering me, Bened?"

"I am not really your equal by birth but near enough now with what I have earned for myself."

He looked at her in confusion when she placed her fingers against his lips.

"Bened, I know that if you offer to marry me that you offer your honors and home and fortune. That needs not be said. What else? Your faithfulness?" It pleased her to see how offended he was by even being asked that.

"Of course. If I did not intend to be faithful, then I would not even ask you to marry me." He pulled her into his arms and whispered. "I want you. I want you in my home, helping me make something fine of it. I want you in my bed. I want you to give me children. I even want you with your foolish dog. You are mine. Knew it the first time I saw you." He slid her hand to his belly. "Knew it in here then." He then slowly slid her hand up to his heart. "Know it here now."

"Then, yes, I will marry you for I have known you were mine, in both places, for a very long time." She laughed when he heaved such a sigh of relief she was surprised he did not keel over.

It happened so quickly that Primrose began to think he was afraid she would change her mind. One minute they were talking about getting married, the next minute they were married. The fact that he had rings for her, ones shoved into his hand by her laughing brother, thrilled her. When he promised to get some of her own, she shook her head. These had been her mother's. By giving them to Bened to give to her, Simeon had shown his acceptance and approval and she cherished it.

Mrs. Jakes served them a hasty feast and the marriage was toasted with both serious and rowdy toasts. Then, Primrose hurried up to her room to pack some clothes as Bened had been serious about needing to get to his home. She realized she was eager to get there as well for it was now her home, too.

"Prim?" Simeon said as he stepped into the bedchamber when the maids left with her chests of clothing.

"Is something wrong, Simeon?" she asked, afraid he was about to prove her assumption about the rings wrong and express his disapproval over the marriage.

"No, I just wished to make sure this is truly what you want. Do not believe I have ever seen a wedding performed so hastily or packing done so quickly. The man came back here when we had thought him gone, helped get you away from that scum, and then appeared to see the pastor and think, well, I might as well get married while I am here. I just was not sure that was what you wanted. What you truly wanted. I do not want you doing this because you have been traveling with him and been his lover."

"And now we are both blushing," Primrose said, and laughed. "I am marrying him for the same reasons he is marrying me. I want him in my bed, I want to share his home, and I want him to father my children. I have known in my soul and my heart that he is mine. That is what he said to me and it is what I agree with. Actually, he said his belly and his heart. I think I can wait for the sweet words as that says more than enough."

"I think, in his way, he gave you a lot of sweet words. As a man, I think I am hearing what he is saying a lot more clearly than you are. You love him, do you not? And that is what you want him to say."

"Of course I want him to say it but what he has said is enough for now. It is certainly enough to get those words I want before too long, I think. Yes, I may have to coax them, but I do not mind." She frowned. "I am, however, running out on you on the very day you actually step into the role of Baron of Willow Hill."

"Do not fret. I will admit it might be good to have you round for a while as I get used to it, but I have been in training for it since the day I was born. As for the household business, I believe Mrs. Jakes and Jenson will suit. And we both know Mr. Sutton is as trustworthy as the day is long. So I believe I will manage." He grinned when she swatted him on the arm and then he hugged her. "I will miss you, though."

She kissed him on the cheek. "And I you. And—oh!"

Primrose suddenly recalled their mother's journal, grabbed the basket with Boudicca sitting proudly in it, and bolted out of the room. A puzzled Simeon hurried after her. Once in the room she snatched the cushion off the settee and breathed a sigh of relief as she picked up the journal and handed it to Simeon.

"Ah, I had wondered if that is where you disappeared to. You may keep it for a while if you choose, Prim," he said.

"Mayhaps another time. I would not wish to tote it for all those miles to Wales and into a house that still needs some work. Too many risks." She turned to go out the door and then paused to look back at him. "Do you think there is something wrong inside me that makes me not shed one tiny tear for our aunt? I even looked at her lying there dead and could only think, 'Finally it is done.'"

"That is much the same as I thought. Go join your new husband, Prim. He is probably getting concerned that you have changed your mind."

Directing the servants concerning her bags, Primrose stepped out of the manor to watch Bened hitch their horses to a carriage even as servants tied their bags on top. Poor Mercury, she thought, and laughed softly. The animal appeared to be comfortable in his new role. Smudge did not look as certain but that could be because she was riding in tandem with a large gelding.

Chapter Twenty

Primrose stole another look at her wedding rings, loving the way the sun glinted off the metal and small gemstones. She was married to Bened. It was a wondrous feeling. The fact that she had come very close to being married to that evil troll her aunt had sold her to made her good fortune even more precious.

She had told her brother she was satisfied with all Bened had said and she was, but on the journey to Bened's lands she had decided she might not be as patient as she had thought she would be.

Primrose badly wanted to hear him say those three little words because she ached to say them to him. She feared they would burst out of her at any time, especially when they were making love, and then he would fail to say them back to her. It was a childish concern, she told herself.

"There it is," said Bened. "Wolfsbane Hall."

"Wolfsbane?"

He grinned. "According to Aunt Dob, the ancestor who owned this first was a little odd."

She stared at the huge manor house built of dark stone. Iron gates were set into a high stone wall that encircled the building. There was even an attractive gatehouse of the same stonework. The place was only a few steps away from being a castle. To her relief height was one of those steps, for the manor was only three stories high. The latest resident had been, it was said, responsible for all comforts and changes that dragged the sturdy buildings out of the dark past.

"That earl gave you a very fine gift, Bened. I think your cousin Modred is correct. The tale of how the place was taken away from your family must have been well recorded and told often. The earl saw a way to remove that small stain from the family shield and took it."

They reined in front of the heavily carved front doors and Bened helped her down from her seat. The young couple who tended the house greeted them with big smiles, the man telling Bened all that had been done and what still needed finishing. His wife, Gwynneth, rushed Primrose up the stairs to a large bedchamber so that she could wash off the travel dust.

Primrose walked around the bedchamber she would now share with Bened and smiled. There was a massive fireplace all readied for the lighting of a fire that was not needed on such a warm, sunny day. Over it hung a large portrait of the Vaughn who had built the manor. Seeing as he was staring at the bed, Primrose thought she might ask that it be removed. Two long windows with beautiful drapes overlooked the side yard. It was not until she got closer that she realized they were not windows but doors that opened out onto a balcony.

Pausing in her inspection, she hastily washed up before the water cooled too much and then dressed in a fresh gown in the large dressing room, which held a tub and a small privacy closet. Another door led into a beautiful sitting room and on the other side of it was another bedroom. The last resident had clearly spent a lot of money to make the master bedroom as comfortable as possible.

With a final check on her appearance she hurried back down the stairs only to meet with Bened starting up them.

"Huh. Thought I would be in time to trap you in the bedchamber," he teased as he took her into his arms and kissed her.

"It is a beautiful suite of rooms, Bened. There is just one thing . . ."

"The portrait. Meaning to move it to the library. Man staring at the bed all the time could make me shy." He winked at her when she laughed and then he took her by the hand. "I need to show you your wedding gift. We can tour the rest of the manor later. I did all I dared to without your opinion but it cannot be full completed until I have it. So, do not be shy in stating it."

As he pulled her down a long hallway, Primrose grew more and more astonished. The woodwork was beautiful and there were a lot of rooms. They would need more workers if they meant to get it down before they found themselves awaiting the birth of their third child. Then he stopped and tugged at her hand to draw her attention from an elaborate tapestry. Primrose stared at the doors he pointed to. Beyond them appeared to be a room that was mostly glass, even the roof, the large thick sheets of glass framed by metal.

"A place for you to grow your plants," he said.

She was speechless and felt her eyes sting with an onrush of tears as she hugged him. "For me?"

"I would love to say I built it for you but I only fixed a broken room, putting in all the glass that could safely be put in it." He took her inside and strode all the way through it to a set of glass doors at the far end. "These lead out into a garden area. The ground has already been made ready for whatever you might wish to plant." He held her close when she threw herself into his arms. "You have a true skill and love of plants, Rose. I knew you would need something to satisfy the hunger to work with them. I wanted you to have what you needed to be happy here."

She hugged him even tighter. "I have it. You. That is all I really needed but thank you. A hundred times thank you. It is a wondrous gift."

He led her around the large room, pointing out what he had brought in for her to do her work. There were tables to work on, shelves for books or potions, and even a set of strong, shiny new gardening tools.

"Simeon is having your plants sent here. Your gardener at Willow Hill is making certain they are packed carefully and the men bringing them well trained in caring for them during the journey. Your books and ledgers, even all your pots. It will be a few days though for the ones bringing them will have very precise instructions so as much as possible will have a good chance of surviving the journey intact."

"I wish I could find the words to tell you how much this means to me." She rose up on her tiptoes to brush a kiss over his lips. "Thank you so much, my dearest husband. I love you."

The kiss he gave her left them both breathless. A quick look around told them their desire would need to wait to be satisfied later. Primrose decided the first thing she would do was to make a private spot, using her biggest plants to shield it from view. It would be nice to make love with Bened in a room where you could see the night sky above you, perhaps be bathed in moonlight, and be surrounded with plants and all without bugs, bats, or anything else that wandered around in the night. It would be better than nice, she decided. It would be magic.

"Rose?" Bened smiled when she blinked clear of whatever thought she was lost in and looked at him. "Where did you go?"

"I did float away for a moment. I was thinking of how to make us a little cove right inside here. Plants to hide us from view, the moonlight all over and around us, perhaps even a view of the stars, the scent of plants and the earth, and, of course, something soft to lie upon. It would be magic."

"It would," he agreed, already eager for the night she described, "but, for now, let me show you the rest of the place." He took her back to the front door as if they had just entered and began the tour room by room, in order. "The parlor for guests. I had my mother do only what was absolutely necessary. She is the one with the best idea of what would be expected by society yet not be too intimidating to those we know who are not of that ilk."

"It looks very welcoming. Why only the necessary?"

"Because I knew it should be left to the woman I brought to live here."

"I am pleased but also rather intimidated. Is that the way you have done it in every room?"

"Nay, the master's chamber needed very little and what I had done was for comfort. I did choose how to finish the library and my office. A few other rooms were simply too confusing for me. I am hoping you know what to do with them. Then there are some that make no sense at all, as if the one who worked on them had half a plan and forgot the other half before he was actually done."

Primrose laughed and, tugging her hand free, looped her arm through his and pressed her cheek against his arm. "We will sort it all out. Even if half the rooms here were unusable we would still have more than enough room to live in great comfort."

"True enough," he said, and grinned. "It is a great deal of home for some man who just kept some idiot from getting a hole shot into his empty head. Leaves me thinking that the way the earl's family got their hands on it was very illegal, and somewhat embarrasses them."

"And so he assuages the shame of that by returning the property to the Vaughns for services rendered above and beyond and all that, by returning it to you."

"I begin to think so."

Primrose had a head crowded with plans by the time he had shown her the whole manor. She was not surprised by the rooms he had worked on quickly to make them more livable. The parlor, the master suite, the kitchen, and the dining room.

They could live quite contentedly with just those comforts for a long while.

She smiled when they entered the bedchamber. A lovely little table was set out in front of the fireplace and it held covered plates of something that smelled delicious plus wine and cider.

"Thank you for doing this, Bened," she said as she moved to sit. "This is wonderful."

"I but ordered the meal served here in the bedchamber," he said as he sat across from her. "Thanks for all else must go to the servants. Of which, I must say, we have many."

Savoring a bite of the rosemary-seasoned chicken, Primrose then carefully cut some pieces and put them on a plate for Boudicca. She urged the puppy back to its bed by the fireplace, set the plate in front of it, and returned to her seat. It was not until she was eating her vegetables that she became aware of how intently Bened was staring at her. He had a faint smile on his face that eased his usual serious expression, softening the harsher lines until he was so handsome he made her breath catch in her throat.

"That is going to be a very spoiled dog," Bened said.

She grinned. "I know but I hope to make her a very well-trained dog, too."

"I think she is very well behaved now. She has been calmly toted about for days and miles on end, in a basket, tied to a saddle. She also stays close to you, no running off when she is out of that basket. But then she would never do that."

"Why do you say she would never do that?"

"That dog will be your shadow, Rose, for the rest

of her sadly short life. She will be, and stay, wherever you are." Seeing her frown and the hint of confusion in her expressive eyes, he patted her hand. "Boudicca is your dog until old age takes her away. Yours was the hand that pulled her out of the water."

Primrose looked at the little dog and smiled. "I did intend to keep her even then so 'tis a good thing."

They idly discussed ideas for what they needed to get done in the manor while Bened had the maids return to clean away the last of the meal. The moment the maids left, Primrose became nervous, no matter how foolish she told herself it was. They had been lovers before they were married so she certainly knew what was about to happen. Neither had they been celibate in the days since they married and then traveled to the manor. When he took her hand in his and tugged her to her feet, she decided she was wrong. It was different. It was their first night together, as husband and wife, in the home they would share from this day onward.

"It was a lovely meal," she said, and stretched up to brush her mouth over his.

"I wished to make our first night here, in this room, in this house, as special as I could."

"And you succeeded."

"Do you know what I thought when I first saw you?" he asked, touching a kiss to her forehead as he began to undo her gown.

"That I was a lackwit for searching so hard for a horse that was standing mere feet away?" She trembled as he ran his fingers up and down her back, the tempting warmth of his touch penetrating her linen chemise and sinking into her blood.

"Nay, I thought you were adorable."

Stepping free of the gown now tangled around her feet, she frowned at him. "Adorable? A woman standing before a man in her shift truly does not wish to be thought of as adorable, Bened."

He laughed. "If you had been standing before me like this on that day, adorable would not have been the first word to come to mind. Nay, it would have been *mine*."

She smiled as he picked her up and carried her to the bed, seating her on the edge. When he knelt at her feet to tug off her shoes, she stroked her hands over his hair and untied the leather strip that held the thick length of hair off his face. Primrose combed her fingers through it, amazed at how soft it felt.

The feel of his hands moving up her leg distracted her from her enjoyment of his hair. He untied the ribbons holding her stocking in place and slowly removed it in a way that was as much a caress as if he was using his hands against her skin. By the time he removed the second stocking she was trembling, astonished by how such an ordinary action could so deeply stir her desires. When he began to kiss his way up her leg, she offered no shy resistance, eager for what she suspected he was about to do. The first touch of his lips in the intimate kiss she had been anticipating almost pushed her over the edge.

As her body weakened from the strength of the passion roaring through her, she fell back onto the bed. Bened took full advantage of her surrender and Primrose lost all ability to even think of how brazen she was being. Then she knew she was close to the edge and called out his name but he ignored her, taking her to the heights with just his clever mouth. She was still sprawled on the bed trying to catch her breath when he stood up and began to shed his clothing.

One thing Primrose had never expected was that she would so enjoy looking at a naked man. But Bened was a pleasure to see in all his glory. Tall and strong, taut swarthy skin stretched over firm muscle. The small triangle of black curls on his chest and the line of hair leading down to his impressive erection. She idly thought that she needed to find a better name for that as it sounded a bit odd. His legs were long and strong as were his arms and she loved to feel all that strength against her, loved to wrap herself around it. It was not even the fact that she had the comforting knowledge of a strong man at her side as much as it was the look and feel of him. When he got on the bed and tugged off her shift she was quick to get as close to him as possible, soaking in his warmth.

Thinking to give him at least a little of the pleasure he had given her, she began to kiss her way down his body. The way he tensed and the faint tremor that went through him told her he liked it. Then she kissed the tip of his erection and he groaned. Chancing a peek at him, she blushed as she caught him watching her but the look in his beautiful eyes encouraged her to be even more daring and she slowly ran her tongue up his length. He buried his fingers in her hair and she decided to keep teasing him, exploring him thoroughly with her tongue and fingers.

"Take me into your mouth, love," he whispered.

Primrose thought about that for just a moment and then did as he asked, finding new ways to drive him mad if the sounds he was making were any indication. Then he grabbed her under the arms, pulled her away, and tugged her up his body. Before she finished the thought that she had done something wrong, he joined their bodies. She sat on top of him for a moment, still somewhat dazed from pleasuring him, and then he placed his hands on her hips and lifted her, then slowly brought her back down on him. He did it twice more before she felt brave enough to do it on her own. He leaned up to kiss her breasts and she lost herself completely in the lovemaking and the delight they could give each other, until the fire flared and swept through her. He held her tight against him as he thrust inside her several more times and joined her in her release.

Primrose toyed with the curls on his chest and worked hard to convince herself that she had nothing to be embarrassed about, but total abandon, even in her husband's arms, was not easy to forget. The way he was gently stroking her back told her he was content and she decided that was all that mattered. Yet, when he set her aside and went through the ritual of cleaning them both off, she could feel the annoying heat of a blush on her cheeks.

Bened grinned as he crawled back into bed and pulled his wife into his arms. Once her desire was stirred, Primrose could be a wild delight in a man's arms, but once those flames cooled she tended to worry that she had gone too far. He suspected it would take awhile before he could convince her that her husband wanted her to get a little untamed anytime she wanted to.

"I did not forget to give you a wedding present, you know," she said, lightly nuzzling his neck.

"You did not have to get me anything."

"Well, I suppose one might say I did not actually get this but was given this."

Primrose wondered exactly how to tell him she was with child. She knew he would be pleased but she did not wish to shock him or make him become too overprotective. They had a home to make together and she did not want him denying her the chance to help in that just because she carried a child, his child.

"Is it some sort of family heirloom or the like?"

"No." She rested her arms on his chest and looked at him. "I was going to be so clever and slip in the information in some clever way but cleverness is failing me right now."

"Then just be blunt. I rather like blunt."

"Your wedding gift from me is that I am with child."

His eyes went so wide and he stopped breathing for a moment. Primrose looked at him in alarm but he did not look angry. Then he began to smile, a broad smile so joyous that she could not stop her own smile from forming.

Bened slipped his hand over her flat stomach. "You carry my child. Our child. You could give me no greater gift. *Rwy'n caru ti*, my rose." He took her face between his hands and kissed her on both cheeks.

"What did that mean?" The feeling that had been behind the words had stirred her almost to tears and she had to know.

"I love you." He brushed a kiss over her lips and then held her close. "When did you know?"

"When I was being forced to marry the swine Edgar and my aunt tried to stab me and was shot for her troubles." She watched him slowly pale and he pressed his hand down a little harder on her belly. "All is well, Bened."

"Were you planning to tell me?"

"Not if you did not wish to stay with me or just stay together, not until you made some decision about it all. I did not wish to be a woman married for what sat in her womb and little else."

He stroked her hair. "It would never have been that but it was probably wise not to immediately run to me and tell me. I probably would have put my foot in it, said or done something Lilybet calls male idiocy." He smiled when she laughed. "It was best to wait until I knew what I wanted. Just one thing, I always wanted you but I had the arrogance to think I could decide what was best for you and did not think it should be me."

"Yes, Lilybet is right. Men can be idiots." She rested her cheek against his chest. "Simeon is going to have so much trouble with her."

"Ah, so you saw that too."

"I have no idea what I was seeing. It could be the rough seeding of a romance, or a true love or of just a truly fine and lasting friendship. That is up to them but she does know very well how to prod Simeon to a temper."

"Are you content with the child coming so soon?"

"Yes, as long as you do not try to build some huge protective wall around me. I want to help build the nest for our baby. I may not be a healer like the ones you know, but I do know a great deal about healing and since I showed a knack for it while still very young, I also know all about childbirth and the carrying of a child, the good for you and the bad for you. I will be fine but if you start smothering me with watchfulness and protection I will get cross."

He laughed but was smart enough not to promise anything. "My mother will be pleased."

"She already has a great many grandchildren."

"'Never too many' is her favorite saying. And if we have a daughter . . ." He laughed and shook his head. "Mother and all the other women in the family will be more than pleased."

"Which do you want, Bened?"

"I just want our child to be healthy, to live."

She nodded, rubbing her cheek against his chest. "So do I but I always thought men wanted an heir and since you are now a titled gentleman, I wondered if you had thought on that."

"I have a great many nephews. Not a direct line to me but one any court in the land would accept." He gently rolled her onto her back and kissed her belly. "You will soon get round here, our child growing inside you. I will love watching it."

"I believe talking about how round a woman gets when carrying a child . . ."

"Might be one of those things that will cause me a few bruises?" he teased.

"At the very least." She murmured with pleasure and burrowed her fingers deep into his thick hair when he began to tease her breasts with soft kisses and long strokes of his tongue.

"I will try to recall that. Lilybet knew."

"Of course she did. She was touching me when Edgar hit me and I fell. She later assured me that all was fine. Hmmm. She might know what we are having, a boy or a girl. I need to decide if I want to know."

"What would knowing help you with?"

"Planning for clothing and all that."

"Ah, I see. I will leave the decision up to you. My mind just freezes on the word. *Child*. I am going to be a father." He pulled her into an enthusiastic hug.

"You are not one yet?"

"Nay, not that I know of and I would. It is impossible to hide a Wherlocke or Vaughn child from his father, or mother as such is the case. It is in the blood, in the very heart of us and we recognize each other."

"That must be helpful." She trailed her fingers down his taut belly and felt it tremble ever so faintly beneath her touch. "So how did ones like Lilybet become lost to your tribe?"

"Our tribe. Hah! I like that. And I have no idea. All we have are some burned or partly burned papers left of a whole family driven into exile or murdered. Getting rid of family records meant they had nothing to take to court. It did not stop the persecutions but it slowed them down. Even when engaged in such horrific persecutions they do love their puzzles. Let us hope Modred and Dob find the answers."

For a while they just relaxed in the bed, enjoying the closeness of their bodies with no fear of societal anger or repercussions. Then Primrose curled her long slender fingers around his erection and Bened smiled. Quiet time was over. He turned to his wife, the woman he meant to spend his life with now carrying his first child, and suspected that any quiet times for him ended the day he found a woman with poor eyesight stumbling through the woods looking for her horse.

More by Bestselling Author
Hannah Howell

Available Wherever Books Are Sold!

Check out our website at
http://www.kensingtonbooks.com